Blood
of The
Fallen

A Novel By

DeQuinton Jackson

BLACKINK
PUBLICATIONS

Blood
of The
Fallen

A Novel By

DeQuinton Jackson

Acknowledgments

I would like to give all thanks to God, the Father in Heaven, and Christ, my Lord, for blessing me with talent and ability.

I would like to also thank a very special and beautiful woman who has made my world a brighter place. There is so much life in you that your smile pulls me away from the darkness and your laughter is a melody that gives me freedom. You are a ray of the sun that penetrated the heavy clouds of my sky and warmed my heart. I will love you until time is no more and my heart will never cease to beat for you.

May you be blessed in your journey and wherever your paths in life leads.

I love you Jenna Marie, as well as little Grayson.

Prologue

Rachel closed the laptop and tossed it to the side of her bed with a flick of her hand. It landed in the spot where a man should've been, but was not. She sighed as she tried to remember the last time she'd woken up next to a man's warm body. She was too young not to be filled with memories of past relationships that she could sometimes reflect on and reminisce over.

At twenty-six she could only recall a small few. She had been pursued often throughout high school, as well as college, so she had no one to blame other than herself. She had chosen to decline the many invitations offered to her by various decent and potentially compatible suitors. Although she had had her reasons for doing so and those reasons were still well founded.

The shortage of men in her life wasn't due to any sense of conceit or any shallow views of herself. The bottom line was that she was different.

She was uniquely different.

She possessed a very unusual mental ability. An ability that had ostracized her from her family and any potential social circles she could've been a part of. That same ability had gotten her recognized by the extremely powerful secret society called The Ancients when she was in college.

Rachel had the ability to influence physical matter with her mind. The scientific term was telekinetic. She didn't care to define herself with such a word despite the applicable truth of it. She had been able to operate in this way since the earliest days of her childhood. She couldn't remember ever not being able to. It wasn't something she learned but was inherent. She was born with it. It was due to her early discovery that she eventually learned how to suppress it and keep it hidden. However, her ability to suppress it didn't exactly equate with her ability to control it.

Her parents had their share of reports from schoolteachers and even daycare workers of mysterious incidents that seemed to occur when their daughter was present. Sometimes it was a toy that had somehow come down from a high shelf that no child could possibly reach. Sometimes a textbook had somehow moved itself from a desktop and appeared at her desk. They would ask her about it and had several talks with her about mischievous behavior.

The innocence of a child could work wonders on the cruelest of parents and she had often used it when being reprimanded. After all, she'd only been a child. How could she be expected to explain such things? Her parents had been troubled by the matter but with five other children, a convenient distraction had always arisen. She had used those distractions to fade into the shadows of her family while she grew into her adult years.

Her parents had known just as her brothers and sisters had known. They just pretended nothing was wrong with the quiet little girl that seemed to attract paranormal activity. She was just little Rachel and when people would look at her and inquire someone would say, "Oh, that's little Rachel. She's always like that."

They knew, they all knew. She could always tell by the look in their eyes. The way they would regard her when the unexplainable happened and she was somewhere in the vicinity. Her ostracism was a subtle and silent one but a real one nonetheless. She didn't hate them for it. She didn't hate them for the unspoken distance they all created with her despite the obvious proximity they all shared. She didn't hate them at all.

There was a bright side to the matter. She had avoided an unpleasant trip to the mental ward, which no doubt would've resulted if her parents had probed a little deeper into their child's abnormality. She had later learned that some children born with this, disease, as it was so termed by some of the experts, ended up being a part of some lab experiment.

She hadn't escaped her childhood completely unscathed. There had definitely been some psychological and emotional damage. She had survived and adapted. From her way of viewing, the matter there had been no other option. She had been characterized as reclusive, an introvert, and even a hermit once but she thought that was a bit extreme. She didn't agree with those assessments. She could admit to being a bit reserved at times, but that was for a perfectly good reason.

That reason being she could literally move a physical object without touching it.

She filled her cheeks with air and blew nosily. She stretched the limbs of her beautiful and athletic body seeking to relieve some tension. It was still early in the morning; her stomach suddenly reminded her she hadn't had breakfast yet. She had been given a new assignment and wanted to get familiar with the details as soon as possible. She blinked her pretty light green eyes at the empty ceiling of the small hotel room and lay perfectly still for a moment.

She didn't want to move, but she knew she had to. There was work to be done.

Her orientation into the organization had been three years earlier and she still didn't have a complete understanding of who these people really were. She had been approached and recruited in her final year of college. She had wrongly assumed it was some type of sorority. It hadn't been that at all. She wouldn't have given the matter a second thought if the recruiter hadn't mentioned he knew of her hidden ability. She had been told about others that were like her and then given a contact card with a number on it. She had heard about the Masons, the Illuminati, the Rosicrucian, but who were these people? And what could they possibly want with her.

They were watchers. That much she could safely surmise. Her orientation had lasted three days. The fact that she could operate outside the laws of physics paled in comparison to what she was exposed to.

Immortals.

The Ancients were the silent watchers of what was called the Bloodline, the children of the Fallen Ones. The idea of a person possessing telekinesis wasn't entirely without scientific grounding, but a person who'd been living for a thousand years? She'd naturally assumed it was all a joke; some elaborate prank planned out by some realty TV show.

If she hadn't seen the live footage and finally seen one with her own eyes, she would've never believed it. Her ability to push things around with her mind was minute compared to those beings. They could defy the very laws of gravity. They were beings of incredible power and yet they were solitary figures, existing in the shadows of humanity.

They were mortal once. At one time, they had lived normal human lives, coming from various walks of life. They were soldiers, priests, farmers, they were fathers and mothers. Sons and daughters who had all been born into this world. A mortal death should've ended their earthly existence but it didn't. Rather it brought them to encounter an even more mysterious being known as a Fallen One. These beings had never been human, to this very day not even the Ancients knew who they were.

Their responsibility, her current assignment, was to watch and monitor these beings who blended so well into the fabric of humanity. She was simply a field agent at the bottom level of some ghost hierarchical system unknown to her. She recorded her information and then reported to her superior. At the center of her wrist was a butterfly tattoo. Upon closer inspection, one would find an eye at the center of the butterfly. This was the identifying mark of the Ancients that only a trained eye would recognize. This had been completely against her wishes but it was necessary.

The secret community was global with an intricate networking system and extremely wealthy. Her salary was substantial. When she was working the field, she was given a credit card that would cover the basic necessities. In the eventuality she went over the limit she could just make a call and the card would be reloaded.

There was one law or rule that was heavily enforced. Never make contact with the Bloodline. That was strictly forbidden. She could admit that on several occasions she'd been tempted to disregard the rule. Rachel wasn't a curious person but who wouldn't want to have a conversation with a person who was alive when the Roman Empire fell. They were trained in the art of surveillance, which strangely didn't deal with a lot of physical tactics but mental tactics. How to shield your thoughts. They were informed that the Bloodline could actually hear a person's thought. She could only guess that was an easy feat for someone who could fly.

After coming off an assignment, they actually had to be psychologically evaluated. She had been told of cases where some agents had become mentally disturbed from working the field. The Bloodline could affect the human mind in unexplainable ways; their energy alone could be radioactive. In other words, she was risking the chemical balance of her brain by following those beings. The fact that she was telekinetic and could move physical objects with her mind was a prerequisite for the job. The sole reason she and others like her were selected and chosen.

It was still the beginning of the new year; the air was cold and chilly. The hotel had its own cafeteria but she wanted to walk and move her legs. She got up and put on some winter gear. The jacket she wore was a little thin but it would do. Rachel wasn't a tall woman; she possessed a light frame with a firm build and healthy body tone. Her years of volleyball in high school and college, as well as her martial arts training from the organization had crafted a very attractive figure and form. Her shoulder length hair was dark and straight, a portion of it tended to shadow a side of her pretty face. Her light green eyes could easily become winter green in a moment of heat and temper. The complexion of her skin tone was a soft white, proper treatment of her skin gave it a healthy gloss.

Her current assignment had her stationed in Atlanta. She wasn't a native but she was familiar enough with the city. The subject she was following had been sighted often in North Atlanta. She was already familiar with the subject's hangout locations.

It took a brief twenty minutes to walk to the breakfast place. After ordering, she sat down on a comfortable stool to do some more contemplating, going over details in her head.

"You headed to work this morning miss lady?" The voice came from her left. "Shouldn't you be a little better dressed? It's in the low thirties all morning."

The voice annoyed her more than it startled her. She knew he was there from the very moment he quietly eased his way over two minutes earlier. Her hope had been he wouldn't want to speak to her, and yet at the same time she knew he would.

"Thanks. I'll be sure to remember that." She glanced at him and then resumed drinking her cup of coffee. She suddenly found herself wishing the cushioned stools were spaced further apart.

He flashed her a smile that she didn't see. He was tall with a solid build, short dark hair, and icy blue eyes. His entire appearance suggested he was a part of corporate America.

"You didn't answer my initial question, but that's ok. I'm headed to the office myself. Not to do any real work of course, that's for subordinates. Just to sign some papers; in and out."

She wondered if he really expected her to respond to that. Her order was brought out and she was tempted just to take the food and leave. He ordered a cup of coffee and took several sips before speaking again.

"Pretty quiet. I take it you don't talk much." He nodded his head as if she'd spoken. "Hey listen, I got nothing else to do this morning after I leave the office. What about you? You wanna hang out?"

She cut her eyes at him while chewing on a mouthful of eggs. A thought flashed across her mind. She could push him clear across the restaurant to the other side without even touching him. A faint smile appeared on her face that she knew without a doubt he would misinterpret.

He visibly brightened with hope of winning her over. "Is that a smile? What's your name?"

"You don't think that's kind of out of order?" she looked at him and asked.

"What?"

"You asked me do I want to hang out first and then you asked me my name." She shook her head at him. "Not many women who have a mind to be attentive will let that pass. You should pay closer attention to what you say. Why should I give you my name when you haven't even apologized for interrupting me?" She took another bite of her food.

He frowned lightly in confusion. "Interrupting? You weren't doing anything."

She tapped the side of her head with a finger. "I was doing something in my head."

He raised a brow; was she serious? "Ah…ok…lesson learned." He recovered quickly, not the least bit undaunted in his efforts. "How about if I start over? My name is Craig; forgive me for interrupting. I happened to see a beautiful woman having breakfast by herself so I figured she was single and could use a little company. Is that really such a bad thing?"

She looked directly at him and did a quick scan. He really wasn't all that bad looking; in fact, he was rather handsome. She was single. She had been thinking about that earlier, but once again, she would have to pass up the offer. She pushed her plate away after another bite and stood.

"I'm sure you're a nice guy Craig, and I'll probably regret this, but the timing is wrong. Always is." She flashed him a friendly smile. "Nice meeting you though."

His facial expression changed so drastically and effortlessly, her rejection forcing his true self to the surface. In a quick motion, he grabbed her wrist and clenched it, bringing her to an abrupt stop. He dropped his voice to a threatening whisper. "This conversation isn't over twinkle toes. You think you can just walk away from me like that? Like I'm nobody? I will put my fingers around your pretty little neck and…"

He never finished. Another reason why she was single was that men simply couldn't be trusted.

In a swift and deft move, she reversed the hold with a quick roll of her wrist. She jerked him forward at the same time turning his hand over, putting his arm in an awkward angle. In a fast maneuver, she brought her other hand up and launched a backhanded chop into his throat. His forward momentum collided with the blow. Not wanting to kill him, she didn't apply full pressure with the strike. Still clutching his wrist, she finished the technique by going into a quick spin and flipped him to the floor. The entire act may have lasted a total of two seconds.

All activity in the establishment suddenly froze as all heads turned towards the commotion. They regarded the woman and then the man on the floor who was in an obvious state of pain. Slowly, movement and conversation resumed.

Rachel knelt beside him and spoke in the same whispering tone he'd used. "I am not the girl next door Craig. I'm not the pretty little captain of the cheerleading squad. I don't hang out with girls named Becky or Amber. You have no idea what I am Craig or what I can do. If I ever see you again I will literally crush the life out of you through a very painful process."

She stood and looked down at him for a moment, thinking how disappointing men could sometimes be. She looked around at the people in the diner. She knew they were whispering to each other about her. She had experienced it her whole life. They would've been looking at her really crazy if she would've done what she'd been tempted to do. After giving Craig a final look, she headed out.

Once she was back outside, she took a deep breath and released the building tension. She shook her head. "Jeez Rachel, at this rate you'll be fifty by the time you find a man," she whispered to herself. She chuckled and shook the incident from her mind. She had an Immortal to stalk that morning.

Chapter One

The car came to a screeching halt as wet tires slid across the rain soaked pavement. The storm was at its worst. Lightening flashed, bringing momentary light to the darkness. It was in that brief flash of light that he saw the figure walking nearly in the center of the road. The headlights worked fine but whatever he saw or whatever he thought he saw was gone. It had appeared as if the figure was brought with the violent flash and then left with it. That was crazy though, it had to be his imagination. He hadn't been going very fast, thank God, when he jerked the wheel hard to the left and hit his brakes. His heart nearly jumped out of his chest as the vehicle swerved in the pouring rain. What had been only a couple of seconds seemed like a lifetime. He grabbed the steering wheel for a moment as he fought to control his breathing and get his heartrate back to normal.

The car was horizontal on the empty road; he'd been able to stop before swerving into a complete circle. He was certain if he'd been going fast enough he would have swerved into a complete circle and flipped. The road he was on was full of curves and sharp turns and gradually inclined its way up a mountainous hill. He was right at the base. To either side of the road was a dense forest area, woods that ran into the bottom section of the north Georgia Mountains. The bright lights of the car beamed into the trees, revealing nothing but rustling branches.

Lightning flashed again, followed by the distant thunder, seeming to cause the sky to shake as the rain fell. He sat there for a long moment listening to the sound of the heavy raindrops beat against the hood. This stretch of road was never thick with traffic so he wasn't in a hurry to move the car.

He watched as the force of the wind made the tall trees bend, as if forcing them to bow to some unseen God. The long branches seemed to be reaching out, giant claws that would snatch up the unsuspecting. As a writer, he could easily imagine some man-eating monster suddenly emerging out to devour him.

"Get a grip Gray. It's just a bunch of trees." He ran a hand across the top of his bald head.

He squinted his old eyes into the blackness of the night, peering through the window for any signs of movement. Even if the road had streetlights, the downpour of the rain made visibility nearly impossible. He was sure he hadn't hit anything or anyone but Gray was a man with a conscious; he wanted to be sure.

The car was still running, he backed up a little and realigned the vehicle with the road. The headlights revealed an empty road; there was no one lying dead on the ground. He was ready to drive off and head home but something was bothering him; something wasn't right.

Someone was out there.

It was true that his imagination could be very colorful and active, always had been. He had made a pretty good living off his imagination. He actually was paid to use it. This wasn't his imagination. This was that innate sense of knowing that all human beings possess to some degree or another.

There was no telling how long it would be before the storm abated and he didn't want to sit there for much longer. It hadn't been raining when he left so there was no umbrella. He shut out the voice of reason and logic that was screaming in his head and stepped out into the madness that was the storm. He stayed within the confines of the headlights, taking only a few steps out in front of the car.

"Hello! Anybody out there?" He cupped his hands at his mouth for effect.

The only thing that responded was the storm.

In almost sixty years of being alive, he was sure this was by far the dumbest thing he'd ever done. He called out again as he looked about. He scanned the trees again half-expecting the man-eating monster to reveal itself. He had a weird tingling sensation. If he could check, he was sure he would find chill bumps on his arms. He stepped out a little further and called out again. No one answered.

He was just about to turn back around when another flash brought the figure back into the visible world and disappeared again. It scared the life out of him. It wasn't his imagination; it was an actual person. He blinked at the spot where the person should've been. It was only a few feet ahead of him and still in range of the headlights.

The instinct to flee was overpowering, the urge to jump back in his car and go was demanding but he didn't. He wasn't crazy...old maybe, but he wasn't crazy. He had seen someone. How the person kept appearing and disappearing was a mystery to him.

"I know you're out there. I saw you. Are you hurt?" He wiped the rain out of his eyes. "If you are I can get you to a hospital."

Maybe the person didn't want any help. He had no idea what he was dealing with. What if it was some psycho who had fled up into the mountains after butchering a family? Wouldn't be the first time. What if...

This time the bright flash brought with it an angry lightning bolt that tore into a nearby tree creating hot sparks that would've produced a fire if it weren't for the rain. The person, the man, was now standing in close range of the struck tree and didn't vanish.

The strike of lightning had been too close for comfort for Gray. So after thanking God he was still alive, he peered at the stranger. Immediately he saw the danger, the huge tree was about to fall and the man was standing in the spot where it would no doubt come crashing down. It would certainly kill him.

The stranger had to see it but he acted as if he didn't. He just stood there in some state of transfixion. His face wasn't clear due to the storm and the darkness. Gray couldn't be sure but it appeared as if the man was naked.

"Heyyyy!" He flailed his arms trying to get his attention. "You gotta move! That tree is coming down nowww!"

The stranger didn't so much as move. What was wrong with the guy? Gray wasn't a young man anymore. He couldn't move as fast as he used to. He could try to run over and grab him, but he questioned the wisdom in that. It wasn't just his age in question; it was also the stranger's sanity.

He called out again. This time more urgently while dramatically stabbing his pointer finger in the direction of the tree. There was no way the stranger didn't see the tall piece of timber descending towards him. He could only watch and witness what would most certainly be the man's death. Suddenly he got that tingling sensation again. The phenomenon that transpired next was too much for his old eyes to behold.

The tree seemed to fall in slow motion. He didn't realize he was holding his breath. At the moment of what was supposed to have been impact; the tree stopped and remained motionless in the empty air.

It was impossible.

His rational mind tried to tell him it was some optical illusion, after all, despite the aid of the headlights, it was still dark and there was a storm.

No, it wasn't a trick being played on the eye, nor was he hallucinating.

It was real.

The tree remained suspended for a moment; suddenly it shifted to the side and crashed into the ground. The stranger never moved. He just stood there, seemingly oblivious of the storm, the falling tree, or Gray. The next thing he did was truly unexpected; he passed out.

Gray had seen enough. It was time to go. Was the guy dead? Maybe the tree did hit him and killed him but somehow he'd missed it. He knew that wasn't the case. His mind was just trying to justify what he'd just seen. Should he leave him there? He could just call the police when he got home, let them deal with it. But what if the guy was hurt?

He sighed and against his better judgment walked over. He knelt down beside the naked black man and checked for a pulse. He was alive. He moved his head a bit and moaned. Gray hurried back over to his car and got an old blanket out of the trunk. He brought it over, covered the stranger, and struggled to get him to his feet. He wasn't completely unconscious.

He half-carried, half-dragged the man to the car and placed him in the back. He got behind the wheel and took a moment to compose himself. He continued to question the wisdom in his actions; this could be a grave mistake. He glanced at his rearview to look at the stranger who appeared to be sleeping. He looked young mid-twenties maybe.

And possibly a serial killer.

He pushed the thoughts away and forced himself to focus on the task at hand, which at the moment was getting home. He was just about to drive off when suddenly the mystery of the suspenseful night got even more mysterious.

Someone was watching him.

In all of his life, never had he received so many intuitive flashes in one night. Was this what it was like to be physic? He squinted his eyes again as he peered out into the night, scanning the trees intently. He really wouldn't be surprised if that man-eating monster decided to come out now. He shook the feeling and drove off, maneuvering around the fallen tree. He already had one psycho in his backseat; he just didn't have the energy for another one.

***

He came out of the woods after the car pulled away. Although it was pitch black, he had no trouble seeing. His powerful vision could easily shame any eagle or nocturnal animal of the night. He looked up into the night sky, allowing the rain to fall freely on his face. He'd been following Michael all night, the mortal had finally escaped the mental intuition that he'd been held prisoner at for so long. The mortal was too powerful to be confined to such a state; he should have escaped years ago.

Julius stood in the center of the road looking in the direction the car had gone. There was something about Michael that snatched his attention. What was it? He didn't normally concern himself with mortal affairs; none of his kind did. There was a certain element about the mortal that nagged at him and pulled at him for some reason. It was true he possessed an exceptional ability to free his energy despite the fact he couldn't control it. However, he was still only human, a mere mortal who would die in the next thirty or forty years. What was that compared to the centuries he'd already been alive?

He had first felt Michael's energy several months earlier and at first, he'd thought it was another Immortal. He was surprised to find quite the contrary. Throughout his lifetime, he'd seen a few humans demonstrate the telekinetic ability to a small degree. It was never anything truly impressive. Once, he'd witnessed a mortal lift a stone with his mind that weighed a ton but that was still nothing. It wasn't so much the strength of Michael's energy that drew him but rather the feel of it. There was some recognizable sense of association that baffled him. Such a thing shouldn't be.

Julius had been a prisoner once, confined to a prison by beings far more powerful than himself. That hadn't been a place of stonewalls and iron bars. It hadn't even been in the physical world. What he had endured in that place no human mind could fathom or comprehend. There was no escaping. There was no anything, just an empty and solitary state of existence...and madness. He almost shuddered at the memory of it. No Immortal ever survived or came back from such a state.

But he did.

So was that it then? Did he feel some sort of sympathy for the mortal? Was there some part of the human in him that identified with Michael's pain? That just didn't make sense to him, but something had definitely attracted him to the mortal.

The storm was beginning to pass. The worst of it was over. He felt lonely suddenly and a person entered his mind he hadn't thought of in centuries. His precious Julia; his mortal love. She had lived and died in the 5th century. The Empire had been divided by then, in Constantinople, Justinian had held hopes of reclaiming the west. That never happened. In his mortal life, he'd been a warrior, a true-blooded Frank and war had been his passion. He had lived for it. Despite becoming Immortal, the loss of his mortal life had been draining. The life of a warrior had been all he'd ever known or loved.

When Julia came into his life, he'd been empty and broken. He'd been Immortal for almost a hundred years when he first caught sight of her beautiful eyes; eyes that had frozen him in time. She had brought him back from the edge of darkness and given him something that not even Immortality could give. She had been deeply moved by the life of Christ and his death; her faith inspired him. He watched as the passing years stole her physical beauty with age but never the beauty of her soul. She had died in his arms.

He released his energy with ease and became airborne, going high up into the night. He spotted the moving car in the darkness. He would keep a close eye on the mortal for now. Maybe it was nothing and the matter would pass. Maybe it wouldn't. The cold wind caused his long hair to blow wildly.

Yes, he would watch…for now.

Chapter Two

Michael awoke with a start on the long brown couch he was stretched out on. He looked about with a confused expression, very unfamiliar with his surroundings. Where was he? How did he get there? The only thing that covered his body was some old blankets. Where were his clothes? He tried to remember the previous night but everything was all fuzzy in his head. He could remember traveling to different places, but how? Had he been on a plane? It was the sudden smell of food cooking that made his thoughts begin to clear. It wasn't food being cooked in a government facility such as the one he'd just escaped from. It was the smell of home cooked southern food.

Someone was making breakfast.

He hadn't smelled that kind of food since he was a little boy. A few incomplete childhood memories flickered in his mind. Home. How long had it been since he was at home? How many years?

"Hungry?"

He didn't see the older man standing off to the side in the entryway to the kitchen. The opening had a dark border of brown polished wood with a high arch. A deer head with huge antlers was mounted at the top.

Gray gave him a warm smile. "Come on. Got plenty to go around." He turned back into the kitchen but then stopped and pointed at the other end of the couch. "They should fit you or at least hold you for a while."

Michael swung his legs down, his feet landed on a warm carpeted floor. He looked at the clothes that rested on the arm of the couch. A white shirt, some jeans, socks, and even underwear. The fit wasn't exact, but it was close.

He made his way to the cozy kitchen and sat at the prepared table. He moved slowly, the whole time watching Gray.

"Orange juice or coffee?" he asked with his back turned.

"Juice is fine." He wanted to keep his eyes on the old man but the aroma of what was before him momentarily stole his attention. Slowly, he began to eat.

Gray brought the juice over and set it on the table. He watched him eat for a moment before sitting down himself. He noticed the stranger seemed to be in good shape. He had a good build and muscle tone. He wasn't quite six feet with short, dark, and curly hair. His skin tone was a light brown and appeared to be healthy. He was obviously hungry.

"Got a name son?" He took a sip of the tea he'd fixed for himself.

Michael didn't realize he was eating like a starved animal. He looked up as he stopped and took a huge swallow. "Michael." His eyes held contact for a moment and then dived back in.

Gray nodded at that. He looked towards the kitchen window above the sink to look out at the morning daylight. "Name's Gray. You remember much of last night Michael?"

"Pieces," he said with his mouth full of food. "It's not really clear in my head yet."

"What do you remember?"

He continued to chew while he debated with himself if he would be truthful or not. It was crystal clear that the old man had helped him; the place wasn't swarming with police. Gray was either incredibly stupid or too trusting. "Two things," he said after another swallow. "I'm being followed. And I escaped from a mental institution."

Gray scratched at the salt and pepper stubble under his chin while taking that in. Who was the young man that had somehow mysteriously materialized out of a storm? He considered himself a good judge of character and thus far, there was nothing telling him that the boy was trouble. At least not yet.

"You being followed by the law? If you are, I won't turn you in, but you can't stay here."

Michael looked at the cup of juice, picked it up, and made a swirling motion several times before taking a swallow. He watched Gray over the rim. The older man was bigger, standing well over six feet tall, with huge arms that were probably the result of heavy lifting. His small head was bald, and he wore his mustache thick. His white skin was rough and patched. It was his eyes that struck him. They were light gray. He didn't detect any danger or threat in them.

"I'm not running from the law. Sure, the authorities are probably looking for me but I'm not running from them. The nature of my escape alone will keep them baffled for a while and probably have the staff of that facility under investigation," Michael said.

"The nature of your escape? Someone on the inside must have helped you?" He placed his fingers on the glass of tea but didn't take a sip.

Michael looked directly at him. "It's complicated." He was quiet for a moment. "How did you find me last night?"

"Find you?" He chuckled lightly. "I don't think that expression would appropriately describe our encounter last night. Perhaps I should ask you how you fell out of the sky last night." There was a bit of humor in his voice but there was also a bit of reasonable uncertainty. That was understandable. He was just about finished with his breakfast.

"I should probably get going. I don't have any money. I can't pay your for the meal and the clothes. At least not now I can't."

Gray rejected that with a slight dismissive wave of his hand but his curiosity wasn't sated. "One does what one can. What makes you so sure you're being followed? I didn't see anyone else last night and…" He remembered something.

Michael frowned at him. "What is it? And what?"

He did recall the strange feeling of being watched last night after putting Michael in the car. Had there really been someone? Everything about last night was strange. Maybe there was a reasonable explanation for all of it. "Nothing. Who do you think is following you? And why?"

Michael shook his head. "You wouldn't believe me if I told you. Look Gray, I'm sorry for all this. I should just get going, the sooner the better. I will tell you this. The person that is following me is possibly very dangerous and can do things that are not exactly normal."

Gray had never been the type of person to scare easily. "Let me guess; he can make trees float above his head too."

Michael was just about to insert the spoonful of grits into his mouth when he froze. So that was real. He remembered it vaguely but he had thought it was a dream. What else had he done last night? And what all did Gray witness him do? Slowly, he resumed eating.

"Michael, I'm fifty-eight years old, been around the world and seen a lot of things. Fought for my country in the aftermath of Nam. The war was over but there were still battles to be fought. I even got exposed to some top-secret government activity once. Military cover-ups, some pretty high-profile stuff. But what I saw last night takes the cake, son. I'm still wondering if my sanity is intact." He squirmed a bit in his chair trying to get comfortable.

"When I brought you in last night I honestly didn't know what I would do with you. I thought about calling the cops but I really didn't have a reason to do that. Couldn't figure out for the life of me how you ended up butt naked on a country road in the middle of a storm." He shrugged. "Figured I'd find out in the morning. I'm not in the habit of bringing naked strangers home, unless you're a woman. But you're welcome to stay for a few days and get yourself squared away. Seems to me you still got some figuring to do in that head of yours. When you get it all figured out hopefully you'll let me know so I can put an end to all this suspense and mystery. I won't turn you in. And I won't advise you to either, decision like that, a man's gotta make for himself. I'm sure you have your reasons for leaving."

He stood and reached for Michael's empty plate. When he picked it up he looked at it and then at Michael.

"I take it you could go for another round?"

He gave a slow nod.

Gray continued to talk as he moved about. "Several extra rooms. Take your pick. I bought this place because Betsy wanted a family home but of course, that means having a family. We tried for years, thought it was me at first, but it turned out she was damaged goods. Her folks were pretty wealthy, paid top dollar for medical science but it just wasn't happening. Thought about adoption. I didn't mind but Betsy girl wanted one of her own. That's what I used to call her, Betsy girl." His movement became slow temporarily as a wave of nostalgia hit him, but he shook it off.

"Twenty years together in this place. I couldn't bring myself to sell it after she died. Too many memories. Besides, Biscuit wouldn't let me sell it anyway." He brought Michael another serving.

"How did she die? And who's Biscuit?" he asked before taking a bite.

"Breast cancer. She fought it for three years." He walked over and leaned his weight against the sink. "Biscuit is the brown Labrador I let out this morning to poop in the backyard. That is one strange dog. He'll let me know when he wants to come back in."

Michael regarded Gray silently while eating. Why was the old man being so nice to him? He wasn't sure if he could ever recall someone being that nice to him. He was an outcast, always had been. People were typically mean to him, most of his life he'd been treated condescendingly, even by his own family. By now, he'd grown used to it and sometimes expected it. Was it possible that the old man had hidden intentions and was planning to hurt him? He doubted it. Sometimes he could pick up on a person's vibe and at the moment, he received no bad vibes from Gray.

"Twelve years."

Gray was fixing himself another glass of tea. "Huh?"

"I went in that place when I was sixteen. That was twelve years ago," he said with a distant facial expression. "My own mother put me there. She told me I would only be there for a couple of days. That they were just going to perform some tests. She didn't hug or kiss me; just dropped me off like a regular day at school and left. I later learned she told them I was delusional and hallucinated. They pumped me with so much meds for the first few years. I can hardly recall ever being conscious. Sometimes I couldn't tell the day, the month, or what year it was. Sometimes I didn't know my own name." He shook his head at the absurdity of it.

Gray was listening carefully. He couldn't imagine being in such a place and was certain he wouldn't have lasted years. His perspective of Michael was slowly changing or evolving rather, obviously the young man had been through a lot. How could a mother do her own child like that? The experience had to be psychologically damaging especially at that age.

Michael looked at his plate as if he wasn't sure if he wanted to eat anymore. "I had these horrible nightmares for years. They got so bad they had to monitor me for a couple of months. I had to go to sleep hooked up to all kinds of machines and wires. It was crazy."

"You still have them?" Gray asked.

"Sometimes. Not as much as I used to. I never got around to hating my mother for what she did, didn't have the heart for it. I'm not saying I approve of her actions, but she wasn't completely without reason for what she did." He decided to take another bite.

Gray disagreed with that entirely. "What do you mean? She abandoned her child. Any woman who would do such a thing doesn't deserve to be a mother."

He could agree with that. "True. In a set of ordinary circumstances, I probably could apply judgement but nothing about my case is ordinary. Some mothers are told their child has behavioral issues, my mother was told her child is probably possessed with the devil. Big difference. Especially when even the teachers are afraid of him."

He was sure he hadn't heard correctly Gray walked over to a far cabinet and retrieved a bottle of Wild Turkey and poured himself a shot. "Possessed with the devil? How could someone reach such a conclusion with a child?"

"I wasn't just a child." He finished with his food and pushed his plate away. He used a napkin that was offered on the table to wipe his mouth. "I was a monster." He took a deep breath and did his best to relax. "Do you really wanna hear this Gray? My life is far from a Cinderella story and if this person is still following me I could be putting you in danger."

"I got a couple rifles, some pretty high powered. I think I can handle any unwanted company. Do you think this person can stop a bullet?" The question was meant to be rhetorical.

"You have no idea," he said plainly.

Gray read the seriousness in his eyes clearly; he wasn't joking. For the last couple of years his life had been quiet, the volume of it had definitely turned down after losing Betsy. That was five years earlier. He had loved to travel and see the world; his early years in the military had given him an edge. He had never considered himself an adrenaline junkie but he appreciated a good rush every now and then. Biscuit wasn't the ideal hunting dog but he still brought him along when he went out to hunt. A fair portion of his life had been spent in some adventure or another.

He hadn't even written in a while. Betsy was the one who had convinced him to get his work published. He didn't think he was good enough, but as always, she was right and he'd become very successful. Twelve of his books had made it to the New York Time's bestseller list and one was being considered for a movie.

Had he lost his spark? Nothing could replace Betsy girl but maybe this would wake up in him whatever it was that had gone to sleep.

He poured another shot of Wild Turkey and consumed it with a quick toss. "I'm listening."

"Scientifically speaking, I have telekinesis. I can move physical objects with my mind but never mind that. I'd rather start with the guy that's following me," he said.

"Why? What makes him so important?"

"He's been alive for over a thousand years."

Gray put the glass down and drunk from the bottle. He was certain by the end of the conversation it would be completely empty.

Chapter Three

Victoria sat alone in the expensive and fancy restaurant in downtown Atlanta, gazing out the window in deep thought. She rested her chin in an open palm with her elbow propped on the table. The sun was setting. The nightlife of the city was slowly coming to life as people milled about. Atlanta was a nice city but despite its many attractions, she could've cared less. She'd seen cities all over the world.

She was a woman who could boast of walking through the city of Rome, the most majestic city of all while St. Augustine was writing his City of God. She could still remember the year 476 AD when Romulus Augustulus had been dethroned by Odovacar. The great city had long begun to deteriorate but that event had been a defining moment. The Eastern half of the Empire had remained intact for many years after but it soon also began to decline. How many cities had she witnessed rise and fall? Too many.

She was elegantly beautiful, her long limbs were slender, and her movements were often slow and graceful. She could mimic a cat the way she moved. Her long and silky dark hair was pulled back from her face and descended into a single braid that glided down her back. She wore a revealing purple gown that left her shoulders bare with a lot of exposed cleavage and a high slit that revealed a shapely thigh. Her heels had straps that allowed her pretty toes to breathe; her nails were painted a glossy black. She sat with her long legs crossed.

"Excuse me, may I join you?" the voice was heavy and southern.

She twisted her head to him slowly and smiled like a Cheshire cat. "Sure."

He was well over six feet and easily weighed 210 pounds. A white male with short brown hair and finely groomed. His appearance was rather neat. He sat across from her. "Thank you. Are you alone?" He knew she was alone; he'd been watching her for the last fifteen minutes.

She tilted her head a bit at him. Her smile still faintly lingering around her mouth. "Yes…and would you please be so kind to tell me how my being alone concerns you." Her tone carried a hint of amusement.

He looked her over, it took all of his willpower not to leave his eyes on her breasts, and then there was the shape of her mouth. He was a man that was accustomed to beautiful women but of the creature that sat before him was a totally different species of beautiful.

"Point taken," he shrugged. "But I've never been the type of person to mind my own business."

"You don't see that as something dangerous and incredibly stupid?" She slowly traced a finger around the rim of her glass.

He gave a nod of admission. "It's gotten me into trouble a time or two but it's also gotten me some um…how should I say this? Rewarding moments." He gave her a smile that gave clear understanding to what was implied.

How cute, she thought and almost said his name, but then he would wonder how she knew. She didn't want to ruin the moment by telling him she was Immortal. "And your name would be?"

"Matthew." He extended a hand across the table. It was more in hopes of touching her cream-colored skin than expressing some form of polite behavior. He was rewarded at the moment of contact, it was electric, and instantly he wanted to touch her whole body.

"A pleasure." She pretended not to notice his roaming eyes. "Victoria."

"A beautiful name for a beautiful woman." With extreme reluctance, he retracted his hand. "So what are you doing here this evening Victoria? Alone I mean. Because if you are single then I have just discovered the 8th wonder of the world."

She smirked at the compliment, both of them. "How charming. Does that come natural for you? Or do you surf the net all day looking for impressive phrases to use on lonely women?"

"Lonely?" He signaled for a waiter. "Now you're just being insulting."

"Oh? How so?"

"I would say that's the biggest lie I have heard all year but the year has just started. If you're lonely I'm a woman," he teased.

She couldn't resist the laugh; he was cute and funny.

The waiter came over and he ordered something to drink. "Looks like you're in trouble Victoria. You know what the experts say don't you?"

"No, what would the experts say?"

He leaned in for effect. "If a guy can make a women laugh within three minutes of meeting her she'll have sex with him."

"And where did you get that information from?" she asked.

"Surfing the net."

She laughed again lightly.

He glanced over at a near table where a young couple was enjoying each other's company. The volume of the overall conversations was at a low buzz with an occasional burst of laughter. The light was dim, the music being played was faint and soft, the entire atmosphere was relaxing.

She had been nursing a margarita that she began to absently finger. "I am here alone because I needed to do some thinking. I really wasn't looking for a social night." That was true; something had been bothering her lately. She had been trying to ignore it but no matter how hard she tried, she just couldn't shake it. "As far as being lonely," she sniffed and looked away, "I'd rather not discuss that."

Her eyes were a powerful blue, electric, captivating. She had to be by far the most beautiful woman he'd ever laid eyes on. "Are you from Atlanta?"

"No." She looked back at him. "I'm sure you are and you would love to show me around sometime, right?"

"You have got to be a psychic," he stated.

She smiled. "I doubt any psychic abilities are needed to know what's on your mind Matthew."

"Is it that obvious? My tongue isn't hanging out of my mouth is it?" he asked in a playful tone.

"Not at the moment, but I'm sure it soon will be."

The sexual innuendo wasn't missed on him at all. Even if it was, the act of her rubbing her heel against his leg was clear enough. He could've sworn he was melting. He wanted to take her right there on the table; he was sure they would be finished before security ejected them from the place. The woman was like a magnet; he'd been drawn to her the moment he spotted her. He was going to explode if he couldn't get his hands on her.

She finished her drink. "Would you like to join me back at my suite Matthew? It has a lovely view of the city."

"It's not the city I want to see."

Several hours later, she lay on her back looking up at the ceiling design next to a sleeping Matthew. She had used him. Wasn't she supposed to feel bad for that? He wasn't complaining and wouldn't be so why bother with her conscious? In truth, there was nothing that a mortal man could do for her in the name of pleasure. Immortality affected a person's physiology, especially a woman's hormones. An orgasm simply wasn't the same.

A mortal had no idea.

Only another Immortal could satisfy her and yet such a union was forbidden by the Fallen Ones. Immortals were governed by the mysterious beings; they were the lawmakers for their kind. One such law was Immortals were not allowed to produce any offspring.

In the event that an Immortal woman became pregnant by a male, they were all executed, woman, man, and child. That was something she had hated since becoming Immortal. The Fallen had given them immortality but what had they taken? What had been the price? They were forced to live in the shadows of humanity and the freedom to love was stolen or at least came with a dangerous risk. She hated the Fallen for that.

In a defiant act, she had fallen in love with another Immortal three hundred years earlier. Those years had been some of the best years of her long existence. He was gone now; taken by the self-righteous beings that had confined them to their existence. Her hate for them had grown even stronger; she no longer cared how they viewed her. Let them come for her; she had been alive nearly two thousand years; she would embrace her death with open arms.

She was tired of life. Not so much of living but rather of having a non-ending existence that seemed to be void of purpose and meaning. It was better to live a mortal life of purpose and die than to be alone and empty with immortality.

Her sigh was soft and light. She had needed this temporary distraction. It had taken her mind off what had been bothering her. She turned her head to look at Matthew. He was sleeping on his stomach with his arms hugged around the pillow. She envied the state of peace he was in. she liked this one; like so many others she would probably keep him for a while. It was forbidden but she didn't care. She was done with living in fear of her self-absorbed creators. She wanted to anger them. Outside of another Immortal the Fallen were the only beings that could end her existence.

She prayed they would.

She quietly removed herself from the large bed and dressed herself. She regarded Matthew one more time; the lower half of his body was exposed. She could see his muscle tone.

"Rewarding moments," she smiled.

She stepped out to the balcony; the cold air meant nothing to her. Although she was well over a hundred feet above the ground, her keen vision allowed her to see movement below clearly. She scanned the night slowly. Someone was out there watching her; that was the thing that was bothering her. She had known for a while now and the feeling was getting stronger. Maybe it was another Immortal; maybe it was something else. Either way, she didn't care.

With a brief release of her power, she leaped off the balcony and dived into the darkness.

***

Rachel had almost lost her. She was sitting down with her headphones plugged into her Galaxy Note watching "Titanic." How many times had she seen the movie? She could probably recite it line for line. She was s sucker for romance movies, especially the old ones. She had allowed her eyes to linger on the sinking ship scene a little too long. She was seated at the food court; her target had been about five tables down. They were inside Lenox Mall. The place was huge; it could take hours to find her again if she lost her.

Her particular subject was in the habit of coming to such public places. It was a female. As was their custom, she remained solitary, staying away from groups of people. The Immortal was an observer; she appeared to enjoy watching things as if she was constantly fascinated with the activity around her. Rachel had watched her stand for nearly an hour in front of a women's clothing store before going in.

Rachel stood and looked about her; scanning the moving faces. The weather and the lingering feel of the holiday kept the mall from being packed. That was something that had definitely worked in her favor. It was already hard enough keeping up with a being who in the blink of an eye could virtually disappear. It was the optical effect their speed had on the human eye; they simply could move faster than what the eye could follow.

She also had to remember to keep her thoughts guarded. It was a strange experience to have your mind assaulted in such a manner. It was an inhumane invasion of the most sacred privacy. She had felt it once and even though she'd been able to repel the attempt it had still left her feeling…stunned, violated. She never wanted to experience that again. As a person who could push her mind again against physical objects, she'd been trained to release that same energy against such an attack.

It required advanced skill and technique to accomplish such a feat because it had to be done in a subtle fashion. They were told that if the Immortal became aware that their probing was being consciously repelled they would unleash their full power. Such an event would be no contest.

She wore a pair of tight fitting, dark blue jeans, a thick black leather jacket with brown fur around the edges and a pair of black boots. Her hair was tied back, and her hands were covered in a pair of white gloves. She had caught the glance of several men and had quickly turned away, not wanting to invite unwanted company or repeat another Craig episode.

If she was honest with herself, the idea of having someone in her life had been orbiting her thoughts but she refused to pay any real attention to it. Truth be told she was lonely. She didn't want to admit it to herself; it made her feel desperate. That was part of the reason she was sitting in a mall watching "Titanic" while she was supposed to be working. She longed to love and be in love like any other woman. Maybe even have a family someday. As always, she pushed those thoughts aside to focus on the job at hand.

She finally spotted her target moving away from the food court, possibly headed for the exit. She quickly followed in pursuit. She was right, the Immortal was leaving; the tour of window-shopping was over. Rachel followed her out into the huge lot. Her target didn't own a care, didn't really need one. Who would when you could fly? There had been no phenomenal activity with this one today. She hadn't been following her for long and so far, there hadn't been a lot of activity to record. That didn't mean there wouldn't be, all it took was for the right situation to develop. To that very day, there were a lot of unsolved criminal cases that were the result of Immortal activity.

She followed her target for another couple of hours with no significant change. Finally, after six hours she called it a day and headed back to the motel to do her report. The instant she entered the warm room she breathed in relief; the January cold air was brutal. She fixed herself some hot coco, activated her laptop, and began her brief report.

One of the important things to log in was whether or not an Immortal had made any mortal ties or associations. An important arm of the Ancients was to prevent any strong human relations from developing. Immortals could be trusted not to attempt to formulate any plot to take over the world, they were solitary by nature. The same couldn't be said to be true with humans. If the right person with world domination ambitions developed ties with an Immortal, there was no telling what that person would endeavor to do. It was rare but some Immortals did develop mortal relations but for the most part, they were harmless. In most cases, the mortal didn't even know the nature of the company they kept.

Another important thing was any public display of their abilities. That was also rare. They were careful to conceal such acts. They were not concerned with the mortal attention. It was always amazing to watch an Immortal take off into the air or move an object weighing a ton with their bare hands.

After finishing her report, she heated up some leftover pizza and continued to watch "Titanic." Why not? Since she didn't have a love life of her own, why not watch a movie about a tragic romance that ends with the guy freezing to death in the North Atlantic Ocean. At least Rose had met Jack before the ship sunk. The way she was looking at it, her ship was sinking and there was no Jack in sight.

Chapter Four

"Be quiet Biscuit," Gray ordered the energetic dog in the backseat that was barking at every passing scene.

As if in defiance, the dog barked at him.

Gray shook his head. "Exactly why I don't like to bring him out in public."

Michael reached back and gave the animal a playful rub. He'd spent the last couple of days getting acquainted with him; he'd always wanted a dog. The creature was very active, hardly ever a dull moment with him.

"Traitor," Gray said as he glanced in the rearview.

They were headed out to get Michael some clothes and other necessities. It was a good half an hour drive. Gray lived at the edge of a rural area with a lot of hills. He had never liked living too close to the city.

"So you have no family that can be contacted? None? Uncle, auntie, brother..." he asked as he adjusted the volume on the country music that was playing.

Michael gave the dog a final pat. "Nope. I never even met much of my family. My mother was too ashamed of me to let me become involved with them. They were told all kinds of things, horrible things about me and I could always tell when they came around. You would think that I had a contagious disease of something."

"Seriously?" Gray hadn't come from the perfect family but he'd been raised to be family oriented. The treatment Michael had received from his family was senseless. "So you never got a visit while you were in there? Not one?"

"Nope."

The older man gave his bald head a rub. "Can't imagine. I grew up with a younger brother and an older sister. Both of 'em 'bout drove me crazy."

"Where are they now?" he asked.

He was making a turn on to a street that would take him into town. "My brother died back in '89 in a car wreck. Mama took it pretty hard, never was the same after that. She passed a few years later. My sister married some Chinese guy after college and moved to China, been there ever since. I hear from her from time to time. I got family all over the place; they have get-togethers and whatnot. Sometimes I go, most times I don't."

Michael couldn't relate to the idea of such family functions. Maybe one day though.

"What about your father?"

Michael was looking out the window. "Dead before I was born. I asked my mother about it once, said she didn't want to talk about it. I never asked again."

Biscuit barked again, obviously feeling left out of the conversation.

"Oh give it a rest will ya," Gray said over his shoulder.

A few minutes later, they pulled up in a small shopping plaza with several stores. It was about two in the afternoon. It wasn't as cold as it had been and the wind was low. They had both agreed that Michael should stay in the car. It was possible the news coverage was still showing his face.

He was playing with Biscuit when he first saw the man walking towards the car; at first glance, he thought nothing of it. Suddenly the dog began to bark aggressively. His gaze was on the approaching stranger.

He got the strangest feeling and it was in that instant he knew the stranger was coming for him. He was about to open the door when the entire structure was snatched right off. He was pulled from the car so fast and thrown against the side of another he couldn't follow the movement. The impact nearly knocked him unconscious and the world almost faded as he blinked several times.

The stranger was tall with dark skin and long braided hair; he wore loose dark clothing. "You do not have the blood of the Fallen but yet your power level is significant. Get up mortal; let us see who is the strongest."

To his surprise, Michael found he was able to stand, considering the huge dent his body had made in the steel he figured his back should be broken. It wasn't. He was also surprised to find the sudden anxiousness in his blood to fight; clearly, this wasn't a normal human.

"What are you?" Somehow, he knew this man had outlived a normal mortal lifespan; he could sense it. Was this the same person who'd been following him? "Why are you following me?"

"Following you? I didn't know you existed until a few moments ago." He flexed his fist. "But your existence is about to end."

The speed of the fist coming at him was beyond human capability. He shouldn't have been able to register it but he was. The Immortal had covered a distance of several feet in the blink of an eye. Michael blocked the attempted strike but couldn't stop the one that followed. The blow knocked him back into the car he'd

41

already damaged. He kept his senses about him enough to see the flying knee that was coming towards him. He rolled off the car and moved causing the car to receive another dent. People were beginning to look their way, taking notice of the disturbance. Some moved towards it, and some moved away from it.

The art of fighting wasn't new to Michael. He'd been practicing martial arts since he was a kid. The one thing he was actually grateful to his mother for. What was new to him was his ability to move just as fast as his opponent was. He had no idea how he was able to keep up. Unfortunately, the Immortal was a far more seasoned fighter.

Michael moved towards him with coordinated strikes that never landed. He launched an elbow at his opponent's face. The Immortal shifted to the side and countered with a sidekick to the head. He was hit in the side of the face and sent flying out into a more open area away from the parked cars. As soon as he stood, he had to duck a powerful spinning heel kick that was rapidly followed by two more. He could literally feel the force of wind the kicks generated. The fourth time the Immortal swept low and took Michael off his feet.

He hit the concrete hard. A wave of anger flooded him, he stood quickly, and before he could even think, he rushed the Immortal. His opponent, the smarter fighter, waited until Michael got close enough and rammed his knee into his chest. Before he could fall, the Immortal grabbed him by the throat, lifted him clear off the ground, and then became airborne. He went about ten feet up into the air and like some old rag doll slung Michael to the ground. At the sight of the flying man, many of the spectators had seen enough.

Was he dead? If he wasn't, he was supposed to be. How was that possible? Michael was positive a human body couldn't survive that kind of impact; every bone in his body should be broken. He laid there on his back looking up at the hovering Immortal, while listening to Biscuit barking.

"How disappointing." The Immortal remained hovering in the air. "You fight like a mortal and now you will die like one as well." He extended his arm out a little and opened his hand with his fingers spread wide. His palm developed a dim glow and flashes of a small electrical field appeared around his hand. He was building energy.

On his back looking up at the unfolding scene he could feel the Immortal's energy rising. The power of it alone threatened to lift him off the ground. He allowed his head to roll to the side, not wanting to see it coming. His eyes fell upon a red pickup truck parked not too far away and something made him focus on it. He was tired and breathing hard but he forced himself to focus and slowly he began to release the energy in his mind directing it towards the truck. Instantly the steel and metal began to protest as the unseen force came against it, bending it, and cracking the windows.

The Immortal's energy was nearly at its apex; he was only a moment from releasing his blast.

Michael had done this several times before but there was something different about this time. This time he was largely motivated by some sense of power that was alien to him. The truck lifted off the ground a few inches, wavered for a second, and then continued to rise.

The very moment the Immortal was about to release his energy, as if thrown by a giant, the truck was slung into him. He was knocked clear out of the air, and the truck crashed onto several cars before hitting the ground.

Michael stood weakly and looked around. He was certainly no stranger to the looks people were giving him. He spotted Gray standing by his damaged car holding back a barking Biscuit. The instant he started to walk over he felt the Immortal behind him; he had gotten back up.

The Immortal was furious. A low growl came from his throat. He was busted up real bad but to Michael's utter surprise, he was healing quickly. He was a good twenty feet away and in a blur of motion, he moved. His fist was drawn back; he had every intention of punching a hole right through Michael's face.

He never made it.

He came to a sudden stop, as Julius appeared before him right in his pathway; it seemed as if he just appeared out of nowhere. Instantly recognizing the power that was before him, he turned and fled, having no desire to fight this one.

Julius turned to face Michael. "Hello Michael, I think it's time you and I have a little chat.

***

Isabella hovered thousands of feet above the city of Atlanta in the cold air of the night. Her attention was north. She had felt the energy of an Immortal earlier and another but she couldn't quite place it. It was probably a new Immortal. The Fallen hadn't been seen in centuries and it was commonly believed that no more Immortals would be made. Maybe that wasn't true; maybe the Fallen had returned.

If two Immortals had been fighting earlier then it had to be the result of what was called the Great Desire. That was a state of mind that an Immortal entered when one stayed in the company of another for too long. They were created to be solitary and were

44

forbidden to reproduce. To be sure, this was so; the Fallen had instilled within their children a lethal magnetism of one another. This magnetic attraction would eventually drive an Immortal to kill his fellow kin. The Great Desire was a fatal disease among their kind.

There was no cure.

However, there had been Immortals who had fallen in love and taken their chances; they had paid the ultimate price. The race of beings wasn't completely anti-social with one another but many of them weren't willing to linger in each other's company for too long either.

Isabella had been twelve for eight hundred years and would remain so until the end of time. She hated the Fallen for this. They had confined her to this eternal state of youth. The body she was in was an Immortal prison and she hated it.

Immortals become stronger with time and despite her child-sized body, she was extremely powerful. She'd had her share of battles. It was in their blood to fight, regardless of what they were in their mortal lives. She was often picked on as an easy fight; the opponent would soon realize differently. She wondered again, who was fighting earlier and why one of the fighter's energy felt so different. She shook the matter away. If a fight came her way, she would be ready.

She always was.

There was another matter that had been nagging her that she wanted to tend to. She placed her sharp eyes on the city below and then moved in the direction of the motel Rachel was in. It didn't take long to get there.

She landed and headed straight for Rachel's door. She released her power and unlocked the door without ever touching it before walking in as if she had paid for the room.

Rachel was in the shower; she sensed the intrusion immediately. She stepped out on to the rubber shower mat, grabbed a towel, and wrapped it about her. She grabbed a shorter one and began drying her face and hair. She opened the door and stepped out barefoot. She found herself looking at her target.

Isabella was very pretty. She was built with a small frame and probably would've been petite as an adult woman. Her dark hair was long with waves, her face was heart shaped, and her skin was a beautiful golden brown. Her hazel eyes possessed the focus of a grown woman; they held a silent depth. She was dressed in a gothic fashion, black jeans and a tight black t-shirt that left her belly button exposed. She wore a lot of silver jewelry, black boots, and had more than one piercing.

She regarded Rachel with a look of scrutiny.

Rachel knew in that moment that all of the mental preparations she received in training were invalid against such beings. They knew they were being watched. They were beings of incredible power, of course they knew. She looked at the phone that was on her bed. She needed to get to it.

"I would rather we leave them out of this Rachel," she said perceptively. "Besides, they're not telling you the truth."

She was about to die; she knew it. She had insulted the Immortal child and now she would pay. Her death would be sad and unfortunate. She had no child, no lover, and she hadn't spoken to her family in years.

Isabella giggled. "Stop it. You're being silly. You're not about to die. Don't be such a pessimist."

She could hear what she was thinking? Who were these people? She reacted involuntarily; she didn't realize she was doing it until after she'd done it. She released her energy, directing it towards the Immortal.

Isabella's body suddenly jerked back as if she'd just received a hard push from a bully. She recovered easily. "Pretty impressive for a mortal girl." She took a few steps towards her and took in the sight of her body. "You have a beautiful body Rachel. I'll never have one like that." Her demeanor took a sudden change; she appeared to sulk and actually looked like a twelve year old. She turned her gaze back to Rachel and looked about her. "It gets lonely out there. You don't know what it's like; you really have no idea."

For the first time since she'd been aware of the Immortal's presence, she began to relax a little. She touched her face with the towel in her hands a few times; she was in no way prepared for this. This wasn't supposed to be.

"Your name is Isabella. You were born in the year 1348."

She turned her head to look at Rachel. "What else did they tell you about me? Did they tell you that we weren't aware of being followed? And did they teach you those little mind tricks to keep us from knowing?" She gave a quick shake of her head. "If you really want to know how to use your energy Rachel I will show you but not now. That's not what I want."

Rachel angled her head a little at the girl. "What do you want?"

Isabella dropped her head for a moment before turning back to fully face her. "What any twelve year old girl would want. I want to be friends." She smiled lightly.

In that moment, whatever this child was, Rachel caught a glimpse of the human she once was. She probably could fly and bend steel with her hands, but deep down, beneath the surface, she was still that little girl. She remembered her childhood and how things had been. Maybe things weren't so different for Isabella. She still wasn't ready to completely trust her but maybe she could see exactly where this thing could go.

Her superior probably wouldn't be too pleased with that but from the look of it, her superior had some explaining to do. There was always two sides to every story; maybe it was time to hear the other side.

Chapter Five

Victoria was curled up in the huge, warm, and comfortable chair in her apartment in south Atlanta. She had the place under one of her pseudonymous identities. The black chair was thick with a soft furry material and had a heating system within it. She was enjoying a romance novel while eating ice cream.

Her thoughts had still been troubled lately and she had also been aware of the Immortals fighting the other day. The energy of one of them was different. She didn't give the matter much thought because it was of no concern to her. It was probably the work of the Great Desire, the genetic disease the Fallen had so graciously blessed their kind with.

She had also given Matthew another thought; he was a convenient distraction, a pleasurable one too. There had been so many mortal lovers she'd indulged herself with over the centuries she couldn't begin to count. There had been some who had given her a worthwhile experience. They were brief moments and never lasted long enough to satisfy her inner longings and desire for true companionship. She could only take from those moments the short-term pleasure that was offered.

She had his number and decided to give him a call. He was busy but of course, he didn't mind if she came over. She got dressed and actually thought about flying over but she would arrive too soon and that wouldn't be a good look. She drove her car instead. Matthew lived out in Roswell in a nice three level home that was luxuriously furnished and had a top of the line security system.

Victoria was stretched out on Matthew's bed with her head propped on a huge pillow. She was enjoying the foot treatment she was receiving as his strong hands squeezed, rubbed, and massaged her feet. A lazy smile rested on her mouth.

"I take it your enjoying this?" he asked.

Her blue eyes lit up for a moment. "I think the enjoyment is mutual."

"Oh really?"

"Um hmm, really."

He kissed her ankle gently. "I think maybe you're right. I really have to like a woman for me to rub her feet."

"You just kissed mine so you must be in love."

He chuckled at that. The woman was truly electric. Everything about her seemed to spark a fire in him. She was mystifying. He was very accustomed to beautiful women; his father had passed the skill on to him. Since his earliest days of school, he'd been able to entice and even manipulate women with his words and charm. He was always in control…except for now. He could tell himself he was in control but it would be a lie and he knew it. He couldn't quite figure her out. She was a puzzle he couldn't put together.

"Victoria you still haven't told me where you're from. Or what it is that you do. I feel like I'm rubbing the feet of a total stranger."

She looked at him. She could hear the questions in his head just as easily as if he'd spoken out loud. The man had spent his whole life bouncing from woman to woman. Now was not the time for him to get serious. She used her toe to rub his chest. "I like you Matthew. I think what we have right now is a good thing. I like what we have. If I was to provide you with any truthful answer to those things you ask, believe me, things would change."

"I just want to get to know you better. I can't even buy you flowers because I don't know your favorite color of if you even like flowers." The contact of her touching him was turning him on and it was very distracting.

In her mortal life, she had loved flowers. "You should regard me no differently than the other women you've lain with in this same bed."

Why did he find that insulting? "You are not those women."

She traced her toe up to his throat and made slow circles. "What makes me different?"

Her voice was naturally husky. The sound of it was music to his ears. He watched her. She was wearing a red dress that stopped short just above the knees. The leg she had extended was long and beautiful. Her glossy black hair was tied back loosely.

"When I woke up the other day and found you missing I didn't mind at first but then I couldn't stop thinking about you. I had already given you my number but I didn't know if you would call or not. I wanted you to and that's the thing. After sex, I normally lose interest, a woman calling me or not doesn't even register. Mission accomplished. I know how cold hearted that makes me sound, but I'm just being honest. It should've been that way with you but it wasn't. It wasn't at all."

How sweet, she thought, but also how empty and pointless. She allowed her eyes to scan the room. It was very spacious with bright colors; there were several large portraits of beautiful women hanging on the wall. There was also a gigantic fish tank filled with various forms of aquatic life. "Touching. Sounds like you're having a change of heart."

"Sounds like I'm losing my heart." He took her foot back in his hand and kissed her big toe.

"You should be careful with who you lose your heart to."

He was quiet for a moment, his hands continued to move and he kept his eyes averted. "Have you ever been in love Victoria?"

That was the wrong question to ask. She was enjoying the present moment, the sight of him, the smell of him, the soft music that was playing. The question related too closely to the matter that had been bothering her lately, love, an old love. She had been sensing something of late that reminded her of a past lover. She didn't like to think about it because it was too much; the memories that assaulted her when she thought about him were draining. The memories also angered her when she remembered how it had ended, how they had come for him and snatched him away from her.

Matthew looked up to see the tears falling from her eyes. "Hey…" He changed position, moving up to sit beside her. He leaned in towards her with his feet still placed on the floor. "What's wrong? I didn't mean to make you cry."

She turned her head away. "You didn't make me cry. Someone else did; a very long time ago."

She turned back to face him and he traced a finger down the side of her face. She took his fingers and kissed them softly. She hated herself for this, for what she was doing. She couldn't love this man and she was wrong if she allowed him to believe that. He was filled with romanticism, which would really be a beautiful thing if she were a mortal woman. His infidelity and indiscretion were of no concern to her; even as a mortal, she knew how to tame a man. This was a strange development of conscious for her. In the past, she wasn't concerned with such matters; mortal men were for pleasure only.

So what was this? A change of heart maybe?

She touched his face and ran her fingers up to his short bangs and lingered there. He was handsome, he was in his thirties, but his face still carried a youthful appearance. "Promise me something Matthew. Promise me something and I will consider sharing some of my secrets with you," she lied. She had no intentions of telling him anything.

He sighed. "I'm listening."

"Promise me you won't fall in love with me."

"Ok, I won't," he lied.

She laughed and gave him a playful shove. "Liar."

She was smiling and the world was alright again. This was so new to him; he wasn't used to being so affected by a woman. Her smile could make all the difference in the world to him. "You willing to negotiate?"

"What are your demands?" she asked.

He kissed her lightly. "As long as I can kiss you when I want, touch you when I want, and have you in my bed when I want then I give you my word I won't fall in love with you."

She pretended to think about it. "I don't think I have a problem with that. Sounds like we have ourselves a deal. Wanna celebrate?"

"What do you have in mind?"

Her smile was pure seduction. "Wouldn't you like to know…?"
***

In another part of Atlanta Andrew was getting ready to head out. He'd had enough of Susan's irritating voice. The woman was impossible. She lived in a half a million dollar home and drove the finest cars, which she hadn't paid the first dime for. She lived the life that many women dreamed about or only saw on TV and all it had cost was some wedding vows. She had nothing to complain about. What woman wouldn't want to be in her position? The woman was ungrateful. So what he slept with other women? What did that have to do with anything? At least he was discrete about it and kept it away from home. What more could she ask for?

Their marriage had been nothing more than a convenient arrangement; it was all about appearances. They looked good together. The sex was a bonus. The kids were great when they came along but they were all in grade school now and would be off to college soon. The woman waited nearly twenty years into the marriage to start nagging him about things he'd been doing. Why pay attention now? Maybe, just maybe, if she'd paid attention in the beginning their marriage would've been salvageable. He was in far too deep to retreat from the situation. Susan was never supposed to know about the other woman. If he were forced to choose, it probably wouldn't be his wife.

It had all started with a bunch of rumors. If he was honest about it, he had no one else to blame but himself. He had allowed himself to get too comfortable around his mistress. Years of never being exposed had made him careless. All it took was one slip and finally that slip had been made. A friend of Susan's had seen him with his mistress out in public and the word had spread like a sexually transmitted disease. He'd managed to keep his cool about it when Susan confronted him but beneath the facade, he'd been sweating bullets. How much did she know? Who was the source? Were there any pictures? He was relieved to know it was only a rumor; there was no concrete evidence.

If he could just keep his cool for a few more days he was sure it would blow over.

It was getting late and he needed to get out for a while before he strangled his wife to death. He pulled out of his driveway and drove off a little too fast for a residential area. There were still children running about and playing in the street trying to take advantage of the last remaining minutes of daylight. After stopping at a stop sign, he turned and practically pushed the pedal to the floor. The sudden rush of speed felt good; he needed it. The street was empty; he would arrive at the next stop sign without accident or injury.

Or so he thought.

Isabella seemed to appear out of nowhere. She was in high spirits; her talk with Rachel had gone well. She had herself a new mortal friend.

It was just a blink, all he'd done was blink, and there was this little girl dressed like she was a part of some new age cult. She was just there all of a sudden; no one had been there a second before. At the speed he was going, he knew he was going to hit her; it was inevitable. He experienced a strong flush of fear. His reaction was natural as he hit the brakes but he knew it was useless. He fought with the wheel as the tires howled and the car swerved. The back end swung around and collided with the child. The impact took her off her feet and sent her body flying into a brick mailbox.

She was dead. He knew without a shadow of a doubt. There was no way she could've survived that. From the angle the car stopped in he had to look back to see the wreckage. The sky was a hot orange as the sun was finishing its slow descent into darkness. He was certain of two things. The child was dead and he was going to prison. He cursed and punched the wheel several times.

Just go, he thought to himself and hated himself for it. Was he really that cold? He should just leave, just drive away, and never look back. The loud screaming of the tires against the asphalt had alerted the residents who were beginning to stir. He couldn't go to prison, not now; he was only days away from being promoted to Vice President of his company. What was more important was his mistress was pregnant. He was going to be a father again.

Just one more glance back out of some twisted sense of respect maybe that would count for something he thought vainly. He was sure it was a trick of the eye but he thought he saw movement. One of her legs protruded out from the debris of crumbled bricks. The movement seemed deliberate. It had to be nerves; those last responses of the brain but something told him it wasn't. He experienced a moment of confusion, what should he do? The remaining fragments of his broken conscious urged him to stay.

He looked about; people were slowly edging towards the scene. Whatever he was going to do, he had to do it fast. In a hurried motion, he stepped out of the car and headed towards the body. He had only taken a few steps when he stopped abruptly. He was positive he was hallucinating when the girl simply rose to her feet as if she had just fallen off her bike. Her curly hair gave her a Shirley Temple look but it contrasted sharply with her gothic dress appearance. She was too young to be in an occult. The only signs of the accident were her torn clothing. There wasn't a single scratch on her, not a broken bone or broken nail. How was that possible?

This couldn't be happening.

"You were going to leave?" she asked calmly and took a single step toward him. "I'm just a little girl; you could've killed me."

What was he supposed to say? He had a bad feeling that something wasn't right with the child. She was no child. "What are you? You should be dead."

She tilted her head slightly and narrowed her eyes as a brick levitated off the ground and positioned itself next to her. "I died eight hundred years ago Andrew."

He didn't know which was more shocking. The floating brick or hearing his name. He stumbled backwards a bit. "How do you know my name? And what do you mean you died eight hundred years ago? That's impossible, you're only a child."

But he knew she wasn't'

"Am I?"

At blinding speed, the brick launched out and cracked into his shoulder, immediately dislocating it and shattering part of his collarbone. The pain was explosive. He leaned over but didn't fall as he screamed out. When he was able to look up again he was horrified at the sight of several more floating bricks.

As he turned to flee to his car for refuge, he was hit high in the back. Instantly the wind left him and he was certain he would pass out. He barely made it inside before the onslaught and barrage of missile bricks destroyed his car. There was nothing he could do but try to fold up and cover himself as fragments of glass flew everywhere. He pleaded for her to stop but his screams fell on the ears of an angry Immoral.

When she finally stopped, he was still screaming.

She walked out in the middle of the street and stood in front of the car. She appeared to observe her work. The hint of a smile touched the corner of her mouth but she wasn't done. The entire neighborhood was watching, some amazed, some afraid.

Andrew was in extreme pain. He viewed the child through the broken and cracked glass. Was she gone? She had to be, he couldn't take anymore.

He was wrong.

He heard the metal of the car groan as an invisible energy came against it, immediately he went for the doors, but they wouldn't open. He felt it as her power snatched the car from gravity and lifted it off the ground several feet into the air. It didn't take him long to realize what she was doing. She was crushing the car with him in it. He beat against the window, hitting at the areas that were badly cracked from the bricks. There was a loud grinding noise as pressure came against the metal, forcing it to bend and cave in.

No one standing around could believe what they were witnessing. They watched in absolute horror, as the car was smashed into a thin strip of metal. His helpless screams soon died out and the car dropped back to the ground.

Isabella looked around at the spectators. She looked at the children and briefly remembered being a normal child. That was centuries ago. She had the sudden urge to destroy them all and she knew she easily could, but she'd done enough. It wasn't their fault; she couldn't hate them for what she'd become, for what the Fallen had made her. It was true that mortals could be cold at heart, so willing to shed blood with no regard for the sanctity of human life. She was a child who had witnessed more destruction by mortals then a mortal man who had lived a full life could dream of. This was why they were always in need of a savior, someone who could save them from themselves.

She came off the ground at such a high speed it seemed she disappeared. Her mood had been disturbed; she would stay off the ground until her anger completely subsided. She didn't like using her power to harm; as long as she wasn't pushed, she was ok. If pushed too far, she could do far more damage than balling up a car. She could do a whole lot worse.

Chapter Six

Julius stood with his hands behind his back looking up at the huge deer head as if the dead animal reminded him of something. He observed it quietly. He wore a very expensive gray business suit with cuff links; the scent of his Italian cologne filled the area. His long hair was tied in a ponytail. He was tall with broad shoulders and very muscular. His eyes were dark as the night.

Michael stood not too far behind him watching him carefully. He doubted Gray was aware of it, but he could literally feel the strength of this Immortal's energy. Who was this man? And why had he saved him?

Gray was squatted next to Biscuit giving him a rub. "I'll let you two talk if you're ok Michael." He suddenly felt like a stranger in his own home.

Before Michael could respond, Julius spoke. "Stay."

Michael didn't know if he agreed with that. Gray shouldn't be involved in this but he already was. He was responsible for that.

There was an awkward silence before Gray stood. "I'm going to take Biscuit out back, make yourself at home."

"Do you have something to drink?" He was still looking at the deer head.

"Got some Wild Turkey. You're welcome to a glass."

"That'll be fine." He turned to face him. "Gratitude, for your kindness."

Gray grunted and headed off.

"Who are you?" Michael asked suspiciously.

Julius sat down in the single seat sofa, rested both of his arms on the arms of the chair, and crossed his legs like a gentleman. He nodded at the opposite extended sofa, the same one Michael slept on just days before. "Have a seat and try to relax Michael. I'm not your enemy."

He hesitated before moving. He sat down but he clearly wasn't relaxed.

Julius took a moment to look around. He had arrived at the home before Michael and Gray. The place was nice and cozy; it had a cabin feel to it. There were several other stuffed animals about and some family photos over the fireplace. "My name is Julius. I've had my eye on you for a while."

"I felt you back at the institution. You're following me. Why?" he asked directly.

"I don't think I can provide you with a truthful or a satisfactory response at the moment." His eyes continued to roam. "But there is something far more important I need to discuss with you."

He sounded like an old friend. Michael didn't trust him; he could still feel Julius' energy and he briefly wondered just exactly how powerful he was.

Gray returned with the bottle and two glasses filled with ice cubes. After pouring his own, he handed the bottle to Julius along with the glass. "Pour your own." With that said, he found himself another seat.

Julius did and then sat the bottle on a thin high table that stood near him. He took a drink and then studied the glass for a moment. His expression was distant. "I'm sure you're eager to hear what I have to say. Very well then. But once I'm done, you will have a decision to make."

He had heard it before, but Michael thought he could detect a French accent. He nodded his head in acknowledgement.

He took his eyes off the glass and looked at Michael. "My father was German and my mother was a French slave that was captured by a raiding party across the Danube River. This was before the House of Merevig or Meravech; this is the bloodline primarily responsible for the rise of Frankish power. At the time, the word French didn't exist, my mother was a Frank. I was born almost four hundred years after the death of Christ. At this time, the Roman Empire was suffering from a very bad strain of religious and political conflict. As I would assume you already know my people were barbarians, nomads who lived for a long time in the shadows of the civilized Roman world."

"I will not bore you with all the details, some of the information in your modern historical books is accurate, and much of it is far off the mark. The year 476 is recorded as the official year the Roman Empire ended and that my people were responsible for its fall. Neither of these is entirely true. You have heard tales of Huns in you history books I'm sure, an Asiatic tribe of nomads who were rather a little too bloodthirsty. The origin of my Immortality begins with my people having small battles with these strange horse riding warriors. The Germanic tribes, my people, lived north of the Roman world. These battles with the Huns pushed my people farther south, right up to the doorstep of the Roman boarders. Whoever the Huns were, they were fierce fighters and in truth, they are the actual catalyst for the decline of the Roman world.

"Historians would later term us as the Visigoths, coming from the west. We fought with the Huns for several years before our tribes began to weaken. It wasn't because we were afraid of these

Asian warriors, Imperial troops began to allow certain tribes to cross the Danube and take refuge within the borders of the Empire. It was due to division that was created by the illusion of comfort. Many Germans began to abandon the fight in hope of getting across the river to a more civilized world," he said it with obvious sarcasm. "There was nothing wrong with our own world. I think sometimes in our raids we brushed shoulders too closely with Roman ideology and culture. Too many of the Germans began to see the Empire as some kind of utopia. The ones that crossed over discovered rather quickly the futility and emptiness of such hope when the Romans began to express their racism towards them."

He took a drink and reflected on something for a moment. He regarded them both; he had their full attention. He placed his eyes on the fireplace and watched the fire.

"I believe to this very day we could've pushed the Huns back and who knows? Perhaps the Empire would still be intact..." He shrugged indifferently. "Funny. It was some of these same tribes that the Imperial troops let in that later revolted with Alaric who killed the Eastern Emperor Valens. Life can have such unexpected turns; wouldn't you agree Michael? He didn't wait for a response because he wasn't expecting one.

"I was thirty-five when my parents left with some of the other tribes to cross the river. It was my mother's idea. She begged for me to come but I was too much of a patriot. I would fight to the death and that is exactly what I did. That was the last time I saw my parents." Something passed in his expression, it could've been sadness it was so subtle and brief. Absently he turned his glass about.

"We fought them deep into the Romanian forest but as our numbers weakened theirs seemed to increase. I was placed in command of a small unit of men. We all fought bravely and we all died. I'm not sure if I am able to describe the experience of death, it's not a memory I cherish. I have never really had a need to put words to it. There is a sense of falling as some people have written about but there is something close that happens that mere words will do no justice for. It was while I was having this experience that the Fallen One appeared to me."

"Fallen One?" The questions seemed to burst out of him as if he'd been waiting to ask something. "What is a Fallen One?"

"The true question is not what the Fallen Ones are but who they are. What they are is something I nor the oldest Immortals I know have ever known. But who they are..." He tipped his glass in the air as if making a toast. "That is the true question. Aliens? Gods? The fallen sons of the Great Rebellion? To discuss such things now would deviate us entirely." He waved a hand dismissively. "Another time perhaps."

Gray was very intrigued with Julius' mannerisms and demeanor; he was the perfect gentleman. He took a quick drink from his glass.

"I will say this," he continued after a brief pause. "I can attest to the fact that much of what modern man considers to be myth is something much more. I have spoken with Immortals who lived before the Flood; they give a very different description of the ancient world than what your scholars do. They know nothing. The historical lenses they use to view the past are badly distorted with modern skepticism."

"There really was a flood?" Michael asked.

"Of course there was." He sounded as if he was shocked Michael would ask such a question. He continued with his narration. "The Fallen One came to me while I laid on the ground bleeding from more than thirty wounds. I was fighting off adrenaline and pure patriotism, my enemies thought me mad and perhaps I was. I wasn't conscious of the pain. I don't think I was conscious of anything but killing. Maybe this is why this mysterious being came to me, maybe it was madness that pulled him towards me that day. No Immortal truly knows why they are chosen for the gift of Immortality."

Michael didn't want to believe what he was hearing. Immortals. Fallen Ones. How were such things possible? He couldn't deny what was right before his eyes.

"I personally believe that it is something about mortal death that attracts them. I couldn't guess what that is, some Immortals died in battle, some died in their sleep. There is no recognizable pattern," Julius said.

"So how did he make you Immortal?" It was Gray. He rested his chin on his fist with his elbow in his thigh. "Did he do something to your body?"

Julius regarded him for a moment. "When I first saw him standing over me I thought it was another enemy making sure I was dead. But then I realized this wasn't the enemy or even another man. His appearance was far too bright and radiant. I remember thinking I was dead. He spoke to me and told me to get up but his voice was in my head; his lips never moved. When I got up my physical body was still on the ground. I had the most unnerving sensation as I stood there looking down at myself. He told me he was going to give my life back and make me Immortal. I was eager to have it done so I could return to the fight. But that wasn't the plan; that wasn't the plan at all."

"As if we were taking an afternoon stroll we began to walk right through the battle. I was infuriated as I watched my people get slaughtered and there was nothing I could do. I tried to attack him or at least I thought about it, but I couldn't do it. And it was then I began to realize the power this being possessed. The lesson he taught me that day wasn't realized until years later and that was the fact that mortal death no longer had any power over me. It is the first lesson that every Immortal learns."

Michael caught direct eye contact with Julius and found himself looking deeply into those two eternal holes of darkness. He caught a flash of something, something he recognized and could identify with. There was pain there, a deep pain. It was far deeper than his own but it was still the same. His entire life he had lived alone in his own mind, and had unknowingly become a prisoner. It was this pain, the pain of being alone and confused that he recognized in this Immortal.

Why was this so? Michael wondered.

Julius broke the connection and rotated his head in a circle while massaging his neck with his free hand. "I have seen the rise and fall of several Empires. I witnessed some three hundred years of a senseless crusade in the name of religion that accomplished absolutely nothing but bloodshed. I watched the Black Death nearly kill half of Europe. I watched the Reformation of the Protestants wound the corrupt powers of the Papacy. I stood in the shadows, as the ideals of men were reborn and expressed throughout the Renaissance. I even watched as this great sacred land was taken from its native people and become a world power."

"I nor any other Immortal has ever even attempted to be involved in these great moments of history. Do you know why Michael?"

He did. "Because it is forbidden by the Fallen."

Gray looked at Michael with a frown.

Julius gave a light nod. "We are given Immortality by these beings which would be considered by most a gift. It is this same gift that chains us to a solitary existence. It is not a gift and a curse; it is the gift that curses us. We cannot expose who we really are to humanity, at least not on a grand scale we can't. There will be no superheroes among us. The Immortal that attacked you today took a great risk, which was a foolish thing to do."

He had some questions about that but he would wait for Julius to finish. "But you have each other. Immortals I mean. So you're not completely alone," he reasoned.

Julius sighed heavily. "You would think. That would certainly be the case if the Great Desire didn't discourage it."

"The Great who?"

His smile was light. "It's genetic, an Immortal disease that we carry in our blood. If an Immortal stays in the company of another for too long he will become magnetically drawn to him, to the point where he will be forced to steal his life force."

Michael's frown was deep. "How do you steal a life force?"

"You kill him," he answered plainly.

"What? So you can't hang out with other Immortals because you get tempted to kill each other?" That was insane.

He spread his hands wide. "We do not get to choose what we are Michael. Immortal or mortal. We can choose who we are but not what we are. What do you suppose would happen if another sun entered our solar system?"

"That's impossible. Too much power and gravity existing in the same space; they would destroy each other," he said.

Julius lifted an eyebrow. "Not so hard to understand then, is it? The difference is the same. We are suns, and if enough time is spent around one another, we will become pulled towards each other. We are threatened by this so one sun must cancel out the other; it will boil down to which sun is the strongest. It is mostly true that which sun or Immortal is the oldest that determines the victor."

Even Gray was beginning to understand.

"There is one more final element to this genetic defect of ours. Once an Immortal enters the Great Desire, whether he kills another Immortal or not, he will gradually begin to lose his sanity." He paused. "In other words, it drives you into madness. There is no returning from it. This is the true reason we remain apart."

"Immortal insanity," Michael said it as if he was tasting something.

"Yes, that is definitely a way to phrase it. When this becomes the case the Fallen Ones themselves will come for that Immortal and take him."

"Take him where?" asked Gray.

The Immortal cast his eyes on the man for a moment and then with a quick toss finished his drink. "It is not important." He looked back to Michael. "I have shared a small portion of my story with you and now you know why my kind isn't recorded in your history books. We remain unknown, only the Ancients know of us and that is only because we tolerate their existence." He held up a hand to halt the question in his eyes. "You will learn who the Ancients are soon enough. I'm sure of it. Now is not the time."

"What is crucial for you to understand right now is my people will see you as a threat and they will move towards you to challenge you as you witnessed today." His tone changed. It wasn't conversational anymore; it was slightly ominous. "That Immortal hasn't lived a whole century yet which makes you fortunate. If he would've been half my age, he would've killed you with his first strike. But there will be others."

"Why me?" He was desperate to know. "What makes me as special? I'm not the first person to have telekinesis; they've been studying it for years."

Julius shook his head. "I can't answer that. Something like this has never happened before but one thing is certain. There is something uniquely different about the energy you possess. You don't know how you escaped from the Institution, do you?"

"It's still not clear to me. I only remember pieces." He leaned forward. "How did I escape?"

"You teleported. I know of no Immortal who can do such a thing."

He could remember traveling that night but he'd just assumed he was in a vehicle of some sort. "I can teleport?"

"Obviously so." Julius grinned. "And I intend to find out what else you can do. But first I must teach you."

"Teach me what?"

"How to fight an Immortal."

Chapter Seven

Cain was at his favorite Hawaiian resort. He was stretched out on the fold out pool chair with nothing but some colorful shorts on. He was bare foot and bare chested allowing the sun to rain its rays of warmth on him. He wore a pair of dark shades and in one hand, he held a fruity drink with actual fruit in it. His other hand was propped behind him. To his right a very beautiful Asian female reclined as well with a set of small earphones in her ear. She was just a tag along; he cared nothing for the woman.

"Sir."

He blinked out of his reverie to regard the house worker standing before him with a phone. He gave the man a nod and took the phone. He didn't appreciate the interruption and was ready to express his irritation but all that changed a few moments later.

"Are you positive?" he asked the person on the other end.

Cain ended the conversation and looked over at the female; he couldn't even remember her name. He waved his hand and snapped his finger at her.

"Hey…"

She gave him a disgusted look before pulling the speakers out of her ears.

"Take it in for a minute," he ordered with a toss of his thumb.

She was clearly mad but did as she was told.

He sat up and made a call. "We got a new development."

The other man was on the other side of the planet, it was in the middle of the night. He'd been asleep. He was a very temperate man but he was also a very dangerous man. "What is this about Cain?" His voice was thick with a Spanish accent.

"Michael K. Flint."

There was a pause followed by some stirring. "Estas Seguro? Are you certain?"

"Just got the call. He was spotted by a Watcher. He reported a fight." Cain scratched at his chest.

"A fight with who?" he asked.

"An Immortal."

Another pause. "He's getting stronger. Where is this Watcher now?"

"Still in Georgia," he responded.

"I want him on a plane to me within an hour. Who else do we have out there?"

Cain hesitated; he didn't want to involve her in something that could be potentially dangerous. He had plans to marry her someday; she just didn't know it. He couldn't lie to Lucas either. "Rachel Anthony. I'm not sure she has the experience."

"Contact her," he cut him off. "Tell her to stand by for a change of duty."

Cain silently cursed. "Got it."

"And Cain…Your vacation is over. I want you in Atlanta by tomorrow morning. If this is really our Michael, we'll need every resource available. See it done."

Cain sighed deeply after the call ended. He looked at his fruit drink and thought, Oh well, so much for this. He stretched back out on the pool chair. If his vacation was being terminated prematurely, he would at least enjoy it.

He would use this time to think about his future wife.

***

Victoria was relaxing in a tub of hot water and bubbles, looking very much like some mythical goddess. She squeezed a rag over her out stretched arm and watched as the water cascaded down her arm. She was back in her apartment. She would go out again that night, maybe even pay Matthew a visit. She smiled to herself as the smooth 1930's jazz music played from a nearby speaker that had been installed. That was something of a ritual for her, her sacred time of reflection over the endless string of years. Sometimes she would think about a mortal affair in the 12th century with a crusading knight and at other times a soldier in the Civil War.

She hadn't been bothered lately with that strange feeling of sensing someone she knew and she was glad. The matter made her heart heavy. Perhaps Matthew had helped with that. It was a pleasant thought to have that she was having such an effect on him but it was also an empty one. He was falling in love with a shadow.

Her sigh was audible when she sensed the other Immortal approaching. "Hello Isabella," she said without looking up as the child entered the bathroom. "You could've at least knocked and pretended to have some form of mortal manners."

Isabella took in the scent when she stepped into the large black and white bathroom. It wasn't the smell of soap or the soapy bubbles and shampoo; it was the scent of a woman that grabbed her. A scent that would never come from her own body. She regarded herself in the mirror. She was wearing white colors today that didn't fit her normal gothic appearance.

Victoria watched the Immortal child; she was so pretty and would have grown into a beautiful woman.

"Am I pretty Victoria?" she asked while looking at herself.

"Of course you are dear." She resumed squeezing her rag over her arms, enjoying the feel of the dripping water.

"But not like you. Men want you. They want to touch you and feel you." She turned to face Victoria, leaning her back against the marble sink. "How does it feel Victoria? How does it feel when Matthew is inside you?"

"Isabella!" she said sharply.

"What!" she fired back. "I'm not a little girl! I'm eight hundred years old and no man has ever looked at me the way they look at you except for child molesters. I have never felt heat between my legs. They did this to me. I didn't asking to be saved from the Black Death. I didn't ask for anything. They gave me Immortality but look at what they took. Look at what they took Victoria."

Victoria regarded her while rubbing her limbs. The child's anger made her hazel eyes appear golden. She had known Isabella was following her, she always was. She had long since given up trying to get her out of her shadow. She would always be somewhere near.

Her heart went out to the child and she hated the Fallen for what they had done to her. "Honey…we can't change what we are. None of us can. I do not smile upon the Fallen for what they have given us. My heart grows colder towards them as the centuries turn. But we must accept our fate. Unless another Immortal kills us, we will live until the end of time; that is too long to hate what you are. Calm yourself, you shouldn't allow yourself to be troubled with such things."

She crossed her arms across her chest and looked away. She was angry and she needed to vent but she knew Victoria was right.

She tried to blink away the tears but they came and slowly she began to break down.

Victoria rose up out of the water, reached for a towel, and wrapped herself before wrapping her arms around Isabella. She held her while she cried; the child turned into her embrace and buried herself. She stroked the back of her head and rocked her a little.

She held her for a long moment.

Victoria cared something for the little girl who she'd known since the 15th century. As a mortal woman, she'd always wanted to be a mother but after becoming Immortal, the idea had perished. She didn't want to see herself as a mother to the child because for one this was no child. This wasn't motherhood but it was probably the closest she would ever get.

Victoria had been drinking on a glass of red wine; she retrieved it and offered it to Isabella. "Here."

Isabella took it and backed up to the marble sink where she composed herself. She laughed suddenly. "I feel like an old woman."

The moment had passed. Victoria grinned and sat at the edge of the marble bath. She dipped a hand in the water and made circles. "We are both old women." She waited a moment. "You ok?"

She kept her eyes on the water; she knew what she was talking about. "Yes, but I'd rather not talk about it. I have told you many times Isabella, you must be mindful of coming around me or any other Immortal that's older than you are. It's dangerous."

"I know. I've felt it too but I wouldn't let it make me hurt you."

She looked at her. "You wouldn't have a choice in the matter," she said it very seriously, but then she had a sudden change of mood. "I have an idea. You wanna go out with me tonight? Just us two Immortal old women?"

She brightened at that. "Really?"

"Sure. I can show you how easy it is to break a man's heart." She frowned at her suddenly.

"What?"

"Have you seriously dressed like that for the last eight hundred years?"

She regarded herself. "What's wrong with the way I dress?"

Victoria shook her head. "You've got a lot to learn sweetie, but don't you worry. I'm almost two thousand years old; I think I can show you a thing or two."

***

Rachel was riding on 75 north headed to northeast Georgia listening to some light rock. She was still wondering why her orders had changed, did they know she had violated standard procedure? She doubted it. Cain would've mentioned it; she was sure. She could've taken Georgia 400 but she wanted to extend the time a little to do some thinking.

She had enjoyed her talk with Isabella. There was really nothing mysterious about her at all, despite her unbelievable age, she was still just a child. She had listened to her talk about two hundred-year-old memories that she had read about in historical books. They had talked as girls. She couldn't believe how human these people were. Behind the mystery of what the Fallen had done to them, their humanity was still intact. The picture the Ancients painted of them made them seem like gods. They were humans trapped in Immortal bodies.

There was a quality of isolation that was associated with them, to a very small degree she could relate to that. She knew what it was like to be different and to exist outside of the popular social stings but their case was a bit more extreme. They had developed the skill of living among mortals in such an incognito fashion. She wondered how far up they went in a hierarchical sense. Did some of them work in government? She didn't think so and even if they did, the only line of work that would best suit them is espionage.

Isabella had warned her of the Ancients. She had told her they were not to be trusted. She had called them a bunch of clumsy scientists who were trying to play God. What exactly did that mean? And she still couldn't understand why the Immortals tolerated them, why not do away with them? If she were Immortal, she wouldn't allow someone to follow her around all the time.

The child had only wanted to talk. She wanted to talk to another female without having the unwanted desire to kill her. It had taken her a few minutes to relax in the company of the Immortal but she eventually did. In her three years of working the field, she had never been that close to one, her energy had been so dominant. She still couldn't believe she'd attacked her and Isabella had merely shrugged it off. She offered her a chance to learn how to use her ability better and she was actually considering it. She would have to be careful with that. If the Ancients discovered her secret involvement with an Immortal, there would be consequences.

Rachel was aware of Cain's feelings for her. She knew he was attracted to her. After her orientation, he had practically abducted her to be her mentor. He had made his efforts to impress her obvious with his easy access to the organization's funds and his extensive knowledge of the bloodline. Her classroom setting had been more romantic than formal. Cain was also a powerful telekinetic and on several occasions she'd felt him releasing his energy against her. At that time, she didn't know telekinesis could be used in such a manner. Cain was good, for a mortal, he had good control of his ability, which he also tried to impress her with.

On one occasion, he'd subtly tried to release his energy against her more private and secret areas. She had released her energy so violently it sent him clear across a room into a brick wall and broke his arm. The situation never really bothered her. To her, it was no different from the women who were hit on in some corporate office by a top executive. She could complain about it but as long as he didn't cross any serious lines, she could deal with it.

She was sure he would try to shield her from any serious reprimand or punishment if discovered but she still wasn't sure, how high up his influence went. She still wasn't exactly sure how high up the society went and who was in charge. She wasn't sure if she wanted to know.

Her hotel room was already booked. She had the location on her GPS. This area was near the mountains. She would be away from the city for a while but she didn't mind. She was told she would be looking for a mortal this time.

Michael K. Flint

Who was he? And when did a mortal take priority over an Immortal? She would do as she was told. Her annual vacation was coming up in a few months. She could go wherever she wanted and she was looking forward to it.

"In the Air Tonight," by Phil Collins came on. She loved that song. It took her mind off current matters. She wondered what she was waiting on as the song played. Phil said he'd been waiting on that moment all his life, maybe she was too. Maybe she would soon find out; she certainly hoped so.

***

Julius hovered thousands of feet above the ground over north Georgia. His clothing and hair flipped about in the wind. His mind was clear and focused. He was facing east, looking towards the Atlantic. There was something stirring on the other side, no doubt being drawn to Michael's unique energy. It was an Immortal he knew too well.

His Immortal enemy.

He had no desire to see this Immortal again because they would fight and they would fight to the death. One of the very reasons he'd been careful not to raise his energy too high is because he didn't want this Immortal to sense him. That was also a part of the reason he stayed off that side of the planet. This made him consider Michael more carefully. What was his relation to this mortal? The magnetic effect Michael's energy was having on other Immortals was puzzling, nothing like this had ever happened before.

Those of his blood were naturally drawn to energy but this was something else, something more. It was as if Michael's energy was literally calling them. This could be a dangerous thing. It was believed among his people that if enough Immortals came together and raised their energy they would awaken the Quiet Ones.

These were the very first Immortals ever made.

These Immortals had been put to sleep before the Flood by the Fallen Ones themselves. They had become far too powerful. They also had been mortal once. It was believed that the cell structure of their physical bodies couldn't contain the power it received. Their bodies had mutated into incredible proportions; these humans became a monstrosity.

He saw a plane coming from the south heading north. It would come near him but he wasn't concerned in the least. The stars were out, the sky was littered with them, and he glanced up at them as he heard the engines approach. He sighed deeply after it passed. This legend was so old many Immortals wondered if there was any truth to it. Was this merely a scare tactic invented by the Fallen designed to keep them from gathering? What would truly happen if his people came together?

He looked again toward the Atlantic. "It seems we may get to battle once more old friend," he said with a light flex of his fist.

He wouldn't think of it now, his focus would have to be Michael. He was only mortal. He would have to bear that in mind as he trained him. He would push him and he would push him hard. One or two things would happen. Either he would die as a mortal or he would become the first mortal to kill an Immortal.

Now that would be a slap in the face to the Fallen. He smiled to himself and raised his power.

Chapter Eight

Gray tossed the Frisbee out one more time in his backyard. Biscuit gave a bark before running after the flying object. It was the beginning of February; it was cold for this but the dog had seemed to insist. He brought the Frisbee back faithfully, tail wagging anxiously, and dropped it at his master's feet.

"No, I'm done. You can hang out here if you want. I'm headed in." He gave him a quick rub on the head.

He walked up to the back door, opened it, and gestured for the dog to go in. Biscuit sat on his back legs and looked the other way. If the dog could talk, he would certainly call him a traitor.

"Suit yourself bone head."

Gray headed up to his room and went to his workstation where he worked on his books. He sat down in the chair with wheels and tapped a finger on the mahogany desktop while staring at the blank screen of his laptop. The recent events of the last few weeks had his imaginative juices flowing. A good writer always used what was factual to write a good fictional story. The things he'd recently discovered were real and were unbelievable. He had actually met a man who was alive before America was discovered. Idealistically, he could write in any direction he wanted to with such facts. The only real challenge would be the change of genre. He wrote murder/mystery but this would have to be a fantasy story.

He had already called his agent earlier to find out what was popular in the market and what stories were having the best sales.

His agent had emailed him a couple of popular fantasy book to give him something to go off. He would scan through them later.

There was a picture of him and Betsy at a ski resort in Colorado. He had his arms around her. They were both smiling and waving. The memory hit him hard.

"I miss you Betsy girl. You wouldn't believe what I've gotten myself into. I met a man that can move things with his mind and evidently teleport. He has a friend who was alive when they were crucifying Jesus and doesn't look a day over thirty." He smiled at the picture as he held it in his hand.

A strange impulse hit him and he was certain it was Betsy's ghost. She was always bugging him about staying in contact with his sister and now he had a sudden urge to call her. He hadn't called his sister in years. He looked at the time; it would be early in the morning where she was. He picked up his cell and played with it a few moments before he realized he was stalling.

"Ah, get it over with Gray."

He called.

"Hello?" There was a hint of agitation in the high-pitched voice.

"Hey it's me."

"Gradie?" The agitation dissolved into disbelief and shock, resulting in excitement. "Oh my God! I can't believe it; my little brother is still among the living."

"It hasn't been that long." Had it?

"It's been six years Gradie," she informed him. "I'm sorry I couldn't make it to Betsy's funeral. I never got a chance to tell you that."

He had never called and given her the chance. After losing Betsy, he didn't have much of a desire to keep in touch with anyone.

"It's ok Alice. It's not as if you live on the other side of town. How have you been? How are Bruce Lee and the kids?"

She laughed at that. "It's Hong Lee and the kids are fine. Actually, they're planning a trip to the states. They've never been, maybe you could show them around? I've always told them about you. You wouldn't believe how excited some half-Chinese kids can be about having an American uncle. They've wanted to meet you since they were little."

"Really?" He had never thought much of being an uncle with his sister's kids so far away and his brother had never had any. "When are they coming?"

"Sometime around the summer. It's all they talk about."

"Where will they be staying?" he asked.

"New York first, then Atlanta. They'll leave from California."

"Maybe I can catch them while they are in Atlanta?"

"Great." She sounded hopeful. "Is this your number?"

"Yeah."

"And what about you Gray? How you been? Are you still writing books?"

"Actually I've got a few new ideas I'm playing with now. I'll probably start writing on it sometime this week. And yeah, I'm ok. Not much going on these days," he lied. "I went up to Johnny's grave on New Year's, celebrated most of the day with my kid brother."

"You two were always close. I miss him and mom." Her voice was touched with a bit of emotion.

But not Dad, he thought. Neither of them ever missed their father and never spoke of him.

83

What was only intended to be a brief call turned into three hours. He was a bit surprised to discover he missed his sister. He was glad he had made the call. He had never been good with his emotions, he placed fault on his father for that. He didn't consider himself emotionally unavailable or dysfunctional; he'd just rather not deal with them. Betsy used to nag him to death about that. She knew that underneath it all there was a man with a good heart and that was exactly why she had married him.

He would be looking forward to meeting his nephews and nieces. Alice had five children and he had none. Did he regret that? Of course, he did but there was little he could do about it now. He promised his sister he would call more often and keep in touch and he actually meant it that time. After hanging up he began to jot some ideas down. He was in a better mood and ready to write. Considering his sources this would have to be the best book he would ever write. The characters weren't exactly fictional; they were living in his house.

***

In a small town right outside of Nashville, there was an old plaza that had been alive once with commerce. There were several department stores. The architects responsible had a vision when the economic status of the small town seemed to be rising. At the time, the area was experiencing an influx of diverse people but for some reason, it died out as things usually happen and business began to dwindle. Eventually the place shut down as the owners took their business somewhere else. Now the area was empty and abandoned. A couple of stray cars were parked in the vacant lot along with the tall light poles that were in bad need of maintenance. The plaza sat at the end of a main street.

Devon remained in the air until the sun finally disappeared. He came to the ground slowly, landing in the center of the empty lot. He was tall and lanky with long, thin hair. His loose clothing was pearl white while his skin was a dirty white. His triangular face sported a finely trimmed mustache and goatee. He knew he was being followed; he'd sensed the other Immortal three states back.

He wanted to battle.

He was six hundred years old; he had fought and won many battles against his own kind. He could raise his energy to high levels. Every Immortal took a risk when they began to raise their energy, if they couldn't contain it, it would destroy their physical bodies. The challenge was to raise it high without self-destructing.

He was well aware of the other Immortal landing several feet behind him. A strong gust of wind suddenly brushed against the ground near him as he released his power; his clothing flapped like the American flag on a pole. He turned to face him.

"You seek a fight. You must be in the Great Desire?"

There was no required time limit for the Great Desire to take effect. It could be a matter of months, or it could be a matter of minutes. It depended on the Immortals involved. The other Immortal was bigger and taller. "No. I was drawn to this region by a strange energy. I thought it was you but I see clearly I was wrong." His voice was a deep baritone.

So he had felt it too, Devon thought to himself. "And what do you suppose is the meaning of this strange energy?"

He shrugged. "Perhaps the Quiet Ones have been awakened." He released his energy. "But at the moment, that is not important. We have business."

In a blur of motion, Devon attacked; his body seemed to disappear from the sheer speed. The charging fist was blocked by the larger Immortal. The impact created a light shock wave. In a matter of seconds, he launched fifty more, driving his opponent back. The force behind each strike could've easily went through a brick wall. He followed his final punch with a lightning fast spinning heel kick. He missed as his opponent ducked. He continued his spinning motion and dropped into a sweep but the Goliath saw the move and came off the ground, going twelve feet into the air.

Devon looked up at him. "We can fight up there or we can fight down here. Doesn't make much of a difference to me."

His body shook with a chuckle. "Your immortality will end tonight little man. Come on up."

Like a missile he came off the ground and launched another assault but the Goliath remained defensive, either dodging or deflecting blows. An electrical field began to build around them, the glass of nearby cars began to creak, and the light poles that were working began to flicker. He took careful note of how huge his opponent's biceps were. He knew he couldn't afford to wrestle with him. The Goliath could probably squeeze the life right out of him. He would have to use his speed until he could get a chance to release a blast of energy. He wasn't using his top speed, not yet.

The Goliath suddenly began to take the offensive approach but it was controlled, he knew he couldn't match his opponent's speed. His strikes were incredibly powerful, to make contact once could be fatal, and eventually he did. He caught Devon in the lower rib with an elbow strike. He grabbed him with one hand and slung him down into a car.

Pain exploded in his body as he crashed into the vehicle completely destroying the metal frame. He growled angrily and tore himself loose, in a fit of rage he kicked the badly damaged car several feet over.

The bigger Immortal descended. The two faced each other; they were both breathing hard and sweating. Devon was bleeding.

"I am as old as you Immortal. I am Kalieth." He pointed to himself. "I stood at the side of Genghis Khan when the Mongolian people knew no equal."

"You will know one today Mongol."

The battle intensity reached a new height as Immortal aggression was released. Their energy manifested explosively. Devon suddenly winked out of existence or at least appeared to. When Kalieth saw him again, he was seeing ten Devons or so it seemed. Like strikes of lightning, he assaulted Kalieth from every possible angle with his fist, feet, knees, and elbows. He came at him with everything but still holding back, not wanting to empty his tank too soon. He was landing some solid strikes but his opponent was a giant of a man. It would take a lot to bring him down.

Finally, with a defiant roar, moving with a speed that defied his enormous size, Kalieth blocked an incoming kick to the face and responded with a powerful hook. Devon's body sailed into a company pickup truck and caused it to slide several feet over. He exploded with a roar of his own; he grabbed a hold of the badly smashed door and slung the entire truck at him. The giant easily dodged it but barely weaved the fist that followed.

The battle raged. Kalieth snatched Devon and tossed him into the air only to fly up above him and beat him with powerful punches back to the ground. The pavement cracked, sending debris and loose rocks flying in all directions. The Goliath remained on top, raining down groundbreaking punches. Devon deflected some; some he didn't.

Devon knew he couldn't stay in that position, with a grunt he managed to roll while delivering a sharp elbow to Kalieth's face. He was on top but he had no desire to ground wrestle with this behemoth. He pushed off, going high into the air but then descended after creating some distance.

Kalieth rose to his feet, he spit blood from his mouth. "I tire of toying with you. I will break you Immortal! Tonight the Fallen will come for you."

"Then let them come." Devon began to visibly raise his energy, creating a storm around him.

Kalieth watched for a moment as his opponent's energy began to build. His low growl escalated into a full-scale roar. His body lost its definition as he moved towards Devon with a drawn fist that now flashed with electrical currents. He had to fight through waves and waves of Devon's exerted energy, with a vicious snarl he pushed through.

The second his fist landed where Devon's face should've been he knew it was over. Devon was directly above him with his arm stretched out towards him and his hand open. A beam of light shot forth into Kalieth and exploded, killing him instantly.

He descended back to the ground and prepared himself for what he knew was coming. He dropped to one knee and bowed his head.

A portal of light appeared before the fallen body of Kalieth. Before the otherworldly being stepped through Devon could feel the divine presence. He kept his head down while Kalieth was taken, knowing he couldn't stand it if he wanted to. If he so much as tried to move an inch the Fallen would take his life without a thought.

He stood when he was alone again.

He sighed deeply. There would be more battles to fight, some he would win, some he wouldn't. He wondered briefly again about the strange energy that now he knew they had both sensed. What was it? Whatever it was, it was drawing Immortals to it. That wasn't a good thing; it certainly wouldn't end well. He would eventually die, he knew that, but after being alive for six centuries, he couldn't complain.

Chapter Nine

It was a beautiful day. There was a chill in the air, but it wasn't freezing out. The sky was clear with an occasional cloud drifting. They were in a huge clearing, in the lower region of the Appalachians. The area was full of wildlife. It was home to black bears, bobcats, rattle snakes, as well as a host of other creatures. To their east was a dense forest that gradually rose into a sharp incline. South of them, cut deep into thick woods, there was a rapidly flowing river that snaked its way into a northeastern direction.

"You ready?" Julius shouted to Michael, who was at least fifty yards away.

He placed a little more pressure on the bow he held and slowly exhaled as he released its arrow.

Focus, Michael told himself moments before the projectile was released. He had to clear his mind and concentrate. His focus needed to be completely on his ability. His heart began to beat in a steady cadence with each beat taking him deeper into the clarity of his own mind.

His objective was to control and stop the arrow with his mind. He wasn't sure if he would be able to do it. The fact that he had already attempted to do so nine times and failed convinced him even further that he couldn't do it. He didn't share the confidence that Julius seemed to have in him to control his ability. When the arrow was released he attempted to focus the energy in his mind directly on the miniature missile. At the last possible second, with the arrow being only inches away from his face, Julius quickly moved.

Crossing the distance in a blink he stopped it and held his pose for a brief moment before stepping back.

"You just died again, Michael. Counting this time I've managed to kill you a total of ten times. You need another cat." He grinned and said.

"What is that supposed to mean?" Michael asked, his voice dripping with frustration.

Instead of answering Julius dismissed the joke with a wave of his hand.

"Julius, we've been at this for hours and I haven't been able to do it! I just can't release what's in my mind that fast. Unlike some people I haven't been alive since King Tut was a kid. I need more time."

"Me either. That was B.C., I was born in A.D.C" He replied in a sardonic tone.

"Whatever. The point is you've been doing this a lot longer than me." Michael said as he stuck his hands in the pockets of the brown slacks he wore along with a gray thermal. Unlike Julius, the cold actually bothered him.

Julius tapped the side of his face with the arrow before saying, "The problem is you're still thinking like a mortal."

"Because I am a mortal. A bullet will kill me as will a speeding car, a strike of lightening... You get the idea."

Julius pointed the arrow in his hand at Michael. "The night you escaped from the institution how did you do it? What did you do in your mind?"

Michael frowned as he tried to remember. "I don't know. I had been looking at some magazines of different places in the world. Japan. Egypt. Just a lot of different places. I remember thinking about those places later; wanting to be there and then suddenly I was bouncing from place to place. I couldn't stop it, nor could I control it. When I finally stopped I was standing naked in the middle of the street." His eyes roamed as he talked before they settled directly on Julius as he continued to speak, "Somehow, don't ask me how, I sensed you."

Julius didn't understand that part either.

"The other day when you were attacked by the immortal, what did you do in your mind?"

Again Michael frowned as he tried to remember. "Nothing, I just reacted," he finally said.

"Precisely. In both cases your mind simply reacted to what it perceived as a threat. You didn't think about it, you just responded." Julius explained and continued speaking. "You could've escaped that place a long time ago, but you didn't because it didn't bother you. As time progressed the confinement and containment began to threaten your sanity. When the threat become credible your mind reacted. The same happened with the Immortal. It didn't take as long for your mind to react because the threat was more immediate."

Michael remained silent as he attempted to digest what he was hearing.

"It's all about perception. Perception is everything." Julius continued as he looked around taking in the beautiful scenery of nature. A group of birds suddenly took flight from some distance trees.

He sat the arrow down and tied his long hair into a knot. "Let's try a different approach." He said elevating himself ten feet into the air, as he came up from the ground with ease.

Michael groaned, "I seriously hope you're not considering what I think you are. There's no way I'm coming up there!"

"Did you know that after Constantine became a Christian he was no longer a god?" Julius asked as he looked down at Michael.

Michael stretched out his hand and said, "I don't get it, Professor."

"Constantine was never a god to begin with. He was perceived as one due to pagan beliefs. Pagan perception made him a god, while Christian perception made him a man. The key word here being perception. Truth is not always relevant. As a matter of fact sometimes a thing is true only because a person perceives it to be and not because it actually is. Do you know who Nicolaus Copernicus was?"

"The cousin of Christopher Columbus?"

Julius shook his head helplessly. "He was one of the men who were responsible for changing a major perception about the earth. Before his time people believed that the earth was flat and that if you sailed to far out you would fall right off the face of the planet. If you would've told a navigator in the 15th century that he could just sail across the Atlantic Ocean to the new land he would've thought that you were mad. The simple truth wouldn't have been enough. A single truth can be perceived ten thousand ways, but in a manner of speaking only one will get you across the ocean.

He's a scholar, Michael thought. There was undeniable reasoning in the Immortal's words that he couldn't dispute. "So in the language of the common people, you're telling me that I'm looking at this all wrong?"

Julius nodded his head and said, "Exactly. Although you're not an Immortal you seem to possess the power of one, so you need to think as one."

As he observed Julius' form suspended in the air he could feel his energy resonating. "Okay, Einstein. How do I get up there?"

He folded his arms across his chest and replied, "What's holding you down there?"

"Gravity." Michael said as he looked about as if he could see it.

"So, focus on it and release yourself from it." Julius said, making it sound so simple.

"I can't see gravity, so how am I supposed to focus on what I can't see?"

"Reality is not always defined with visibility. You have never seen gravity, yet you've never attempted to walk off a bridge or a tall building. Why? Because although you've never seen gravity you still know that it exist. The fact that we can't see gravity doesn't change the fact that it's real. You don't need to see it to focus on it, you just need to acknowledge its existence. Now, Michael, focus on that which you know exist."

Deciding to at least give it a chance, he took a deep breath and closed his eyes. His breath evened out as he focused on what he knew to be real instead of that which he couldn't see.

When he wanted to move an object with his mind he simply pushed his thoughts towards that object. He began to do the same with gravity. He clenched his fist and flexed his fingers causing the muscles in his arms to tense as he pushed against the invisible force that held him to the ground with his mind. The sounds of nature became fainter as his mind centered in on the task at hand.

He emptied his energy into that single thought as he pushed with everything inside of him to free himself from the control of gravity. He'd never attempted something that required such an intense focus, therefore it took all of his concentration to maintain his focus. He thought he felt something but couldn't be sure. He didn't dare consider it and risk breaking his concentration. It seemed as if hours had passed when in reality it had been only a few minutes. Starting to feel as if he was going to pass out he opened his eyes and immediately swung his arms out to maintain his balance when he realized that the ground was no longer beneath his feet.

"Look, I don't..."

"O ye of little faith."

Michael wobbled a bit in the air while looking around in disbelief. "Whoa! Am I really doing this?"

"Of course you are! You're not hanging from strings. Now you just need to find your sense of balance without gravity and adjust your equilibrium." Julius informed him.

Looking worried he asked, "How do I do that?"

"I watched as you fought the Immortal and noticed that you have experience with Martial Arts."

While fighting not to wobble he responded, "Yes, since I was young. I continued to practice while at the institution. Why?"

Julius just smiled.

Even if Michael would've seen Julius' flying fist coming towards him he doubted that he could've dodged it. Normally he would've fallen to the ground, but being that the dynamics were different, considering he was ten feet in the air he couldn't. Instead he found himself shifting backwards. Julius hit him several more times before he was finally able to get a block up. However, when he attempted to throw a punch of his own he wobbled again. While momentarily distracted by doubts of whether or not a punch, if landed, would have any real effect on him Julius suddenly grabbed him by his shirt and tossed him in the opposite direction causing him to fly out a good fifteen feet.

As Julius glided over to Michael he stated, "The rules change when you're fighting off the ground. As a fighter, you should already know that fighting is all about balance. That being said you don't have the same balance up here as you did down there." He pointed to the ground. "Up here you have to assimilate your balance. In other words, you have to create your own."

Breathing hard Michael said, "Create my own? Are you serious?"

"What does gravity do, Michael? It holds you down which allows you to find your balance. Up here you have to depend on what we consider as artificial gravity to find your balance. You have to find your balance up here or you can't fight up here. If you can't fight up here you'll never be able to fight an Immortal and win."

He couldn't follow Julius' movement when he moved. He sensed the Immortal behind him, he turned to block the strike he knew was coming and wobbled again. He was hit square in the face. He did his best to defend himself against the assault that followed, but failed miserably. He simply couldn't find his balance. Every time he managed to deliver a strike it was ineffective. Julius laughed at several of his attempts which only infuriated him.

This continued for two hours. For Julius it was two hours of amusement, for Michael it was two hours of frustration. Finally, Michael collapsed and crashed to the ground.

Julius descended with ease to the ground. "Well, that was absolutely terrible. If you was fighting with the weakest Immortal he would've destroyed you despite the fact I believe you would be stronger." He sighed deeply. "Focus. You must find and master your ability to focus. Immortal or not, you will not be able to channel what's in you until you do."

Lying on his back, Michael gave the thumbs up sign, as he looked up at the sky. "Can we leave now?"

"Sure we can." He smiled as he floated back into the air. "After one more round."

***

"He's one of our own." A skinny female store worker said.

Rachel glanced slightly over her shoulder and said, "Excuse me?"

The store worker moved a little closer and replied, "That book is by Gradie Bentson. He lives here in Martin, up near the mountains."

Rachel looked at the book she held. It was titled 'A Killer's Motive'.

Today was only her second day in the small town. The bookstore wasn't far from the hotel she was staying in and since she had always enjoyed reading she decided to check it out. She normally kept a good novel with her anyway when working out in the fields, there was nothing like a good story to pass the time.

"Oh. I usually read romance, but decided I'd give something different a try."

The girl smiled, displaying a set of pretty pearly white teeth. "Oh, he's good. I'm sure you'll like it. He's a funny old guy, with a crazy dog. He was married, but his wife passed on a few years back. She was such a sweet lady. You just missed out on a chance to meet him. He was just in the area a couple of days ago, with a black guy. There was some kind of crazy fight. Everybody's talking about it. They say some guy showed up and ran the other guy off. My friend Lisa was there and she claims a car even moved by itself. I don't believe it. Cars can't move by themselves. What planet does she think we're living on? She…"

If it was one thing that Rachel hated it was a female who couldn't shut her mouth, but in this case she didn't mind the woman's loose lips. She looked at her name tag and cut her off. "Jessica, when did you say this all happened?"

"Maybe two days ago?" She said unsure of the exact day.

"And this Gradie, he was with a black guy? You're sure they were together?"

The store clerk's head was bobbing before she even spoke. "According to my friend Lisa they drove off together, probably headed back to his place. She said that she had never seen the black guy before, that she didn't know who he was. Said he was cute too, but she thinks my brother is cute also so…" She made a face of disgust. "That don't mean nothing."

She was probably the gossip queen in high school. Rachel thought as she listened to the woman carry on.

What was this all about she wondered. Who was this Michael person? If he was just a mortal than why was he so important? "Let me ask you something, Jessica. According to your friend how exactly did the car move itself?"

She placed a hand on her hip and shifted her weight from one foot to the other and said, "Lisa said that they were fighting and that the black guy wasn't doing so good. Somehow he ends up on the ground, right. Now, here's where the story gets crazy. She said the other guy jumps really high in the air and like... stays up there. I mean seriously, who can do that? Well, next she said this car or was it a truck? Yeah, it was definitely a truck. Well, anyway, it comes off the ground and hits this guy who's still in the air. Being hit by the car knocked the guy down, but it also pissed him off. He got up, but before he could retaliate the new guy arrives and he ends the fight. Go figure, huh?" She gave a short laugh at the absurdity of it all. "Lisa was probably high cause ain't no way that happened."

From the sound of things Michael was fighting an Immortal. Rachel wondered why Cain had failed to mention this tidbit of information. It was becoming obvious to her that Michael was no ordinary mortal, which had her becoming more curious about the matter. Cain hadn't told her much and her new instructions on how to proceed had been brief. She was told to contact Cain immediately once she located Michael. As usual she was given strict instructions not to engage, only to follow and watch.

There was something going on that he wasn't telling her, which didn't surprise her since she wasn't a part of the inner circle. She was just a field agent, a watcher. She realized that Jessica was still talking and wondered if the woman ever stopped.

"Thank you, Jessica. I think I'll buy this book."

Before heading back to the hotel she went and bought her a bunch of snacks and junk food that she would probably jog off later. The hotel had an inside gym with all sorts of exercise equipment.

Dressed in purple with her hair pulled into a tight ponytail Rachel also had on a pair of white sneakers and some tinted glasses to shade her eyes from the brightness of the sun. As she leisurely strolled back to the hotel she took in the small town. In her observation she noticed that it was a typical small town where everyone appeared to be friendly and everybody seemed to know everybody. She also noticed that there were a lot of Hispanics.

Making it back to her room she welcomed the warmth inside, as the temperature had began to drop with the setting of the sun making it a little chilly outside. After putting away the things she had purchased she settled in on the bed with the book she had gotten. She skimmed through it briefly before reaching for her laptop and typing the author's name in.

"Let's take a closer look at you, Mr. Gradie. Maybe you're an Immortal too."

When she was finished checking him out she would then see what she could find out about Michael. If he wasn't Immortal than what exactly was he? She didn't know, but she intended to find out.

Chapter Ten

There were some Immortals who took their chances with The Great Desire and fell in love. Even for beings such as these the power of love proved to be incredible. Such cases were rare, but they did exist. When The Great Desire began to take effect they would separate for a great length of time, sometimes for a span of a hundred years, just to weaken the effect of the Immortal disease.

Victoria could sense them before she saw them.

She was on 285, after spending all morning with Matthew, headed back to her place. He had been able to charm her again and had placed her in a rather pleasant mood; until now. This strange new energy was affecting Immortals all over the globe, even she had felt a slight pull from it. What was this? Whatever it was it was getting stronger and stronger. These two Immortals approaching her now probably thought that it was coming from her. She shook her head at the bad timing. Not only had she just gotten her hair and nails done but she also had on tight clothing. She wore a pair of black leather pants with a matching short t-shirt that left her belly button exposed along with an expensive pair of boots.

It was just a little after noon and traffic was still light. About a mile up ahead of her Jason was running towards her. He maneuvered with ease through the traffic. Some of the vehicles swerved as drivers jerked their steering wheels to avoid hitting the Immortal. An eighteen wheeler suddenly appeared before him and he quickly shifted around and slid under its trailer. A blue Nissan was waiting for him on the other side. Barely pushing his feet against the ground he sailed up and over it. As he landed another car was there, then another, and another. He moved off reflex, dodging the oncoming traffic effortlessly while leaving a wake of colliding vehicles behind him.

Spotting Victoria sitting about five cars away Jason used his mind to release a burst of energy that sent the cars in his path flipping to the side of the road. Like a bull seeing red he charged full speed ahead at the two door sports car she drove. Upon reaching her car he dropped his shoulder and rammed it into the front bumper instantly sending the car flying over him. High in the air the car flipped over several times before slamming back down into the concrete and continuing to flip over, causing traffic to go into a bigger frenzy. Brakes were slammed on in an attempt to avoid colliding with the fallen car. Through it all Jason stood in the center of the road waiting for Victoria's tumbling car to come to a stop. Although the structure of the car was completely totaled he knew that she was alive and well inside.

He couldn't help but grin when the badly damaged door suddenly without warning flew from its hinges and she emerged. No Immortal ever backed away from a fight, no matter the odds, it simply wasn't in their blood to do so.

The call to battle was urgent so without any preliminaries it began.

He knew that older Immortals were stronger and faster, but he was still caught off guard when the fist, that he never saw coming, slammed into him and lifted him off his feet sending him crashing into the door of a car. He slammed into the car with such force that it caused the driver inside to flee as the door's window shattered.

There was a car near Victoria, its occupants long gone, that had been flipped on its side during all the commotion. She reached over and snatched its front tire off with one hand, as if she was tearing off a piece of tissue, and launched it at Jason. If not for the sudden appearance of his lover, Valenia, and her catching it the tire would've taken his head completely off.

Valenia threw the tire back and followed closely behind it with her attack. The tire was easily dodged and her attack was greeted by a strong defense. She continued to press her attack as she waited for Jason to recover and join in on the offense. She attempted to deliver a high kick to the face, but Victoria caught her by the ankle and slung her away.

As soon as Victoria released Valenia's leg she was met by Jason jumping in the air with a forceful kick intended for her neck. It never landed. Instead she dived to the ground and rolled right under him. Keeping her momentum she came off the ground with a flying kick of her own. By the time Jason realized what was happening, her kick was connecting with the back of his head sending him crashing down again.

Out of her peripheral vision she saw Valenia flying towards her fast as a rocket. Glancing at a vacant Toyota she released her energy and brought it up in the air and positioned it in front of her like a shield. Valenia crashed into it head first at a high rate of speed causing her to crash to the ground next to her lover.

Rising off the ground Victoria floated into the air several feet and poised herself ready for battle. She looked in the direction of the fallen Immortals, knowing that they would get back up, and waited. As she waited she decided to raise her energy level up. She knew

105

that it was dangerous and that she could possibly kill herself if she wasn't careful.

She felt that she had no choice.

Although Jason and Valenia weren't as old as she was they were each close to a thousand years old, which meant that she would need the extra energy to defeat them both alone.

She closed her eyes and began breathing evenly. In her mind she concentrated all her energy causing it to build and grow stronger. Her increased energy manifested itself instantly and a sphere of electricity enveloped her. The sphere grew in diameter and intensity until it enclosed her completely in a bubble of power. The air around her generated an incredible wind speed and pushed at all the cars remaining nearby causing them to slide back and away from the surrounding area. A low growl from deep inside of her rose until it was a powerful scream, which was followed by a powerful sonic boom as her energy level surpassed another barrier. The electric field that she was creating had consumed so much gravity that it began to lift the scattered vehicles in the vicinity off the ground. She was pushing the levels of her energy so far that that her body was fighting not to rip itself apart.

Jason and Valenia both stood as they attempted to resist the push from the force of Victoria's power. Ascending into the air they begun to raise their energy as well, but it didn't manifest itself in the same manner as Victoria's had.

With Jason taking the lead and Valenia attempting to shadow him they attacked. Victoria allowed them to approach. She blocked and weaved away from the strikes he threw at her as she reserved all her energy for Valenia. Looking for a better angle to attack the two lovers circled her trying to find an opening.

The human eye wouldn't be able to monitor the fight that was going on in the sky. They would only be able to glimpse brief flashes of light that were followed by a thunderous booming sound.

Jason managed to get behind Victoria. Valenia immediately took advantage of his new position and rammed her knee into her opponent's stomach. The pain she caused was blinding, but Victoria refused to fold to it. Instead she let out a feral growl as she snapped an elbow behind her to Jason's face. Reversing the motion she did a complete spin and hit Valenia with the same strike. Jason shook the blow off, but his lover tumbled to the ground.

Wasting no time Victoria turned her offense on him attacking with a flurry of strikes. Jason knew that there was no way that he could keep up with her. By himself he knew that he was no match for her. In a consecutive succession he managed to block twelve of her strikes, but when he finally was able to fire one back she wasn't there. Unawares to him she had moved behind him. Once there she dropped her body low and she shot an open palm strike into his lower back causing him to drop to the ground like a fly that had been swatted with a fly swatter.

She sensed Valenia's approach from behind and gathered her energy into her hand causing it to light up like the light atop of a Christmas tree. With the grace of a professional pitcher, she turned and slung a ball of energy at the Immortal knocking her back a hundred yards.

Again Victoria was left floating alone in the air posed for battle.

Appearing torn and disheveled Jason fought his way back to his feet. His battered and bruised body was bleeding from several deep wounds Victoria had inflicted upon him. Looking around his eyes spotted an eighteen-wheeler carrying a chained down load of huge tree logs, further down the interstate and an idea came to him.

Slowly he ascended back up into the air and spoke. "You are a powerful Immortal, Victoria. The blood of the fallen is strong in you."

"You shouldn't have challenged me. I am not the source you seek," she said watching him intently.

He shrugged and said, "We are Immortals. We were created to kill and destroy one another, much like the mortals below us." He looked away from her and noticed Valenia in the distance getting back to her feet. "Something is happening. Some Immortals believe that The Quiet ones are awakening. If so we are all doomed."

A smile cracked her mouth and spread across her face. "You are doomed now."

Valenia approached and for a brief moment there was a standoff, since no Immortal would ever back down. Jason telepathically signaled to Valenia to attack and without hesitation she did. Before joining his lover he used his energy to release the thick chains that held the tree logs down. A single log levitated up and aligned itself with its target.

Victoria was well aware of the movement, she knew that she was in trouble, but she couldn't afford to divert her attention.

Valenia understood her lover's intent. He was trapping Victoria in her position then they both would press her until he was able to fire the log.

He timed it perfectly.

As he fired the log he slightly shifted his body creating an opening for the log, which was aimed directly at the back of Victoria's head.

Victoria's reaction was pure instinct. She turned and intercepted it with a fist causing the wood to explode and shattered leaving her entire hand throbbing. The move cost her dearly as both Valenia and Jason rained blows down on her before she recovered and quickly got back on defense. She tried to position herself so she could keep the tree truck in her line of vision, but her opponents prevented it.

She sensed the release of energy before she saw another log levitating up in the air. Things were about to go bad and she knew that there was nothing to do to stop it. In light of the fact that Immortals lived for several centuries, death was never really a scary prospect. If this was how her Immortality was to end, so be it.

It wouldn't be easy. No, it wouldn't be easy at all.

***

Isabella was walking the streets of Manhattan, New York. She came here often just to get lost in the multitude of people. There were so many different groups and races of people here. She enjoyed being able to just disappear in the sea of faces like she was just another face. She also liked the fact that everyone seemed to be headed somewhere important and that no one would stop her to ask her where she was going. Walking the streets of New York made her easily remember when she walked the crowded streets of London in the same manner two hundred years ago.

She had often used her beautiful young looks, not to mention the powers of her mind, to deceive the rich into adopting her. She had even lived in the castles of some of England's most famous royal families. Of course it never lasted. How long could you be twelve before people started asking questions? She couldn't honestly say that she'd enjoyed those brief moments of luxurious living, well at least not in the way that a human would. She was an Immortal, the blood of The Fallen that ran through her veins wouldn't allow her to form any real social bonds with mortal women, except for Rachel. She really liked her. She was different and was closer to understanding what it was like to be Immortal than she even realized.

She didn't like the fact that she was a member of the Ancients nor did she understand why her kind allowed their existence. If it was up to her, she would destroy them all. She made note to remember to speak to Rachel again when she returned to Atlanta.

She spent some time looking in the windows of the different fashion stores at the items that were on display, visible for all to see. She watched as beautiful women laughing and giggling, sometimes even gossiping with one another, as they did their shopping. She thought about how that would never be her; she would never possess a body that she could show off or flaunt while hanging out with her friends.

She thought about Victoria and how beautiful she was. There were times when she had viewed her as a friend, something like a mother figure. She had met her in during the 15th century in Europe when it was recovering from the devastation of The Black Death and The Hundred Years War. She'd been living in different small towns along the Baltic Coast, where at the time the fishing business was plentiful and flourishing. Sometimes she would even journey on the trade ships, traveling on the open seas for months at a time.

Often some of those ships had carried expensive furs from the East along with other luxuries of that time. Victoria would drain the ships of their goods while they were far out in the deepest waters of the sea. Isabelle happened to be present on one particular ship one night. She had sensed Victoria before she even got near the ship. She originally thought that she would have to fight, but quickly found out that Victoria was only interested in robbing the ship. That night they talked long into the night and it was then that their friendship was sparked.

She didn't feel alone anymore after that. She had wanted to return to Southampton, England, which is where Victoria lived at the time, with her, but of course she couldn't. So instead she made it a habit to always go out on the ships in hopes of encountering Victoria on one of her raids. Eventually she did follow her back to England.

She had been in her shadow ever since.

As she stood looking into the window at the latest designs of Victoria's Secret she thought she felt something, but dismissed the feeling as quickly as it came. She was standing wondering what the sexy material would feel like against her skin when she felt it again. Recognizing what the feeling was she raised her energy level causing a powerful violent burst to explode and shatter the entire store front window.

***

Deep up in the mountains, near Virginia, Julius hovered like a cloud at a summit above a particular region. The cold air of the high altitude had no effect on him whatsoever as he meditated, trying to keep his mind clear of something that was always threatening him. Something he'd come into contact with years ago. It was like the lingering remnant of a disease. It would've destroyed most Immortals a long time ago. The only reason it didn't destroy him was because his focus was too sharp and powerful to allow his mind to bend to it.

Immortals were beginning to stir around the globe and Michael was the cause of it. They were drawn to him for some reason. He still hadn't figured out his connection to him or why his energy was so different, stronger than theirs. That Immortal shouldn't have had any problem defeating him, yet he did. There was something in him, something powerful.

He wasn't really concerned with his people fighting, they would always fight each other. They were designed that way. It was a matter of disturbing The Quiet Ones. Did they really exist? There was no immortal walking the earth that had ever seen one; they thought that it was a legend. What if it wasn't? Many years ago he'd once met an Immortal so old that he could raise his power level so high it could draw meteors to the earth. He spoke of The Quiet Ones, but he had never seen one either. Was it possible The Fallen ones themselves had planted the legend to keep their children from raising their energy to high? It was highly unlikely. The Quiet Ones were real.

He sighed deeply as the inevitable had finally come, he had been avoiding this day for over three hundred years. She needed him and he would have to go to her. He didn't want to because he knew what this would mean. He knew that once he saw her beautiful face, looked into her eyes, and heard her voice he would be snatched back into her world. There would be no walking away. He would be taking the same risk he'd once took three centuries ago. It would be dangerous to be that close to her, was he strong enough to resist it? Was he strong enough to resist the Great Desire?

Had three hundred years of separation been enough time to build a sufficient barrier against it?

He had met her in Paris in the early part of the 17th century. Louis XIV, the Sun King, was the ruler of the time. He had just moved the capital from Paris to Versailles. It was a dozen miles away and he had a vast palace more than a third of a mile long. It had taken forty-three years to build. Julius had fought the entire thirty years in the Thirty Years War. He wasn't supposed to but he had literally watched the French Nation form from its embryo stages. He had felt compelled.

They had traveled Europe together, appearing to be a normal mortal couple. They went everywhere and had visited all of the great works of the time. The Adoration of the Magi by Botticelli, The Last Supper by Leonardo da Vinci, and The Frescoes for the Sistine Chapel by Michelangelo Buonarotti, and even the famed St. Peter's in Rome. They had to separate often and he hated not being able to smell her hair or touch her skin for the briefest moments but it had been necessary.

But it hadn't been enough.

He couldn't see it but he knew she was fighting and the two she was fighting were no different than what they had been. The Great Desire was a powerful thing, but nothing could compete or compare with the power of love. He felt the rise of her energy and knew she was probably in trouble. It was dangerous for an Immortal to raise their energy to such heights. She had been in fights before and he had avoided getting involved, but this time was different. She wouldn't win.

Slowly, his eyes open.

He began to raise his energy and the very sky above him began to darken. The Beast had awakened.

Chapter Eleven

Michael looked up from the list of groceries he'd been instructed to get, someone was following him. It was amazing how you could tell when someone was doing that. It was almost as if you could literally feel their eyes on you. He looked down the aisle he was currently standing in. There were three other people in the aisle with him, an elderly lady, who was looking at some oatmeal, and a mother and child looking at the cereal.

He wasn't in the same exact area where he'd fought the Immortal, but he was close to it. Had someone recognized him from the other day? It was a small town after all. He doubted it. Plus Gray had sent him down in another car while the other one was being repaired.

He was wearing a white sweater, some faded jeans, and some white sneakers. His facial hair was neatly trimmed and groomed. In front of him sat a portable shopping cart that was already half full. He glanced back at the list and noted that he only had a few more items to get. He hadn't been grocery shopping since he was a kid.

He moved on. Pretending to look at the list he held in his hands, he kept his eyes lowered as he watched people as they shopped. He wasn't as good as Julius, but he could extend his energy out without causing a catastrophe and drawing any unnecessary attention. He had just about convinced himself that he was overreacting when he reached the checking line and saw her.

He stood rooted to the spot as he gazed upon her standing near the exit pretending to read a newspaper a portion of her hair slightly covering one side of her face. On the other side her hair was pushed back behind her ear. Her skin was the color of cream and she had a small frame with perky breast. Dressed in dark green colors, a light jacket, some boots, and a pair of designer shades on her face she stood with one legged propped up behind her against the front glass of the store.

She wasn't Immortal, like him she was telekinetic.

She looked up at him and even with the shades concealing her eyes there was an instant connection. Michael couldn't move, for him it was a quicksand moment. He had never looked at a woman and experienced such feelings. What was actually only a brief second seemed like an eternity as they looked at each other. Without a word she snatched her gaze away breaking the connection and left.

He nearly forgot to pay for his items in his attempt to follow her. He quickly grabbed his bag of groceries and rushed out of the store. Once outside he scanned the small crowd of people in the parking lot, easily spotting her heading to a car parked at the rear of the lot. He took note of the distance. If he ran he could catch her, but then he decided that there was even a better way to catch up to her.

It was time to see if his training was paying off. The trick to teleporting was maintaining the thought of the location until you actually arrived at there. If at any time, even the last second before arriving, the thought was interrupted you could end up anywhere. Teleporting could be a difficult thing to do if one didn't focus. The other day, for instance, he was supposed to have teleported ten feet in front of where he originally stood, but somehow he had ended up in Africa instead. He'd had a few successful attempts, but not enough to say that he had the hang of it. He could end up by her car, but then again he could end up somewhere in the Atlantic Ocean.

Narrowing his eyes he relaxed his breathing, and quickly ingrained the desired destination into his mind before closing his eyes completely. Slowly he began to raise his energy and released it as a thought of teleporting. He felt a tingling sensation followed by the sound of rushing wind as the gravity around him began to change. The sensations lasted a few seconds and then he was gone. Just as she was reaching for her car door Michael suddenly appeared behind her.

Sensing an intruder she reacted instantly without thought. Spinning she delivered a sidekick to his throat causing his back to hit the side of a van parked next to her car. With her balance remaining perfect she eased the pressure of her foot on his throat without removing it.

Michael could have easily blocked it, but he decided not to since he was the one intruding on her space. "Sorry, I didn't mean to alarm you." It was hard talking with her foot to his throat.

While still holding her position she asked, "Who are you Michael?"

She knew his name? He thought with a frown. "How do you know my name? And can you please remove your foot?"

She didn't budge.

How had he just done that?

He was just about to say something when he suddenly looked off and saw a woman walking towards him. He groaned loudly instead. The woman was Immortal.

*****

Victoria was badly hurt and she knew it. The huge log had crashed into her upper back breaking and shattering bone. The

117

severity of the damage caused her power level to drop and Valenia instantly took of advantage of it. She vehemently attacked, hitting her with several vicious blows, but still Victoria did not concede. She refused to give easily.

As Valenia continued to press her attack Jason backed off and prepared another wooden missile with the intention of killing Victoria with it. He aligned the giant log with perfect precision as he allowed his energy to build to an even greater level. Seeing his lover was getting the best of her he released the log ready to deliver the final blow.

The fight certainly would've ended if not for Isabella appearing and intercepting the log with a powerful blow from her fist. With a scowl on her face the child Immortal flexed her energy causing it to flash visibly as debris from the exploded tree log fell around her.

Who was this? Her sudden appearance confused Jason, but he didn't have the time to consider it as the young Immortal exploded into action. In a blur she rushed him. Screaming wildly she forced him back with her viciously powerful strikes. She landed several blows to his face, dodging a hook from him she continued to batter his body with multiple combination of hits from her clenched fist. She moved about him with her assault. Her small frame made her lighter and faster causing his attempts to hit her to being futile.

Somehow Jason managed to maneuver himself behind Isabella and locked her in a choke hold. As he attempted to choke the life from her she positioned them both horizontally and used her energy to push off the air causing them both to fall to the ground. With him on the bottom his back crashed into the pavement causing it to crack and collapse to the indentation of his body.

She drove her elbow into his side, which allowed her to break free as he loosened his hold around her neck. Once free, in a frenzy, she literally tore a huge chunk from the Interstate's divider and operating off pure rage she pounded him with it.

There was no reasoning left in her, only madness.

At the sight of the child fighting to defend her something happened inside of Victoria's heart. The part of it that was still mortal was touched. She was so deeply moved that she was at the point of tears.

Victoria was badly wounded, but she couldn't allow it to be a factor. She had to fight pass the pain. A rage began to rise inside of her giving her the strength to block another strike from Valenia. In a mad rush she took the offensive. This was it. Having nothing else to give except anger she gave it with all that she had to give.

Isabella probably would've done some real damage if she had been an adult, but being that she wasn't the blows that she delivered to Jason had no lasting effect. Growling deeply he grabbed her by her throat and with incredible force he rammed her against an upturn car. As she struggled to break his hold he continued to ram her against it until he felt her body grow weak.

Victoria wanted to rush to her aid but couldn't. She was hard pressed herself with the attack that Valenia was lodging against her.

Valenia hit Victoria with a spinning heel that shattered her jaw. The blow was so powerful that it caused her to drop down in the air as her energy faltered. The staggering blow was followed by a brutal knee to the face, which almost rendered her unconscious. With her world growing dark Victoria knew that The Fallen would be coming for her soon.

Just as her world was coming to an end she felt him. The feel of him alone almost caused her heart to stop. She knew in that very moment that it was him. He was the one that she had been sensing and he had been there all along.

Time itself came to a slow crawl as every Immortal present felt his energy. Although they all felt his energy she was the only one who knew who and what was being felt. She smiled from the knowledge of knowing that at least if she was about to die she wouldn't be alone, both Jason and Valenia would be joining her.

Without warning the sky began to darken.

***

He would question his instinct to protect her later he thought to himself as he shoved her foot from his throat and stood in front of her. While standing in the small space between two parked cars, which didn't worry him since they would probably be used during the fighting, Michael prepared himself for battle as he watched the Immortal approached.

The female Immortal was tall with broad shoulders and short hair. She was dark as the night with a very muscular, also manly, build. Her energy was already raised as she moved with deadly intent. Her strides were short and slow.

Rachel took note of his protective stance. Furious because she didn't need a man to protect her she hissed, "What do you think you're doing? She's an Immortal. You can't fight her."

Tossing her a quick glance over his shoulder he responded, "If we survive this I would love to know two things from you. One, how do you know about Immortals? And two, how do you know my name?"

Shifting to get a better view of the woman she replied, "I… am going to survive this. She doesn't want to fight me. You're the only mortal that these people seem to have a problem with."

Who was this woman, he thought again, and how much did she know?

Suddenly realizing that he still held the bag of groceries in his hands he set it down. "Don't get in my way."

"You may need my help. I hear you didn't do so well with the last one." She said to the back of his head.

Yes, he would definitely be having a chat with her when this was over. Taking a quick look around the parking lot he suddenly become conscious of the people there. There were both kids as well as elderly people. There were even entire families entering and exiting the grocery store. They couldn't risk having a battle here, too many innocent people could get hurt. Also with this Immortal he could sense her age, and he wasn't sure that he could beat her.

Once she reached hearing distance the Immortal stopped and said, "Move, Mortal. This doesn't concern you."

Michael blinked in confusion. She wasn't there for him? She wanted him to move?

"I know who you are, Michael, but I have no interest in the energy you possess. My business is with Rachel." She stated and pointed at her target.

Rachel was just as confused as Michael. What could this Immortal possibly want with her?

Turning to Rachel he asked, "You know her?"

"No." She snapped back.

He scanned the area again before letting his eyes rest back on the Immortal. Without taking his eyes from her he said to Rachel,

"Get the bag and grab my hand." In a subtle fashion he extended a hand back to her.

Rachel regarded the hand with a raised brow wondering what he was planning on doing. Was he going to try to make a run for it?

He was asking her to trust him. Rachel couldn't remember the last time that she had trusted a man. However, he had stepped protectively in front of her, and she hadn't asked him to do that. She couldn't remember the last time a man had done such a thing for her; that's if one ever had.

She felt something then that she would later identify as the first real emotion she felt for him. Slowly, she reached out and grabbed his hand after picking up the bag.

"If we end up in Japan, we'll take a plane back." Despite the immediate threat there was a bit of humor in his voice.

She didn't know what he meant, but she didn't like the sound of it.

When he didn't move the Immortal shook her head and said, "So be it. You may fight like one of us, but the blood of The Fallen does not flow through your veins. You are nothing more than a mortal man." That being said she moved quick as a bullet with her fist drawn back.

He had absolutely no idea how things would turn out. They could be terribly wrong or exceptionally right he thought as he watched her approach. Focusing he pictured Gray's home in his mind before releasing enough energy to teleport both himself and his passenger. He felt the normal sensations and then they were gone.

The Immortal's powerful fist swung through the empty air and hit nothing.

*****

The forecast for the week had said nothing of a thunder storm so many of the residents of Atlanta were surprised by the fast changing sky. Moments before the skies had been clear with no clouds gathering which meant no rain. Now the entire sky above the northern end of the interstate looked electric.

The light of the Sun was dim in comparison to the radiance from Julius' form as he descended in a dynamic fashion over the bridge. His energy illuminated his appearance and made the area around him explosive. He appeared otherworldly, as if he'd just stepped through a dimensional portal, with his hair dancing around his head and the fabric of his clothing flapping about.

The center structure of the bridge exploded suddenly with the concrete, metal, and iron fragments moving up in the air instead of down towards the ground. The gravity of his energy grabbed at the materials causing them to float over to him and remain suspended about him. Bolts of lightning flashed above him.

He placed his eyes on Victoria and instantly his heart broke from seeing her body battered and bloody. Her clothing was ripped and torn on her body while her hair was loose and scattered wildly all over her head. She appeared worn. Her breathing was heavy erratic as she was on the verge of collapsing.

The word rage couldn't begin to describe the feeling that was building inside of him. There was no word that could ever describe such an intense emotion.

Jason dropped the nearly unconscious Isabella and charged up in the air at Julius. Valenia followed from another angle. In unison they attacked him coordinating their blows to create an opening for one another. Julius, however, was far too skilled for either of them and he easily maneuvered between the two while keeping them both in his line of sight.

Jason brought another log up with his mind, trusting Valenia to know his intentions he fired it instantly. Julius never broke his stride, at the last instant he released his energy and re-directed the log. It struck Valenia across her upper body and Julius followed behind it with a spinning elbow to her face dropping her right out of the sky.

Jason became enraged. Three vehicles suddenly came off the ground and positioned themselves in a circle around Julius. Jason released his energy with the intent of smashing Julius with the vehicles, but it didn't happen. Instead Julius flexed his power level and sent the cars crashing back to the ground below. Jason snarled and rushed toward him and found himself forcefully colliding chest first into the open palm of Julius' hand. He grabbed his chest as he crashed to the ground from the force of the collision.

Julius followed him down, landing just as Valenia was getting up. Giving a wild scream she sped towards him with the intention of hitting him with everything she had.

Deciding that it was time to end this Julius raised his arm and opened his hand. A white light appeared as he released a blast of energy into her knocking her to the ground. She was dead.

Julius lowered his power level before dropping to one knee with Victoria and Rachel following suit.

Frozen in utter mortification Jason didn't move an inch.

When The Fallen One came for Valenia's body it sent Jason completely over the edge.

"Don't touch her," he screamed. "Don't you dare touch her!" He screamed again even louder sounding like a raging lunatic.

A moment or so passed before a portal opened near him. Instead of light pouring out there was total darkness. Upon seeing the darkness he attempted to flee immediately, but got sucked in by the inner vacuum that the portal possessed. He screamed as he tried to fight against it, but it was in vain. His screams faded as he was swallowed up by the portal and it faded from existence, his fate sealed with its departure.

Isabella had witnessed the occurrence countless times before, but never had she heard the voice of The Fallen. The Fallen Ones only spoke to an Immortal upon his or her mortal death. She heard the voice telepathically, which seem to be their method of communication, and was highly disturbed by what she heard.

When it was over and all was quiet she stood to see Victoria in Julius' arms and her heart instantly warmed at the sight. They needed this moment of joy she thought because according to what she had just been told dark times were ahead of them.

Chapter Twelve

"What do you mean you lost her?" Cain asked as he held the man off the ground by his throat using his telekinetic ability, since he wasn't physically strong enough to do it with his hands.

The man tried to talk but couldn't, as a matter of fact he could barely breathe.

After a moment he let him go, but kept him suspended in the air with his power. "You were given simple instructions. It's a small town for crying out loud, how could you lose her?"

"I didn't lose her she vanished. She simply vanished. I believe Michael was responsible." He coughed a couple of times. He tried to move but couldn't.

"Michael?" They were together? A wave of jealousy hit him so strong he nearly exploded with rage. He calmed himself instead. He needed to think.

With a glance at the dangling man he released him from his power, he looked away as he fell to the floor. They were at his place at Peachtree Towers, one of his many lavish homes, in downtown Atlanta.

The man crawled to his feet while Cain sat down. He viewed the man a moment with a finger under his nose before calling out in an Asian tongue. The same female from the Hawaiian resort came from a back room.

She was dressed very sensually and provocatively in a sheer nightie. She was slim and thin with legs for days. She appeared to be in a much better mood than what she was in at the resort.

He spoke to her in her native tongue for a moment, asking her questions and then dismissed her. He looked at the badly shaken man still standing and ordered him to have a seat.

"Tell me exactly what happened, Oliver." He interlocked the fingers of his hands together and assumed a thoughtful pose.

Oliver had been trying to explain what happened several minutes ago, but all Cain had heard was 'lost her'. So he kept starting his explanation over.

Cain was a child, therefore he hadn't even been a member of the Society when The Flint Experiment was being conducted. He had been spending the last few days going over some of the records pertaining to the case. He had only been briefly acquainted with it before it was a high profile case. The case had been deactivated years ago since no one held any real hope of ever finding Michael. According to the mother he was dead, which was obviously a lie. He had to admire the woman's stamina. She'd been subjected to all kinds of torture and had never bended nor folded.

The love of a mother for her child, what could possibly compare to it?

If Michael truly was a success, meaning if his blood cells had actually bonded properly with what they had injected into his father, then there was not limit to how powerful he could become. Based on what he was hearing Oliver explain he was already able to teleport, something that no human could ever do.

His superiors were surprised to learn that all of this time Michael had been in a mental institution and that his mother had actually paid to have his admittance removed from the records, which explained why they had never found anything all of the years that they had searched for him. It was definitely a clever ruse on his mother's part.

In truth, he wasn't concerned with Michael. He was old business of The Ancients. His only concern was Rachel. How much longer would she deny him? He had attempted to use his power against her once, but she had repelled him. She didn't realize her potential or how far she could go if she would just trust him. He didn't want to hurt her, but maybe he would have to start dealing with her more aggressively.

Oliver, a pencil thin soft spoken man from the Middle East, who had finished speaking asked, "So, what do we do now?"

Cain looked up at him as if he'd forgotten that the man was standing there. "I need to contact Lucas. He wants to assemble a team to apprehend Michael once we have a definite location on him. I personally don't think that particular course of action is wise."

"Why not?"

"They Ancients are so blinded by their need to retrieve that which they lost that they are overlooking the obvious." After opening and closing his fists several times he continued. "Why would Michael suddenly want to escape from that mental institution after all this time? Also even if his powers are evolving on their own there is no way he's learning to control them on his own; especially not this quickly. The mind is no easy thing to master and control. The Watcher stated in his report that another Immortal intervened in their fight."

"Immortals don't usually get involved in Mortal affairs," Oliver stated beginning to follow Cain's line of thinking.

"So, why this one? If the report is accurate then this Immortal that came to his rescue had to be pretty powerful in order to make the other one flee. It is in their blood to fight! They never back away from a fight, unless they're relatively young." Cain looked off in thought. "What would such a powerful Immortal, one who has to be at least five hundred years old according to energy he was reported to have displayed, want with a mortal man?"

"Someone has to be helping him."

"An Immortal is helping him," he corrected. "Which is precisely why I disagree with Lucas' plans. The situation is doomed. Not even a thousand of us could begin to compare with the power that those beings possess. I have no intention of letting the woman that will someday bare my children become involved in this madness."

Oliver didn't allow his face to reveal the doubt he had for that happening. It was obvious that the woman he spoke of had no such feelings for him. "What do you intend to do?"

"Return to the area and wait. She'll call me to report in, and once she does the system will locate her. I'll send the link to your phone, you'll find her, and let me know who she's with. In the meantime I'll have to create a little leverage because she's not going to come willingly. I hate to play it this way, but she leaves me very little choice."

Oliver didn't know what he was talking about, but he didn't like the implications. He was glad to be dismissed.

The Ancients, like any other secular organization, had its darker side. They were called The Silent Death, a unit of assassins that could kill a mortal without ever touching them. Only top personnel could contact them, but he didn't need that. He had a mole on the inside. He made the call and when asked who was the intended target he calmly replied, "The family of Rachel L. Anthony."

***

Gray tossed another log into the fireplace and then looked at Biscuit who sat on his hunches. "It doesn't get any more exciting than this, does it?"

The dog looked at the fire and sniffed. All of a sudden, as if he was tired, he laid forward so that he now rested on all four of his legs.

Gray shook his head. "Man's best friend, huh? I've had better friends than you pal. There's a twelve year old in my house who can fly across the Atlantic Ocean and you don't want to talk about it? Don't forget who feeds and cleans up your poop around here."

Biscuit whined in response.

"Oh hush!"

Rachel came out of a door that lead to the lower level of the home and shut it behind her. She looked at Michael, who was seated on the loveseat with his elbows propped on his knees while leaning forward. "Victoria is fine and Isabella is still resting. Julius will continue to stay with them."

Michael looked at her still not exactly sure who she was, but knowing that he could trust her. He also still wasn't sure why he'd been so willing to protect her. He couldn't ever recall doing anything like that before. "We need to talk."

Rachel slowly nodded her head in agreeance. Her world was rapidly changing. Old boundary lines were being crossed while new ones were being made. The moment was fast approaching when she knew that she would have to choose a side. "Sure."

"That's our cue Biscuit. Let's give these people some privacy," Gray said.

Biscuit didn't move.

"You don't have to, Gray. This is still your home." Michael said.

He waved a hand. "It's fine. I've started on something and I need to get back to work on it for a few hours. Holler if you need me." He looked at the dog and with a little more authority ordered him to follow. Reluctantly Biscuit followed behind him.

Rachel walked over, but didn't sit down. Instead she looked towards the living room windows and out into the front yard. "In the few years that I have worked for these people I have never seen a mortal take priority over an Immortal. That is until you. For some reason you're important to them."

They had only spoken briefly. Julius had arrived with Victoria and Isabella shortly after them.

"I can't imagine why? I'm nobody. I just spent the last twelve years of my life in a hospital for the mentally insane. I've done nothing significant to have garnered the attention of the secret society that you belong to." It was all frustrating. What could these people possibly want with him? How did they even know of him? None of it made any sense to him. "Are you sure you were following the right guy?"

She focused her attention on something outside as she responded, "I just recently discovered that every Watcher or Field Agent has a photo of you, from when you were younger as well as an enhanced photo of what you may look like now in their data files. They were all told to call in immediately if they spotted you or even thought that they had spotted you. For some reason I was never informed of this and I intend to find out why. Michael, there's only one plausible and logical explanation for this and what's going on."

"This is not about you or at least if didn't start out that way."

He stood up. "What do you mean? If it's not about me then why are they following me?"

She placed her eyes on him. "It's about your parents."

"What?"

She walked a little to change her angle. "I was able to squeeze a little information from the system on you. Did you know that your father's death was medically unexplained? To this day his cause of death is listed as unknown. On top of that your mother has completely vanished. There isn't a single trace of her on file anywhere after she admitted you to the institution. No bank account, car note, or tax return. There's absolutely nothing. And if she's died her body was never recovered. That's rather odd for an ordinary woman living an ordinary life. What's even more baffling is the fact that the only proof that you were even admitted to that place comes from the news coverage of your recent escape. There is no existing record of her ever even signing you over to the state.'

He listened in awe, not able to believe what he was hearing.

"I don't think your mother put you in that place to abandon you. I think she put you there to hide you." She was nearly convinced that that's what had happened.

Memories of that day flashed in his mind. He could remember the hurry that she was in. He had always assumed that she was just in a rush to wash her hands of him. Maybe he had been mistaken. "But why? What could she or my father possibly have gotten themselves involved in that was so important? I went to a public school. My mom had a regular job and normal friends. I don't recall them attending any secret meetings or anything that would even suggest she was part of some silent organization."

"You don't know these people. I've been working for them for the last three years and I still don't have a complete picture of who they are or what they do." She placed her hands in the pockets of her jeans for a moment before taking them back out. "Isabella told me that they can't be trusted. She called them clumsy scientist. I'm not sure what she meant by that. What I do know is that there is a physiology department, but only those who studied in that field in college are allowed in. I also know that they research cell growth, development, and other genetic stuff. Cain has mentioned to me, a couple of times, what they do, but it's hard following the terms and language that he uses."

She needed to talk to Cain. She was sure that he had the answers that they were both looking for.

Michael leaned back in his seat and took a deep breath. So many memories of his mother were flashing in his head. He was going to have to re-analyze every one of them. While he had never hated her, he also had never held her in the highest regards either. What if she had loved him? What if she hadn't been at liberty to show it because of the circumstances at the time that he wasn't aware of?

"Michael?"

He blinked. "Huh?"

"You okay?"

"Yeah. It's just…" He began.

"Everything is changing." She slowly walked over and sat at the other end of the love seat.

His nod was barely noticeable. "Yeah, everything is changing."

Finally getting the chance to look at her up close and observe her he studied her for a moment. She was truly beautiful. He wondered if she even knew it. Being so close to her he was able to confirm his suspicion about her eyes. They were indeed green, a beautiful light green. She was wearing shades when he had initially saw her and he hadn't had a chance to take in her beauty since then. Now not only could he take in her beauty but he could also smell her perfume. It was a light and pleasant scent. There was something about Rachel, something that pulled at him and made him want to know more about her. He wanted to know things like where she was from, what her favorite color was, and what her favorite food was. Although he was sure that there was no man in her life, he still didn't think he had any right to ask her those things.

"What are you gonna do?" He asked her. "Will you tell them you've found me?"

"I think we are beyond that, Michael. The way I see it they are making a mistake if they try coming after you. More importantly I don't think your two thousand year old friend downstairs is going to let that happen. His powers are tremendous and so are his girlfriend's."

"I thought they weren't allowed to do that."

She shrugged her shoulders. "Everyone needs somebody." Including myself she thought.

"Why do you suppose that that Immortal was looking for you?" He asked still feeling protective towards her. The idea of her being in danger just didn't sit well with him at all.

"I have absolutely no idea. This is exactly why I need to report in. I need answers. I've already crossed the line again. I did it with Isabella, but I doubt that they are aware of it." At least she hoped that they weren't.

Becoming very serious he said, "You should be careful, Rachel. These people sound dangerous."

And you sound concerned she thought to herself.

Julius suddenly came through the door that lead to the lower level. "Come, both of you." He said as he turned back around knowing that they would follow.

They glanced at one another.

"They're not gonna start fighting down there, are they? If they do I'm teleporting to China," he grinned and said.

"Make sure you take me with you." She grinned.

He didn't think that was a bad idea at all.

Chapter Thirteen

Immortals healed fast, regardless of how serious the wound. Even a limb that was amputated was restored after a couple hours of rest. Victoria and Isabella were both scratch and bruise free after the naps they had taken. The only remnants they wore from the earlier battle were their torn clothing and their disarrayed hair.

Julius was leaning against the wooden wall close to the window frame. The window set just inches above the ground outside so there wasn't much visibility. Victoria sat on a full sized bed while Isabella looked through an open closet with fold-out doors.

There was an old classical baby grand piano that sat next to the room's entrance way. Rachel sat in the small wooden chair that was intended for use with the piano that Michael leaned against.

"I don't get it, Julius. Why do your people allow these people to exist?" He looked at his mentor and asked. "I don't see what purpose they serve."

"I agree with him." Isabella said without looking at them.

"We have our reasons," Julius responded quietly.

"We are granted access to their main library, as well as their records of some pretty ancient information. How long have they been around?" The question was directed at the three Immortals.

"Since the beginning," Victoria responded. She looked at Julius as if asking for permission to continue. "We allow them to exist because they are the only source that can validate our existence," she explained as she looked from Rachel to Michael. "They document and record proof that we walk this earth."

As if they were in a classroom in school Michael raised a hand. "Umm... okay, I still don't get it. What is that supposed to mean? Why do you need someone to validate your existence when you're real? I can see you with my own two eyes."

He had spoken to Michael, but again Victoria responded. "What is history, Michael? It's nothing more than a collection of human trials, defects, and victories. It's also a reminder of the world's good and bad along with its times of war and peace. History carries the total package of everything that is essential to human life. If another race of beings were to suddenly invade this world they could only develop a proper perspective of what it is to be human through what has been written and recorded. History is a living organism to be studied in order to experience humanity's weaknesses and strengths. The definition of a human is not found in a dictionary, rather it is found in the heroic tales of great men and in the tragedies of weak men."

She looked at Rachel and smiled for no apparent reason other than the fact that she liked her. She could tell that she was the mortal friend that Isabella had spoken so highly of. "As Immortals we will never create civilizations, build empires, or have dynasties, therefore we have no true need to record the present or the past. Nor do we have any desire to.

"The Ancients have always explored the paranormal and preternatural since the beginning of time. As far as human beings are concerned they are masters of the mind. They recruit those who are born with a gene for telekinetic capability, such as yourself."

Rachel raised a brow. "Open gene?"

Julius spoke without looking at her. "Humans were originally designed with the ability to manipulate physical matter without physical contact. Throughout time there has been a successive genetic deterioration that in turn has caused the gene responsible for such neurological behavior to become recessive. People like you and Michael were born with what The Ancients refer to as the Open Gene. This simply means that both of your brains are able to access that lost capability. The Ancients teach you or try to teach you and others like you how to harness that ability."

She focused her eyes on him and asked, "Why do I get the feeling that it's not because of your age that you know that and that you have some sort of relationship with them."

"Except for Isabella we all do," Victoria admitted.

The child frowned at her Immortal friend. "I think we should kill them all!"

Julius chuckled at her outburst while Victoria ignored her.

"Her case is different. Isabella was a child when she died. Although she is older than any mortal woman walking the earth now her mentality is still that of a child. At some point these Watchers will eventually build up enough nerve to approach us, this is how secret relations are created. Your superiors prohibit this to blind you to the truth.

"I told you they couldn't be trusted," Isabella said as she sat with her shoe in hand.

Victoria cast her eyes over at her briefly. "Then there's the very real possibility of some rookie field agent developing ties with a powerful Immortal, which wouldn't be good for their superiors if their Immortal ties prove to be younger or weaker."

A picture was beginning to form in Rachel's mind that she wasn't liking at all. When her recruiters had first approached her this wasn't the idea that they had given her. The picture she'd been painted was one of a community of scientist working together to understand the abnormalities of humanity. The fact that they knew Immortals walked the earth was a bonus. She was beginning to realize that she'd been deceived.

Speaking to Victoria, Michael said, "So, this Immortal that came after her was probably sent by the same people that she works with?"

"Oh, I'm sure of it, dear," She replied. "It's hard to keep secrets from these people. Their network is simply too strong. They don't necessarily need a satellite to monitor you, they have more unconventional methods at their disposal."

"No kidding." The situation bothered him a little more than it should.

"Who needs a tracking device when you have a person who can fly and follow you with their mind? You don't think this is more of a reason to put an end to these people?" When neither of the Immortals responded he suddenly remembered the nature of these beings. "Oh, I forgot. You're not concerned with mortal affairs. You'll be alive for the next two or three hundred years. This is crazy."

Rachel glanced at him, careful to note his growing concern for her. "I can only assume this is about Isabella, but I don't think Cain would do something like this."

"Who is Cain?" Michael asked.

"My boss. He's over the entire Southern region."

"Want me to pay him a friendly little visit?" Isabella asked while walking towards Rachel.

"Isabella." Victoria called out firmly.

Isabella responded by making a face at Victoria and then turning around to explore the room.

"Julius and I would both agree that the focus should remain on Michael," she announced.

"Me?" He frowned at the beautiful woman seated on the bed.

"Everything that is happening now is because of you. Two Immortals just tried to kill me because they were drawn to your energy, we all are." Her tone wasn't accusatory at all. As a matter of fact, it was conversational. "If The Ancients have made you a priority it's for a very important reason. I agree with Rachel, this has to be about your parents. Somehow they are involved in all of this. There has to be something on record that she can look into and find out."

"Whoa. Wait a minute." He said holding his palm up in silence. "You just said that somebody is probably on to her. Is it even wise for her to return at all? There's got to be a better way to find out what's going on."

Rachel was shaking her head. "There system is hacker proof and virtually impenetrable. You won't get in without personnel access, you would have to get pass a retina scan, voice recognition, there is even a required body temperature."

"Body temperature?" He asked.

She nodded. "The computer recognizes a certain temperature. Sometimes abnormally low, sometimes abnormally high. Even if you manage to get pass the first two if you don't meet the required temperature you will be denied access. You have to be incredibly skilled to do that. I can't!"

"Jesus, who are these people?" He looked at Julius and asked. "And why can't you just fly in there and take whatever it is we need?"

Julius had been quiet the entire time that everyone else had been talking. His mood was a bit subdued. Something had been itching at the back of his mind sending his thoughts back into the past three hundred years. "It's not that simple, Michael. I can be beaten. I'm not invincible. These people network with other Immortals."

It was hard to imagine that. "Well, don't you have a contact person? An inside man?"

"I haven't been watched by a member of The Ancients for quite some time now. I doubt that Victoria has either." He was sure of it.

"No." She looked at Julius and noticed that something was bothering him. She then looked back to Michael. "It's been many years since I've been watched as well."

"I was Isabella's Watcher so unless you know another Immortal willing to join our crusade I've got to do this." She stated as she turned to face him front on.

"Crusade," Isabella giggled girlishly.

Michael sighed, "Okay, so what are you gonna do? How do you plan to get this information? And what happens if they catch you?"

"I'll come up with something." She stated indifferently, although that wasn't the case.

What really bothered Michael the most was the fact that they had three super humans on their side and the only one who seemed willing to do anything was a twelve year old.

"You won't be alone," Isabella said. She walked over and sat beside Rachel on the small seat. "I'm not as strong as these two, but you won't be by yourself."

Rachel smiled at the child the way a big sister or a parent would. "Thanks, but hopefully it won't come to that." She ran a finger through some of her hair. "Your hair is a mess. I can fix it. Come on." As she rose to leave she made eye contact with Michael. His eyes were filled with concern, while hers were thick with suspicion. It was still too soon to trust him totally.

"So, what's the plan?" He asked Julius after Rachel left.

"For now we will continue your training." He'd been standing with his weight resting against the wall, but now he stood erect. "Hopefully, she can find out something about why these people want you so bad. Michael, don't lose your focus. The time will soon come when you may have to fight Immortals my age and I may not be there to help you. You have great potential, but this is something you must realize for yourself."

Michael nodded as he considered Julius' words before he left the two Immortals alone.

"So this is the one who nearly got me killed?" She looked at the spot where Michael had been standing before focusing on Julius. "He's different."

"Yes, he is." Julius agreed as he regarded her quietly. The thought of almost losing her was still lingering in his head.

"Why Julius? All these years you have been there in the shadows watching me. I've felt you. I didn't know that it was you, but I felt you. Why did you never come to me before?" There was a pain in her voice that she tried her best to hide, but couldn't. "Was

The Great Desire so strong? We both feel it, yet we fight it. We always have."

His eyes went soft on her. The sight of her even the smell of her he could resist, but he couldn't and wouldn't resist his desire to have her. He walked over to her as she stood. He lifted her chin with a finger as he slowly dipped his face towards hers. First his lips lightly brushed hers. Then he allowed his lips to linger a moment longer before he devoured her mouth with his kiss.

Breathless from their shared kiss she asked, "How? How is it possible Julius? The Fallen, they came for you. They took you away from me. I don't recall you being in a state of madness. I'm sure I would've remembered it if you had been. Why didn't you tell me? We could've just increased our separation time."

Julius looked away from her as his mind traveled back in time. "I did taste insanity and the more time we spent together the more bitter that taste became. But I couldn't show that to you. I didn't want you to see that in me." He looked back at her and stroked her face gently with a finger. "I will never forget the day they came for me. I wasn't concerned about where they would take me. I was concerned about being able to see you again."

"Where did they take you, Julius?" She asked as she returned his touch with one of her own. "And how did you escape?"

He searched her eyes for a moment before turning away and walking back towards the window. "To a place that is no place. It is not this place that you have to escape. It is the insanity. Once you do this The Fallen will return you to this world. It was you, Victoria, it was my love for you that saved me from my own insanity." He turned back around to face her.

The weight of her own immortality paled in comparison to the weight of emotion she experienced as he looked at her. His words hit her with the force of a hurricane. How could she ever love another?

"I love you, Julius! I always have." She said as a single tear fell from her eye. "If I live for another thousand years I will love you every day of it."

The Great Desire raged within him even as he looked at her and considered his love for her. He would fight it. He was stronger now than what he was back then.

She stepped into his embrace and he held her close with his arms wrapped tightly around her. He had waited three hundred years to hold her again and now that he had he held no intention of ever letting her go again.

Chapter Fourteen

In the Spring the weather is nice, fair and moods are generally peacefully, yet it's still a lonely time of year and because of this there were very few peaceful moods for Michael.

Julius was pushing him hard nearly every day. The only time he managed to find any peace was when he was alone or out in the yard playing with Biscuit. If he was honest with himself he'd admit that he was also at peace when he was thinking of Rachel. It had been almost two months since he'd last seen her and he missed her. Sometimes it was too difficult to focus on his training because his thoughts were on her. Of course Julius knew this and pushed him harder because of it.

He pushed him beyond his limits. Several times he was convinced that Julius had forgotten that he was a mortal. The lessons often reminded him of his martial arts Instructor, a thin little Asian man who never used complete sentences, from when he was younger. He was no Immortal, but he was certainly highly skilled as a fighter. He had pushed him and there were times he could even recall where he felt like he'd been pushed too far. This was different. It wasn't the physical push that gave him trouble. It was the mental one. Julius wasn't pushing his body. He was pushing his mind.

There was one thing his childhood Instructor had taught him that remained a part of him and that was how to shut the outside world out. This was something that had helped him cope with the ostracism he had experienced at the time. His peers hadn't been of much help.

There was one particular method of training that Julius would use that was a bit frightening. He would check for severe thunder storms all over the world, once he found one he would transport himself into its atmosphere to train. The first time a bolt of lightning had raced towards him he'd accidently teleported himself to the opposite side of the world. Julius had found it rather amusing, he didn't. The increase of electrical activity made it more difficult to release his energy. His complaint to Julius was how was he supposed to concentrate on releasing his energy with vicious strikes of lightning near you? He didn't appreciate Julius' indifference to his mortality. A strike of lightning wouldn't affect him, but it would certainly turn him into a piece of toast.

Despite this he had to admit that he was improving. He was getting stronger and faster. He was also becoming more accurate at teleporting. It was obvious to him that Julius believed in him, but he didn't know if he was that sure of himself. Immortals were powerful and when it was all said and done he was still just a human.

Michael was seated at the kitchen table, after having showered, getting ready to eat the dinner that Gray had made.

"Got some news." The old man said as he entered the kitchen and headed straight for the cabinet that held the Wild Turkey. "I'm going to China."

He looked up with a mouth full of food. "You're gonna leave me here by myself?"

"Course not! Biscuit will be here with you."

The dog, who was enjoying his own meal, glanced up at the sound of his name.

"Are you serious?" He asked as he watched gray pour himself a drink.

"It's only for a week. I've never met my sister's kids before, and they're coming to the states for a couple of months." He seemed to think about that. "Alice convinced me to make the trip to spend a couple of days with them."

"But, I can't cook." He teased.

"You're almost thirty, I wouldn't tell anyone else that if I were you," he said with a smirk.

"That's great. When do you leave?"

"Tomorrow."

Michael nodded. "Maybe you should learn some Chinese first."

"Sure, why didn't I think of that? Do you know any you can teach me?"

"Nope, but I can show you how to dodge a lightning bolt."

Gray shook his head and chuckled. "I'll pass on that lesson." He took a deep breath and relaxed, taking a moment to enjoy the country music that was playing from the kitchen's radio. "There's nothing like family, Michael. I shouldn't have separated myself from mine the way that I did. I'd change it if I could. If you ever get the chance to patch things up with yours be sure to do it."

He would keep that in mind, he thought to himself. He glanced at the phone, that Gray had gotten him, that sat next to his plate. He glanced at it again when it rang. He hoped that it was her.

"Well, it's not going to answer itself, Michael." Gray said with a grin.

He tried to contain his excitement when he answered and heard her voice. "Hey, how are you?"

"I'm good. A little exhausted, but good. I've been on a plane six times in the last week. Cain is keeping me busy. He knows that I'm up to something," she said.

"Where are you now?" He asked.

"I'm back in Atlanta, for now. I'm at Cain's place. He just stepped out for a minute."

"Be careful, Rachel, I've been worried about you." He openly admitted.

Why was she so suspicious of that? Also why had she thought about him often over the last few weeks? She refused to believe that she held any feelings for him or that he held any genuine feelings for her. They had been tossed together in a situation beyond their control. Yes, that was it, nothing more. She was telling herself that but was wondering whether or not it was true. Yes, she kept telling herself it was, but was it really? "I'm still looking for a way to get into the system. Finding The Holy Grail would've been a lot easier."

The matter still didn't sit well with him. He should be the one out investigating, whatever his parents had gotten themselves involved in. It shouldn't be her. "You don't have to do this. If they find out…"

"If they find out then I will deal with it," she interrupted. "I can't fight an Immortal, but I think I can handle myself against Cain and his people. Plus Isabella, my little angry guardian angel, is always nearby." She chuckled. "I'll be fine, Michael. Enough about me, what about you? How's your training going?"

He couldn't help but notice and admire that she was just as stubborn as he was. "It's okay, I guess. It's so natural for them to move the way they do." He paused. "Have you ever wandered what it would be like to be Immortal? To live forever?"

"They will live until the end of time." She corrected. "To answer your question, yes. Yes, I have and it's something hard to imagine. They will never age or catch a cold. They have no fears. They don't even experience hunger and thirst."

"Would you give up your humanity for it?" He asked her.

She thought about it. "I don't know. Technically, they didn't give up their humanity. They died. It was The Fallen, whoever they are, that made that decision for them. I guess it would be cool, but they seem to be so... lonely. Even when they are around one another they still seem to be alone."

It was their nature. Julius had spoken to him about this several times and he was beginning to get the picture. "Who would ever think that immorality could be overrated."

"Who would ever think Immortals existed?" That reality alone sometimes still managed to amaze her.

Michael absently stabbed at his plate.

Gray had been monitoring the conversation. He put the bottle back into the cabinet and was leaving the kitchen when he spoke. "You can fly. You can actually fly, Michael, but you can't tell a girl you like her or ask her out on a date." He shook his head. "That's just sad."

Michael narrowed his eyes at his friend until he disappeared from his view. "So, um... how long are you going to be in Atlanta?"

"A few days, maybe. He doesn't think I realize it but Cain is trying to keep me away from all of the activity regarding you. He's trying to protect me. If he wasn't such a jerk the gesture would be romantic," she said aridly. "Why do you ask?"

He scratched the back of his head for no apparent reason and responded. "Well... Gray is about to go see some family in China and he'll...be gone for a couple of days. And well, I was just wondering...if you wanted to come up and hang out for a while. If you're not too busy," he said tentatively, sounding very unsure.

For some reason the memory of him stepping in front of her to protect her from The Immortal flashed in her mind. It warmed her.

"By the way, I've got instant air travel. There'll be no jet lag."

Her laugh was easy and light. When was the last time that had happened? When was the first time? "Sure. How about tomorrow night?"

It took a moment for his brain to register her response. "Yeah, yeah that would be great. I guess now would be the time to tell you I have telekinesis. I can teleport and all my friends were born before the Civil War. A mysterious group of people are after me and I spent about twelve years in a mental hospital. Just so you know."

Again she laughed. It was a sound that he was beginning to want to hear more of.

***

Lucas sat the phone down and took a pull on his cigar, taking his time before slowly exhaling. He was seated in the hot tub of the large shower room. The shower room was one of five in the huge multi-million dollar home. A light mist of steam filled the air as the sound of Mexican music played at a low volume and a tall glass of Tequila sat within arm's reach.

Lucas was a short and stocky man with short limbs. Over the years his muscled frame had begun to turn into fat, yet he still maintained himself well. He was almost sixty-five and still had a head full of naturally black hair. His face as always was cleanly shaven.

The Ancients consisted of three branches that operated independently of one another. He was the President of his branch. The three power's heads only met once every three years to discuss current business. The meeting was strictly formal and often carried a lot of pretense. All sensitive and secret information was withheld unless a vote was cast for its exposure. In such an event all three heads would have to open their records and that was something that none of them had any desire to do.

The next meeting time was quickly approaching.

Knowing that his voice would be picked up by the intercom installed he suddenly spoke into the air. A few moments later a tall white man with long hair dressed in a dark blue business suit entered the room.

Lucas stared at the man for a moment before speaking. "I think it's time that we move," he simply said.

The man, whose name was Edgar, nodded his head slightly and then spoke. "We have a location on Michael. We also have locations on every living relative of Mr. Bentson, as well as some of his old Army associates. Cain has a team monitoring the perimeter and we have a team monitoring them."

Lucas had his back against the smooth polished porcelain with his arms propped up. The lower half of his body was concealed beneath a mountain of soapy bubbles. "What about our Allies?"

Placing his hands in his pockets Edgar responded. "We have three from the bloodline with the youngest being three hundred years old. If you intend to engage in an open battle we will need them. This Julius is extremely powerful."

He admired this. "This is the one who was able to somehow reverse the effects of The Great Desire?" He asked although he already knew exactly who he was.

"Yes, As far as the records show no Immortal has ever done that. In addition, there's the matter of the other two, who are also very powerful. I'm not questioning your judgement, Lucas, but I think the odds are against us if we strike against these people. And that's without mentioning the growing abilities of Michael."

Lucas was no fool, he had absolutely no intention of a direct fight. He knew that the Immortal child alone could annihilate them if he did such a thing. It was times like this that he appreciated subordinates like Edgar, who weren't afraid to speak their minds. "I intend to fight, but in a more subtle fashion."

Edgar frowned. "I don't follow you."

Lucas rotated his neck. "We still have his mother. During his last conversation with Rachel, Michael confirmed my suspicions about the two of them. They are becoming romantically involved. Sometimes you have to distract a lion to kill it." Edgar stated perceptively.

"Precisely. I don't want to kill this lion. I just want to catch it. His cell structure may possess the missing element that will allow us to succeed where others have failed." His eyes brightened at the thought. "We only need a sample of his blood."

Edgar, being close to Lucas, was familiar with the Flint Files. A thought struck him then. "You don't think Julius knows the truth about Michael do you?"

"I doubt it. It's highly unlikely. Julius' Watcher was already communicating with him before The Fallen came for him. He stated in his report that when Julius returned he suffered from heavy memory loss. By the time The Immortal got his senses back the Watcher had already carried out the deed." He shrugged his shoulders. "If he would've known I'm sure he would've killed The Watcher.

The taller man thought about that for a moment. "If he learns the truth, or remembers it, it could change things. It could become personal."

He scoffed at the thought before reaching for his glass. "They're Immortals. Whatever reasons this Julius has for training Michael I doubt that they're sentimental. They are incapable of becoming emotionally attached to a mortal. I believe if we remove Michael from the equation Julius will turn away; especially now that he's reunited with his girlfriend. Which again is why I say it's time we move. Go bring the mother to me. Hopefully, she has enough sanity left to remember that she even has a son."

"Should I contact Cain?"

He held up a hand to quiet him. "No, I'll deal with him personally. A man who stands on his emotions is not stable. He has potential to take his seat, but he's got to change his foundation first, and I intend to show him the way."

Edgar gave a nod at that, but his thoughts were contrary. The expression 'take his seat' meant becoming president. How could Lucas be so blind? He was far more qualified than Cain. The man was incompetent and disloyal. He made a mental note to kill him if the opportunity presented itself.

He would then be the next candidate for the seat. Men like Cain were sloppy, so he would slip. And when he did Edgar planned to be sure that his fall was complete.

Chapter Fifteen

"You know we are being watched." Rachel said to Michael as they slowly walked the trail at the park. It was a beautiful day. The sun was resting behind pretty fluffy clouds stretched across the sky. The temperature was nice and the smell of Spring was in the air.

He glanced about looking at the different people as they went about their business. A couple jogged pass them followed by a man with his dog. "You okay? You know they followed us here, right? I can teleport them to India if you want."

She smiled as she laughed. "No, I'm sure that Cain sent them here, so I'm sure they won't try anything."

He looked at her. Her eyes were a clear green sea of mystery and intrigue. Her hair was once again pulled in a tight ponytail that outlined the shape of her face, making it clearly visible. Her skin was so smooth and beautiful that it made him want to reach out and touch it. To touch her.

She was dressed in all white. She wore a tight fitting shirt and jeans with a pair of sneakers. She wore silver jewelry on her wrist and around her neck. Although he stood a few inches taller than her he didn't appear to be looking down on her. They were standing close enough that he could smell her perfume. Again it was light and pleasant.

"They better not. You kicked me in my throat the first time we met," he said as he rubbed his throat as if it still hurt. "Do you do that to everybody you meet or was it just me?"

She shoved him lightly and said, "Oh hush. I didn't know who you were. I'm a nice person."

"Really? This guy Craig you just told me about I wonder if he would agree."

"That was different."

He shook his head at her in a teasing fashion. "You have a history of abusing men. Ever thought about counseling?"

"You know what? I am not listening to you." She said while pretending to walk away.

"Hey, where you going? If I have to fight these people I might need that kick of yours."

She was amused and she was actually enjoying the moment. She hadn't felt like this since high school. She felt like a girly girl instead of like a secret spy.

"So tell me some more about your story, Rachel." He said when he caught up to her. "You've read my file, but I haven't read yours."

She looked up at him for a moment before looking east towards the mountains of Northeast Georgia. "I'm from a small town in North Dakota. I have three older sisters and two younger brothers."

"Serious?" He would've guessed she was an only child.

"I know. I'm not exactly family oriented. My parents both worked and we were well off. At Christmas and Thanksgiving we celebrated abundantly and there were times we even donated to others." Memories flashed in her mind. "My parents were good parents who loved each other and their children. It wasn't their fault I was born with an Open gene. They tried their best to protect me."

"Protect you from what?"

She shrugged. "From everything I guess. They knew something was different with me, it couldn't help to be noticed. I was a walking Bermuda Triangle. Strange and paranormal activity followed me everywhere I went."

"They weren't mean to you, were they? Your family, I mean."

"No," she said quickly, almost too quickly to be truthful. "Not really. They treated me categorically. I think they wanted me to be a part of the family circle, but I just didn't fit in. They weren't mean to me and I never ever hated them."

He studied her a moment while she looked away. There was a strength about her. He saw it in her eyes and he heard it in her voice. It also showed in the way that she moved. He knew that that type of strength was developed when one was forced to be alone. It was internal.

She looked at a guy sitting on a park bench pretending to read a newspaper. "High School wasn't so bad. There were enough loners and weirdos to go around. I had a few close friends. I played volleyball. I was invited to be on the cheerleading squad, but like most cheerleading teams their reasons were superficial. A nice set of boobs and a small waist will get you on any cheerleading team in America."

"Think I qualify?"

She chuckled. "Not quite."

He was falling in love with the way she smiled. "You went to college?"

She nodded. "I wanted a degree in business. The idea was to start my own business. I even wanted to go across seas."

"Really? Where to?" He asked as he caught sight of the man on the bench watching them, he kept his eyes trained on him for a moment.

"I was never sure. London. Maybe Australia." She had never really made up her mind.

"What happened?" He glanced at her when he asked.

She smiled at a kid walking pass with his mom. "The Ancients happened. I met their recruiters in my last year. They knew my whole life story. I didn't believe them at first. I actually thought that it was a sorority joke. I didn't really take them serious until they mentioned my abnormal abilities. The thought of there being others like me appealed to me. I had read up on the ability and the scientific studies on it, but I had never met another person with it. I mean, my high school friends were different, but not like us."

He understood completely. Of course the idea had appealed to her, not many people could understand what it was like to possess such a capability. It automatically alienated a person in every social aspect possible.

She stopped walking. "I gave up what I wanted to do because I believed in what they told me. They used my own abilities to blind me from the truth while distracting me with tales of these mysterious Immortals." She looked at the tattoo on her wrist and absently messaged it.

He saw both hurt and disappointment in her eyes. It moved him deeply.

They had no right to do what they had done to her. Gently he lifted her chin back up with one of his fingers. "You didn't know," he spoke softly. "You did what you thought was right. You can't blame yourself for that."

Tears fell from her eyes before she even realized that they were there. "Michael, I haven't even spoken to my family since college. I didn't want them to know. They don't even know if I'm alive or dead."

The sight of her tears was too much for him. He wrapped his arms around her and held her close. Not accustom to displays of emotion she was stiff at first, but within seconds she slowly melted into him. She buried her face into his chest and closed her eyes. Why did this feel so right? Never in her entire life had she felt like she belonged anywhere until now. A volcano of emotions erupted inside of her causing her to tighten her grip around him. She didn't want to let him go.

He held her out in the open. A quiet anger rose within him towards the people who she worked for. Again he felt an overwhelming need to protect her. He knew that he would, no matter the cost.

A strange thing occurred to him then. These people, The Ancients, seemed to be the source of their trouble and yet they had brought them together. Should he hate them or should he be grateful to them? He decided that he would be grateful later. When it was all said and done he would go to war with these people.

She laughed lightly as she pulled away a little. "I've completely ruined our walk in the park."

"No, you haven't. As a matter of fact, you made it better." He kissed her lightly on her forehead and said. "I'm glad you came early."

She was still in his embrace when her eyes locked with his, and for a brief second time itself faded as she was pulled into him. Her first instinct was to resist it, to pull herself back, but she couldn't nor did she want to. He wouldn't come to her she knew that. She understood that he didn't know how, so she would go to him.

Slowly she brought herself even closer to him. The sounds of the park died away as she moved her lips to touch his. The first contact was light and gentle. It caused her eyelids to flutter. She saw the fire of desire ignite in his brown eyes. It was a sleeping passion that had slumbered too long, one that needed to be awakened and was.

It had been over twelve years since he'd kissed a girl. He had been a teenager. He'd never kissed a woman until now and he quickly found himself filled with the need to have her. He dove back into the kiss like a scuba diver in search of a buried treasure. It surprised him to find his energy rising and he pulled back abruptly.

"Whoa! Tell me that you felt that!"

She smiled. "Yeah... I did."

He brushed some of her hair away from one side of her face. "You know we're still being watched?"

She gave him a sly look. "I had a college roommate who once told me it's always better that way."

"I wouldn't know anything about that."

He placed his arms around her shoulder and continued to walk at a slow pace.

A few streets over Cain nearly punched a hole through the van he was in as he watched the live feed come through one of the miniature cameras being worn by one of his men.

"Ah... sir." It was the driver. "I think we have a problem."

Cain was a bit distracted and he wanted, no needed to hit something. There were five small monitor screens installed along with the other surveillance equipment. He wanted to rip it all out. How dare she kiss him.

"What? What is it?"

The driver didn't want to move. He was pointing towards the windshield. "Ah… you might want to take a look."

Cain tore his eyes from the screen and took a step towards the front of the van. He rested his hands at the top of the seats as he peered out. He froze instantly at the sight before him.

Isabella stood in front of the van, her head slightly tilted to one side. She had resorted back to her gothic look. She had ironed all the crinkles out of her curly hair and it now hung long and straight covering one side of her face.

One of the men in the van, a novice, drew his weapon. Cain looked at him disapprovingly and said, "You'll be dead before the gunpowder explodes. Now put it away."

Cain was no novice nor did he have any bloodline allies with him, therefore, he would do nothing to provoke her.

"What does she want?" The novice asked.

As if in response, the metal structure of the vehicle suddenly caved in a bit as a force hit against it. The surveillance equipment blinked from the interference. The van slowly lifted off the ground. First one foot, then two, and then three. Isabella took a step closer, her hands behind her back, and inspected her work.

Suddenly the windshield shattered and fell away. "Hello, Cain. You wouldn't happen to be spying on my friend would you? How would you like it if I spied on you? Followed you around and took notes on and watched everything you did. Do you know how annoying that is?"

There was a total of six men in the van. Five of them drew their weapons aiming them at Cain. He knew why.

"Are you going to kill me, Immortal?"

The corners of her mouth cracked into a grin. "I should and eventually I probably will, but not today. Instead of killing you today I'm going to leave you with a little warning. If you value what remaining years you have left on this earth I advise you to leave my friend alone."

Cain cast his eyes on the guns that were aimed at him. He was actually capable of stopping one bullet, but five...

She easily read his thoughts and intentions and found herself amused. "Oh, so you'd like to test your abilities." It wasn't a question. "Very well. I will make it easy for you. I will only fire one weapon, but... you'll have to figure out which gun it will be. If you don't stop the bullet..." She didn't bother saying anything else because there was nothing else that she needed to say.

He looked at her with hate in his eyes. She, along with others like her, was an abomination; descendants of some rejected Angelic race. Gathering his concentration he began to breathe evenly. His life would end if he wasn't careful. How would he marry Rachel then?

His men had no neurological control, and he could see the panic and fear in each of their eyes. She probably could've hijacked his brain too. He would've resisted her for a while, but he knew that eventually she would overpower him.

He kept his mind clear preparing it to release its energy.

She waited watching him with mild amusement. She could feel his energy building.

The first shot came from the guy in the passenger seat. Cain instantly released his energy and brought the bullet to a halt only inches away from his head. The man blinked in confusion, having no idea to what had just happened, as he was released from Isabella's hold. The second shot came from the driver with the same result.

Cain kept his breathing even and his ears tuned in to the sound of exploding gunpowder. He was far too skilled to easily lose his focus. The third one fired followed by the fourth and now he waited for the fifth. As he waited he never took his eyes off the Immortal, instead he watched her intently. He used his hate for her to strengthen his focus.

It was all a game to her. If she really wanted to she could kill them all in a blink of an eye. She released the final bullet, but this time she did something different. This time she pushed her own energy behind it.

For the first time Cain began to worry. He succeeded in slowing the bullet down, but not stopping it as it continued on its deadly path towards his head. He knew it was her. He could feel the raw power of her energy as he pushed with everything he had. Thoughts of Rachel flashed in his mind. Thoughts of her being with Michael and his fingers flexed absently into a fist. His muscles twitched as a light sweat began to build on his skin. The bullet slowly inched its way to his skull, even though it had lost some of its velocity he knew that she could still drive it right through to his brain.

He was close to passing out from the effort and strain, but he refused to give up. If he was going to die it wouldn't be without a fight. He nearly screamed out as he felt the hot burn as the bullet made contact with his flesh. The pain was excruciating. It felt like he was being branded with a hot iron. At the exact moment that he thought the bullet would penetrate it dropped along with the van back to the ground.

She walked up to the van, placed a hand on the front, and said, "If we have to do this again it will end differently." And then she was gone.

Cain took a moment to relax. It was time to put an end to it all. This wasn't his war. Lucas was wrong, he would lose in whatever fight he started with these people. Who could win against such strength and power? Lucas was fighting for power while he was fighting for love. He wasn't willing to die for this, but he was willing to die for her… even if it meant her dying with him.

Chapter Sixteen

Gray's home had a custom built-on open back porch that provided a clear view of the mountains. The backyard was clear of any trees. There was a shed and several iron log racks that he kept mostly for the winter. There was a dog house for Biscuit that he didn't frequent much. Betsy had always wanted to create a garden and there was enough room for that, although she never got around to using it. There was never any need for the installment of a fence since the nearest neighbor was several hundred yards away.

Michael sat with Rachel on the wooden porch swing watching the sun dip into the darkness. The powerful bright lights on the porch were already in use. They both sat quiet enjoying the view along with the smells of the country.

"Reminds me of home," she said without looking over at him. "I grew up around farms with big fat dairy cows." She smiled to herself in memory.

He studied her face from the side while enjoying the light and soft sound of her voice.

"Ever milked a cow, Michael?" Making a face of disgust as she asked. "It's nasty business."

"I can't imagine you milking a cow."

"I couldn't either. I'm glad they sell it in stores."

He chuckled at that.

They got quiet again. They had already had something to eat, having eaten out since neither had much experience in the kitchen. After eating they had walked around town a little. While doing so Rachel had run into Jessica, the girl from the bookstore, again. It was a small town, there hadn't been much to see, but they had enjoyed it.

"Think they got tired of following us?" He asked.

They both had known when Cain's men had pulled out.

"Hard to say. " She said with a shrug. "If they pulled out they were ordered to."

"You ever felt anything for this guy? He seems to be pretty taken with you."

She made a face at him. "No, I have always kept things professional with Cain. He convinced himself to come on to me, I didn't offer him any invitation. About a year ago I requested to transfer to a different region, of course he denied it. I don't know what his thing is. I tolerate it because he signs my checks."

He waited a beat then said, "I get it."

"You get what?"

He smiled at her. "You're beautiful, Rachel. It's hard for any man not to see that. I saw it the first time that I laid eyes on you when you were pretending to read that newspaper. I saw it when you put your life on the line for me by crossing those people. I see it now as I look at you, it's hard not to. I'm not making excuses for him, this guy is obviously a nut job, but you are beautiful."

His words were spoken softly since they were sitting close enough for their shoulders to touch. They rocked just a little bit.

Her heart warmed again at his words. He seemed to have a way of affecting her despite her defenses. She had told herself that the kiss earlier was just a slip, a blind act during a vulnerable moment. She knew that she was lying to herself, that this was what she wanted; what she had been waiting for. It wasn't just emotions,

168

it was a connection. The memory of him willing to protect her, to fight for her circled in her head continuously like vultures over fallen prey.

He would fight for her.

This time he was too anxious to be hesitant. He leaned in to kiss her, having tasted her once he needed to taste her again. When his lips were on hers he was alive in a way that he had never been before. She fueled a fire that burned deep inside of him. He stood, lifting her in his arms and took her inside.

She reached for the bottom of her shirt lifting it and pulling it off over her head. He froze at the sight of her. His hands explored and roamed over her flesh followed by his mouth. Her breast were so firm and fit that they sat up. Her stomach was tone and flat. Hungry for her he kissed his way back up to her mouth to taste there again.

He stopped long enough to lift his shirt from his body, getting the same reaction from her he dropped his shirt.

Her eyes bulged slightly at what she saw. The shirts that he normally wore were big and loose so she was shocked by what she found beneath. Never would she have imagined all that was beneath it. His muscles were so defined, it had to be from all the training. She just had to touch them before tasting them. She hadn't realized that it had been so long. The volcano building inside of her was begging for its pressure to be released. It was like a caged animal clawing and scratching to be freed.

Lifting her he brought her mouth back to his as he gently laid her down. His fingers fumbled with her jeans while his lips were still on hers. Once he got them unfastened he slid them off of her only stopping to remove her shoes and socks. If the sight of her naked breast hadn't slapped him the sight of her legs delivered the killing blow. They weren't long, but they were shapely. He was mesmerized by them. He didn't move with the experience of a seasoned lover, instead he moved with the curiosity of a novice. Gaging her body's responses to how and where he touched he followed her sounds of pleasure.

Her body convulsed as his lips found the inside of one of her thighs. "Michael..." Her breathing was becoming rough and her eyes were closed. She didn't need to guide him as he removed the soft fabric of her panties and tasted her with his tongue. Her vision become blurred and she nearly screamed from the sensation. He didn't try anything fancy, he simply tasted her taking what she offered with his mouth. The first wave of her orgasm hit her and she let go a scream as she locked her legs around his neck. Her fingers dug deep into the bed sheets as her body shuddered with pleasure.

He held her tight until her spasms passed. Something in him caved in when he moved back up to look in her eyes and saw the mist that was in there. Where did she come from? It seemed as if she'd just walked into his life. He had been waiting for her and hadn't even realized it. She gave him passion and desire. Her presence brought him to life. Suddenly he knew. He knew why he'd been so willing and driven to protect her. She was his heart.

She was the breath that gave him life.

His own eyes filled with tears. "You are so beautiful, Rachel." He kissed her tears away. "Everything about you is beautiful."

He'd been fighting the need to be inside of her, but he couldn't fight it any longer. After removing her bra he took off the rest of his clothes and positioned himself between her thighs. She placed her arms around him as he looked into her eyes. Her quick intake of breath seemed to hold forever as he entered her. In that moment everyone else in the world ceased to exist outside of them. Their energy became one as their bodies worked together to achieve the ultimate pleasure. They drifted to a place beyond the physical. Higher and higher they flew on the wings of desire. Their pace quickened then slowed. There was no greater or weaker between the two. They were equal as they rose to a climax. They reached their peak at the same time, a moment of destiny that had been waiting for them.

Later, he held her as she slept. She had mentioned returning to Cain's place, but he wouldn't allow it. It was time for her to sever all ties with him and his people. They had taken his parents. Immortal or not he would kill them before he allowed them to take her as well. Julius believed in him, it was now time that he started believing in himself.

***

Pulling up to the half a million dollar home that he owned in Buck Head, Matthew parked his luxury vehicle, thinking about Victoria he got out whistling a tune. After two agonizing months she had finally called him earlier. She had pulled away from him. She hadn't been answering his calls or responding to his texts. What had happened? He'd went over the matter a thousand times in his mind. Things seemed to have been perfect between them, so it didn't make any sense. The idea that there was possibly another man crossed his mind, but not wanting to believe it he quickly dispelled the thought. Jealousy was an emotion that was as foreign to him as a Korean, but he couldn't deny that that's exactly what was sparked in him.

He was no stranger to beautiful and exotic women, but Victoria was beyond such comparison. She did something to him that was alien to him. The sensations he experienced when they were together were mind altering. He was tempted to believe that the woman wasn't human, but that was crazy. What else could she be? She'd told him that they needed to talk. He wasn't concerned by that. He just wanted to see her again.

He entered his home and immediately disabled the security system. Feeling like a celebrity he headed towards the bar area that was annexed off the kitchen. The lightening there was dim. Suddenly he stopped. What was that? He felt something. The feeling was so strong that it caused him to look about although he knew that he was alone.

Not seeing anything he shrugged it off. He turned the dimmed lights up and turned on the flat screen, which was posted high up on the back wall behind the bar, to ESPN. He tossed his keys onto the marble bar top and checked the fridge. On his way back he froze in sudden alarm at the man sitting causally on one of the bar's stools nursing a drink on ice of some brown liquor. His brown liquor.

"What are you doing in my home? How did you get in here?" He demanded as he balled his fist in anger. He attended the gym regularly, so he was in top shape and he could also handle himself well.

The stranger shifted his head around a bit but his long hair still completely eclipsed the side of his face. "We can do this the easy or the hard way... either way is fine with me."

A gut feeling warned him that something wasn't right, yet he ignored it. He was no coward. Not only had his privacy been violated, but the stranger added insult to injury with his nonchalant attitude and by helping himself to his liquor.

"How the hell did you get in here? It won't take the cops but a few minutes to get here. That's if I decide to call them instead of taking matters into my own hands. I have a permit for my firearm as well as a good relationship with the D.A. I could kill you and get away with it with no problems."

The stranger gave a low chuckle. "Really? Is that so?" He said taking a sip from his glass. "I find all that very amusing. I will say this one last time... we can do this the easy way or the hard way, with or without cops, and as far as your firearm goes..." He waved a hand absently. "I won't repeat myself again, Matthew."

The warning feeling in his gut got a little stronger at the sound of his name. Who was this guy? Why was he here? He didn't have any enemies, as he made it a point not to make them. He could feel something about the stranger. It was the same feeling he'd gotten a few moments ago upon entering his home. He swallowed nervously and looked towards the glass case filled with exotic porcelain figurines. On the top of the case was an automatic handgun. Could he get to it quickly enough? It wasn't so much that he was afraid of a physical fight, there was simply a sense of urgency to get this stranger out of his house.

Julius lifted his head and faced him squarely. He rotated the glass in his hand in small circles. "Gonna go for it?" He asked.

The stranger must have been in his house for a while now and had searched, or maybe he had even been here more than once. How else would he know where he kept his weapon?

"I got an idea Matt." Julius kept his voice at a conversational level. "It's gonna take you what... maybe eight or nine strides to reach it? Then you have to take it down, take the safety off, and then turn around and aim it at me. You have a hunting knife in an upstairs closet in your bedroom, the end room located at the farthest end of the house. How about I retrieve it and put it in your thigh all before you fire the first shot? Then we can talk."

Matthew almost laughed. Evidently the man who had broken into his house was a lunatic. "You're a dead man."

Still there was something about the stranger's nonchalant demeanor and the lazy grin that sat at the edges of his mouth that made Matthew slightly uncomfortable. He could feel his heart pounding inside of his chest. There was no way that the stranger could move as fast as he claimed, it was impossible. However, he still knew that he had to be quick. He stole one more glance at the case. Six seconds. Six seconds is what he estimated that he needed to make it over. It would take him another six maybe seven seconds to fire the first shot. It would take the stranger at least a full minute.

Gesturing with the glass Julius said, "Go for it."

A heartbeat later he moved. He closed the small distance between himself and case and reached up to grab the gun. He immediately took the safety off. It felt like a lifetime had already passed before he turned around. He swung his arm around to take aim, but dropped the weapon suddenly instead when a piercing pain exploded in his leg. He released a loud scream as his vision blurred and blood poured down his leg like water from a faucet. He held his leg as he laid on the floor, his eyes bulging at the sight of the knife protruding from his leg.

Julius was still reclined on the stool as if he'd never moved. He took a final swig of his liquor and then sat the glass on the counter behind him. He got up and slowly approached Matthew. Kneeling beside him he spoke. "Looks pretty painful. I can't remember the last time I experienced mortal pain. I think it was a few years after the death of Constantine." He shrugged. "I guess, but that's not the point."

Matthew grinded his teeth together from the pain. His initial anger had dissolved and was now replaced with fear. This was no man.

"It has come to my attention that you have recently been intimate with my lady friend, Victoria." Actually he had been near the first day Matthew had spoken to her. "Believe me when I say I've been in a relationship with her since before your first teenage crush. She is very dear to me. I literally lost my sanity because of her. You can't even imagine. You are too human, too limited in your scope of time to even begin to understand the hell I've endured for this woman. So, here's the deal, Matt. Whatever ideas you have of the two of you being together get rid of them. You will not call her. You will not even think about her. Are we clear on this?"

Matthew cursed at him. The pain was so excruciating that he couldn't even think coherently. How did he know Victoria? Was he telling the truth? He couldn't believe that she had sent this man. What if she was in some kind of trouble?

Julius laughed at his thoughts. "You fancy yourself in love with her?" He shook his head. "I can promise you she doesn't share the sentiment. Perhaps you believe you have satisfied her sexual cravings? If you do then you are sadly disillusioned." He looked down at his wound. "You might want to let a doctor look at that. Wouldn't want it to get infected."

There were tears in Matthew's eyes as he held his leg and screamed, "Who the hell are you?! Get me some help! I'm losing too much blood."

Julius regarded him with a confused expression. "Hmm... I don't think my point has penetrated... maybe I need to go a little deeper."

The moment he said it the knife dug itself deeper, getting even closer to the bone. Matthew's screams were wild and spit flew from his mouth as he jerked his head about. He was seeing spots as he was slipping into the realm of unconsciousness.

"Stop!" He screamed over and over again as he wept like a child. "What do you want? Please just stop. Stop please!"

Julius smiled. "That's the spirit. Now listen to me carefully, Matthew. I'm in a good mood which is pretty much the only reason why you are still alive. I will allow you to live the next twenty or maybe even thirty pathetic years you have left, letting you die most likely from some sexually transmitted disease. It's your choice. All you have to do is never see her again. Don't even think her name, and trust me I can hear every little dirty thought in your dirty little mind. If you try to contact her I will come to you and we will repeat this process, but I won't be in such a good mood. Are we clear, Matthew?"

His loss of blood was making his wound fatal. His expensive carpet was soaked with in. Matthew fought against the darkness as he faded in and out of consciousness. He finally gave a faint nod of acceptance.

"Don't worry, you'll live. Paramedics are on the way. I already made the call." As soon as he finished speaking the sound of the ambulance's siren could be heard. "Well, my business here is done. Thanks for the drink."

It seemed to Matthew that the stranger simply disappeared, but that couldn't be. He must be hallucinating from the pain. He had to be. Again he heard the sound of sirens and prayed that he wasn't hallucinating. Victoria was crossing his mind as he faded out, but he quickly pushed her from his thoughts. He didn't want to think about her. No he didn't want to think about her at all.

Chapter Seventeen

Tybee Island, in Savannah, Georgia, was a beautiful place. Tourist from all over the country flocked there to visit. People were scattered everywhere on the beach. There were friends, couples, lovers, and even some loners roamed the crowd. Julius stood behind Victoria with his arms wrapped around her waist. They both were looking out across the Atlantic. It was evening and the moon was full and the tides were high. Yet they stood, feet bare, at the shore line the Ocean water swirling around their ankles.

"I have a confession to make." He spoke into her ear and then nibbled on it.

She made a sound of pleasure. "I'm not a priest, Julius. As a matter of fact I don't even like priest."

"Oh. And why is that?" He asked as he took another nibble.

"Because one accused me of being a witch in the 16th century and tried to have me burned alive."

He fought to keep his laughter in his throat. "What an amusing thought. I wonder how that ended. For the priest, I mean."

She leaned back into him and angled her head to look at him. "What is your confession?"

"I've been bad." He mumbled, his nibbles turning into kisses as he moved down from her ear to her neck. "Real bad."

"What did you do?"

He shrugged his shoulders. "Oh nothing, but don't expect any more calls from Matthew. His feelings towards you may no longer be romantic."

Reluctantly she turned to face him. "Julius, what did you do? You didn't hurt him did you? I was planning on speaking to him myself about that," she said while secretly applauding the idea of two men fighting over her. She was still a woman after all.

The brief flash of anger in her deep, dark, blue eyes did something to him. It brought a sudden intensity to her beauty that amplified his attraction to her. "Of course I didn't love. He may limp around for a while but he'll live. I've known you a long time, Vicky Girl, and he wasn't your type."

She narrowed her eyes at him. "My type? And what exactly is my type?"

"You normally date men that are at least a hundred and he's not even fifty yet plus he can't fly."

He tried to kiss her, but she dodged it. "You are a bully."

"No, I'm not." And like a bird catching a worm his mouth caught hers and he melted into her slowly.

"Bully," she moaned softly as she pulled away.

Hungry for more he pulled her back in and drowned her with his kiss. She closed her eyes and fell into the bottomless kiss. She felt a shift and knew that they had moved before she even opened her eyes.

They were about fifty miles out in the ocean. It never ceased to amaze her how effortlessly he could release his energy. They were inches above the water, she looked down to glance at it as her arms wrapped around his neck. "You're fast."

"Under the right circumstances I can be rather slow."

Looking about she giggled like a little girl. She didn't need any convincing of that. She took in the scenery of the seemingly eternal water. "It's so beautiful out here." She knew that they couldn't stay long due to the fact that cruise ships as well as private boats came through this particular area. Her thoughts shifted. "Do you think The Quiet Ones are real? Do you believe that there are Ancient Immortals that are sleep beneath the earth somewhere?"

He waited a moment before responding. "I hope not, but it's possible. The power of such beings would be beyond control."

Her tone become serious and stern. "Who do you think Michael is, Julius? That day we were all at Gray's house, something was bothering you. I saw it in your eyes."

He sighed deeply. He was looking out over the ocean, yet he was seeing the past. "When The Fallen returned me to this world it was my Watcher who aided me. I have never been able to remember much about those first few days, but I know something happened. My memory was severely affected by my insanity. Even years after my return I was still struggling to remember things like my name... who I was... what I was. The only memory that remained intact were those of you."

Her heart warmed at the knowledge, but she was still concerned. "What do you think happened? How long had you known your Watcher?"

"Years. He knew I was slipping into The Great Desire. I warned him to keep his distance." Absently his fingers made small circles on her lower back. "I believe he took something from me."

She frowned. "Took something from you? What do you mean? Like an object or something?"

The fact that he couldn't remember was frustrating. "I'm not sure, Love. When I finally parted from him I felt that something was missing; a part of me was missing. I eventually convinced myself that I was just missing you."

She studied his face. "You think that The Ancients have it," she stated not asked. "Whatever it was he took."

He didn't answer. She dug her face into his face and held him closer for a long moment.

"Why did they chose us, Julius? What gave them the right? They didn't consult with us. This life wasn't offered to us it was forced upon us. What choice did we have?"

"And what would your choice have been, Victoria?" He understood her anger towards The Fallen. He had his own share of it towards them, but they couldn't let their anger blind them to reason. "Immortality is a glittering jewel, Love. No one would refuse its allure upon first sight. Would you have truly walked away from the temptation to live forever? We are no different from Eve. We all crave the knowledge of life and we will accept it, even if it comes in the form of a talking serpent or some fallen god."

It wasn't his words that cooled her, it was the voice of reason his words carried. However, she would not relent with the views she held against them. "They could put an end to everything that is happening, but they don't. They do nothing as they have for centuries. Perhaps these Quiet Ones will awaken and destroy us all. Perhaps that is their plan.

"Shhh. Hush now." He gave the back of her head a light pat. "Don't waste your emotions. Whoever they are they gave us this gift, as well as this curse. We live. That is what's really important."

"Do we? Do we truly live? We can't even have families. What is even sadder is that we don't even want families, or do we? It's not in our nature. We don't desire the company of our own kind. It's genetic. Only a few of us challenge The Great Desire for love."

Her voice was nearly muffled since her face was still buried in against his chest.

He looked down at the Aquatic life drifting near the surface of the water. He had no doubt that they were curious about the intruders above them. He kissed the top of her head. "It is who we are. What The Blood of the Fallen makes us and we cannot escape it. Let us return."

They returned to the beach moments later where they walked hand and hand until night fell. There was a hotel near the beach where Victoria had booked them a room. She was running towards it with Julius chasing her along the shore line. Her hair was wet and sandy from where she'd fallen in the sand several times. He caught her and swooped her up in his arms.

"Where are you taking me now?" She asked playfully as he carried her.

"Where do you think? To your room."

"I have two perfectly working legs I can walk on." She wiggled her legs dramatically for effect. "See?"

"I do. I have plans for those legs tonight."

"Oh. Is that so? Why wasn't I informed of this? They are after all-my legs."

"You just were. Sorry about the short notice." Without breaking his stride and his eyes closed he kissed her deeply.

"Hmm... what was I saying?"

"Nothing important."

She leaned her head back into him and closed her eyes. She felt the pull of The Great Desire, the sudden urge to take the life of her lover. She hated the feeling. She couldn't imagine what it would be like if it dominated and took control over of her. She didn't possess the focus of Julius. The disease could kill her. It was still hard to believe that she had him back. She wondered about this place The Fallen had taken him to. What had happened to him there? Was he completely healed from it?

She didn't want to lose him again. She wasn't sure she could survive it. She didn't share his stoic views on The Fallen, but she respected him even more for it. She would stand by him until the end, whether it was tomorrow or a thousand years from now.

No, she couldn't change what she was, but she could take what was given. She would take it tonight and she would take it all.

*****

She was running through some thick woods and although she was Immortal it seemed like she could only move at the pace of a mortal. Her heart beat was pounding continuously in her ear and she could feel the beat of it throughout her entire body. It was late night so it was dark, but the light from a giant full moon poured out to guide her. She would not break her momentum or her stride. Fallen trees, huge logs, and large pieces of rock were scattered about and she dodged them all. She moved and maneuvered like an Olympic runner through an obstacle course. She couldn't stop. To stop was to die and this night death would be denied. She came upon a short drop and descended into a rapidly flowing creek. She then crossed it and hit an incline without missing a beat.

They were coming.

She hadn't seen their faces so she didn't know what they looked like, but she knew that they were Immortals. She could feel that these Immortals were different, there was something disturbing about them. She could feel it. They were Ancients from before the time of the flood. They were also powerful, extremely powerful which is why she was so confused. Who were they? And why were they chasing her? She knew they could catch her if they wanted, but for some reason they wanted her to run with the illusion of escaping.

There was no escaping.

She had no idea how long she'd been running. Time was irrelevant. Her only focus was on running. She became vividly aware of the creatures of the night, nocturnal eyes, hidden deep in the dark, that watched her as she passed. She was an intruder, a trespasser trespassing in their world.

The Quiet Ones were coming. She had to keep running.

All of a sudden she knew. She knew that it was them. In eight hundred years Isabella had never know fear. She had never been in its cold embrace… until now. The forest seemed to be never ending. With the moon in front of her she kept running towards the light like a child running towards its mother. She was afraid, petrified. She had become a prisoner to her fear. She could almost feel the cold steel of shackles on her wrist and ankles. The weight of it was her reality, a tangible reality. Her body was heavy with exhaustion. She could feel the ache of every muscle in her body, yet she kept moving. They were getting closer, she could feel them. She was tempted to look back, but she didn't want to risk it. She was also afraid of what she would see if she did.

Suddenly she came to an edge and nearly slipped as she came to an abrupt halt. Before her was nothing but emptiness. She looked down into an abyss of grey mist and saw nothing. There was absolutely no visibility whatsoever. She had seen nearly all the known geography of the planet and there was nothing familiar or recognizable about her current view.

It was all a dream. She was dreaming.

She couldn't remember the last time she'd slept. Was it a month ago? Immortals didn't require sleep in the same manner that mortals did. She looked back behind and in the distance she could see the tree's leaves rustling indicting movement, but there was no sight of her pursuers. She turned back towards the edge of oblivion and peered into the darkness. Her conscious became aware of something. Whatever was chasing her wasn't coming from behind her as she had initially thought, it was coming from below her. It was slowly rising, reaching up to grab her right as she awoke.

She understood now. The meaning of it all was now crystal clear. The Quiet Ones were about to awaken.

***

The private jet powered down after landing at Hartsfield airport in Atlanta. The sky was gray signaling the approaching rain, as Lucas stepped down followed by Edgar who had a prisoner, whom was bound at the wrist, in tow.

Cain, with a bored look upon his face, was leaning against a black luxury sedan with his hands in pockets. Instead of watching his superior approach, Cain focused on Edgar; there was something about the man that he just didn't like. He had never gotten a positive or cordial vibe from him. In his opinion he was just the top lackey for Lucas. He was just like a dog that ate the crumbs that fell from the master's table.

Although he knew who the woman was this was his first time ever seeing her in person. He could smell the cologne of Lucas before he got in conversation distance. He was dressed casual but his boss sported a light gray expensive suit.

"Lucas." He greeted him with a firm handshake. He greeted Edgar with a cold stare. He looked at the woman, there was no focus in her eyes. She was probably drugged.

The drive back to Cain's place was mostly quiet. Lucas spoke with someone on the phone briefly in Spanish. His Asian escort had drinks prepared for them when they arrived.

"What do you want to do with her?" He hooked a thumb at the woman.

Lucas was already seated. "Put her in a room somewhere. She won't be a problem. I doubt she even realizes she's in America."

"Kim, see to her." Cain instructed.

Cain was the last to be seated. "So, what's the plan?"

The question was for Lucas, but Edgar responded. "We intend to extract Michael in three days."

He kept his anger in reserve. "And exactly how do you plan on doing that?"

Edgar was seated close to Lucas, he glanced over at him before speaking. "Your girlfriend is going to bring him to us. We're not gonna use a stone to kill two birds, we're gonna use two birds to catch a stone."

Cain almost released his anger, instead he hid his fist as he clenched it tight. He fought to control his tone as he looked a Lucas. "What is he talking about?"

Lucas had already lit a cigar. "Is she your girlfriend? That's not very professional. I expect better judgement from you. You were aware that she made contact with the Bloodline and she received no reprimand.

"The violation wasn't even reported." He watched his subordinate through a cloud of smoke. "Yes, at some point many of us develop secret ties with an Immortal, but she is still just a Watcher. A mere novice. We prohibit this at this level because they lack the experience. She has become a liability. And as such we will use her accordingly. Her life has been forfeited, you forfeited it. Michael is the prize, and if she can be used to help acquire him then so be it."

Cain was about to explode. How could he not know they had been watching him? Some of his best men probably were working for Lucas. He had done his best to protect her, but it seemed his efforts were working against him.

Lucas crossed his legs in a gentleman's capacity and gestured with the hand that held the cigar, as he spoke. "You contacted Silent Death and placed a hit on her family. That order will remain. If she survives this she will know that you were responsible. So, if you have any intentions of trying to salvage whatever it is that you think you have with her you can cancel them. Once we apprehend Michael she is no longer a part of this Organization. If one of our men have an open shot he will take it, her blood will be on your hands."

Cain said nothing. How dare they do this to him? It was time for him to contact some people that he was positive Lucas couldn't monitor. He would play along for now, but they would pay. They both would.

Chapter Eighteen

A week before Lucas arrived in Atlanta, Alianna had finally made the decision to fly out to Georgia. She was in San Francisco, where she'd been all her life. It was time to involve herself with Michael who she'd known about since she was a little girl. She lived a normal life and had done well concealing her own abnormalities from the public. She had her father to thank for that. He wasn't her biological father, but he'd been there since she was an infant.

He'd been there when she first began to discover she was telekinetic and he was the one who explained to her why she'd been born with such an ability. He told her about the Open gene. He had also told her about her mother. She'd known about her all her life. She didn't hate her mother. Her father had explained to her what happened and how her mother had been left with no other option. She was sure her mother would've loved her. Maybe it still wasn't too late to experience that in person.

For as long as she could remember she had felt a connection with Michael. She had sensed him as if he was standing right beside her. There were times where she had missed him although she had never met him. When her father had told her he'd been placed in a mental hospital she cried. She had wanted to go to him then but she was too young. That was twelve years ago. Since then she had graduated and got a degree. It had taken her five years to reach an executive position. She worked in the Traveling Department for a hotel branch. She handled the marketing and scouted for new possible location sites.

She was very beautiful. She had golden brown skin with dark hair; that she kept short. She was taller than the average woman. She was slender, yet full figured with curves in all the right places. Her eyes, which were brown, were usually kept hidden behind a pair of designer shades; year round. The eyes she had were like those of a cat, they could dig into a person's soul and make them feel exposed.

She was taking her vacation, which she normally spent with her daughter, early this year. Her world revolved around her daughter. She was her everything. It had taken everything in her to make the decision to leave her with her father. She didn't know what she would encounter and it was safer, as well as better, to go without her this time. She'd contacted the institution and was surprised that Michael had escaped a few months ago. They were still looking for him. This had bothered her a little and was another reason why she wasn't taking her daughter.

Her father had warned her about a special group of people who called themselves The Ancients. They didn't know about her, so it was unlikely that she would encounter them. They were the ones responsible for what had happened to her mother and Michael. They were the reason he'd been placed in the institution. Her father had told her everything and she couldn't believe the things they were involved with. She wondered if Michael knew the truth. If he knew what they had done. Had they come for him? Had they finally found him?

Her father had expressed his desire for her not to go, but he knew she would sooner or later. He knew that what was in her blood would force her to go. She normally slept or watched a movie when she flew, but this time her mind was too plagued with questions to sleep. She was used to getting on and off of planes, it was routine for her. When the commercial flight landed in Atlanta she then took a smaller plane to middle Georgia. Her rental and motel room had both been handled before she left home. It was a short and easy drive as she followed the GPS to the motel.

She crashed as soon as she entered her room and slept a little longer than what she intended on. It was almost midnight when she woke. The motel had its own restaurant that was open twenty-four hours. She headed over to get something to eat. The place was nearly deserted.

"Couldn't sleep?" The old janitor asked as he approached her from behind.

She was in the process of devouring a sandwich when she glanced up. "Overslept. Hadn't ate much." She said as she looked at his name tag. The name on it read J. Editton. He was an old skinny black man who was bald on the top and grey on the sides. He was pushing a mop bucket. "It's pretty good."

He nodded at that. "That's Darla's cooking. Guarantee you'll want some more. You sure are pretty missy. You from the South?"

She smiled at him. She was a bit amused by his Southern accent. "No, I'm here on business."

"Didn't figure you were. Got that look about you. Fine place, this is." He looked towards the huge glass windows. "Nothing more unpredictable than a Southern storm. They'll rattle you a bit, but once she's passed you'll feel the peace of her in your bones."

She had no idea what that meant. Was a storm coming or was that some kind of southern metaphor? "Excuse me, Sir, but do you know the mental hospital that's out here?"

His frown was deep. "Your business is out there, Ma'am? It's about an hour's drive out. You don't wanna go. Nothing but a bunch of sick folks and spirits in there."

"Spirits?"

"Evil spirits. You ain't never read the Bible?" He sounded as if he would go get her one if she said no.

She had been to the South before, but it was mainly on business and always to a big city. She was out in the country where religious and spiritual ideologies were prevalent.

"Sure. Did someone really escape a few months back?"

He scratched the side of his head. "I believe I heard something like that. Not sure though. If I'm remembering right they didn't never catch him either. Ain't no telling where he at by now. You must be a reporter?"

She shook her head, "No, It was just something I heard." The flash of lightning surprised her and caused her to jump a little.

"There she is, on her way. Well, guess I better get back to work. Enjoy your meal, Ma'am." He gave her a nod before strolling away with the mop bucket.

Strange. People in the South were definitely different from people out West.

The next day she followed the GPS and couldn't remember the last time she'd seen so much open pasture and acres of farmland. The place was literally in the middle of nowhere. She thought she would be pulling up to a building that resembled something from a 1980's horror movie, but she didn't. It simply looked like a hospital with bars. She took in the sight of the facility when she stepped out and got an uncomfortable feeling. To think Michael had spent twelve years of his life living in this place. How did he manage to survive?

She had already spoken with the administration staff over the phone, so they were expecting her. She checked in at the front desk and was told to have a seat. When two detectives appeared and not the staff personnel she knew that something was wrong.

"Miss Andrews, could you please come with us for a moment?" One of them asked after flashing his credentials.

"What's going on? What's this about?" She viewed them both through tinted lenses.

The same man spoke again, "You're not in any trouble Miss Anderson. We just have a few questions. I'm Detective Rains, and this is my partner Detective Johnson."

"I don't know where Michael is. I just came here to ask some questions." She felt the energy in her building, but she kept it under tight reign. She didn't want to hurt anybody; especially not the cops.

"Just come with us please," Detective Rains repeated.

Frustrated she sighed deeply. She didn't think the cops would be waiting for her arrival nor did she want to deal with them. She hadn't done anything wrong. She paused for another moment before standing.

They lead her into an empty doctor's office where credentials covered the wall along with several photos of the doctor and his colleagues. The desk was littered with numerous personal items. Rains carelessly pushed them to the side before having a seat. His partner took a seat in the cushioned chair that set behind the desk. She took a seat on the small sofa reserved for patients.

Rains continued with the lead. "What is your relation to Mr. Flint?"

"I'm a friend of the family." She said as she tried to relax.

Rains looked back at his partner, who was already scribbling on a notepad. They worked as a unit. One asked the questions while the other took notes. It was a system that worked for them.

"I see. Well, the problem with that is he doesn't have any family, at least none that we are aware of. He spent the last twelve years in this place without a single visit. What is even stranger is that there is no record of him officially even being admitted into the facility. It's like someone just pulled up in the parking lot and dropped him off at the front door and kept going. The same year he arrived here his mother also fell off the radar. She just up and disappeared just like that!" He said snapping his fingers.

"So, I have to ask, what family are you a friend of? Because as I stated before he didn't have one."

He had never had a visit? Her father couldn't have been aware of that. She was sure he would've told her if he had been. There was no way she would tell them the truth, that Michael was her brother. Why hadn't Katrina been to see him? Her plan had been to come here, speak with the staff about Michael, and hopefully be given Katrina's address. Where was she?

"I knew him as a child. I moved away before all this happened. We were still kids the last time I saw him. I'm putting together a reunion for old classmates and childhood associates and when I discovered he was here I decided to reach out to him. They told me he had escaped, so I wanted to come out and talk with someone about him. They said I could." She didn't lie naturally, so she chose her words carefully.

"Who did you contact to find out about Michael?"

"The internet." She replied dryly.

194

"And where did you move to?"

"California."

He nodded as he tapped his leg absently a few times. "What kind of family does Mr. Flint come from? A big one? A small one? A dysfunctional one?"

She shrugged. "It was always just him and his mother. They seemed pretty normal to me."

Another nod. "I'm sure they didn't tell you the nature of his diagnosis."

Lifting her chin she calmly responded, "No they didn't."

"Do you recall Michael as a child ever exhibiting any forms of mental instability? Did he have any imagery friends? Did he display any abnormal behavior?" He asked.

"No!" She snapped.

"So, he was perfectly normal the last time you saw him?" Asked Detective Johnson.

"Yes, but that was over twelve years ago. People change." She said crossing her legs.

Detective Rains took the lead again. "Miss Andrews we've been conducting an investigation into Michael's escape and we still don't have any real leads. A few years ago this institution, as well as many other state facilities underwent security reconstruction, which basically means more steel bars, more cameras, and a better security system to replace the one designed back in the '80s. That being said for a patient to be able to escape from here, after the changes were implemented, he would have to be able to do more than just pick a lock. He would also have to have some help. Inside help."

"From the looks of things it looks like Michael Flint simply walked out the front door never to return."

"We have no reason to suspect you of anything. There is an on-going investigation of the staff of this facility. Someone had to have given him a key and assisted him in getting out of here without being caught by one of the many high profile cameras. He couldn't have just got in a car and drove away either. Someone had to have been waiting for him. He had no active contact list, no visitations, no phone calls, and no mail. So, what we're doing here is trying to see if you know of anyone who would've tried to keep in contact with him or even wanted to. These places are infested with cellphones, which makes it possible that he was communicating with someone."

She wanted to erupt with laughter. She saw the picture clearly now. They didn't realize what Michael was capable of. She didn't know how many cases they had solved together, but she knew that they wouldn't be solving this particular one. "I'm sorry, Detective, I am just as much in the blind as you are. I haven't been in contact with anyone out here since I was a kid. All of this is new to me. Sorry."

A few moments after she left, Johnson, still reclining in the chair behind the doctor's desk, turned to his partner and said, "She's lying."

"You think so?" Rains asked as he resumed tapping his leg.

Johnson reached in his jacket pocket and pulled out a picture of Michael and slapped it down on the table. "If they're not related then The Statue of Liberty is really a man."

"You know some people actually believe that." Rains said with a smirk on his face as he picked up the photo. He blinked in shock at the strong resemblance between the man on the picture and the woman who just left. He hadn't been thinking of Michael's picture when he was speaking with her, but looking at it now the resemblance and the chance of them being related were undeniable.

"If she helped him escape then why come back? It doesn't make sense."

Johnson propped his feet up on the desk and crossed his legs. "Ever watched Michael Jordan play? He always had a great finishing move. Doesn't really matter much if you have all that fancy ball control if you can't finish the move."

Rains continued studying the picture. "So you're saying that she came here to finish what she and her possible brother started?"

"Officially it looks good. It's been three months. He's probably on the other side of the planet by now. You can look at her and tell she's got some money. She's probably tucked him away on some remote island in the Pacific somewhere. She knows eventually the link will pop up that they're related, so she came here pretending she's looking for him after she heard about his escape. Her not knowing about his escape, it's just a clever ruse she wants us to believe." He held up his hand mimicking the pose of a basketball player taking a shot. "Swish. Game over."

Rains shook his head at his partner. "But how did he managed to get out of his room?"

"Always a missing piece to be found. Sometimes the only explanation is the only explanation. Someone on the inside helped him." He picked up a little league baseball trophy that the doctor's son had won and gestured with it. "And it's up to you and me to find out who that someone is."

Rains nodded in agreement as his thoughts went back to the picture. What his partner was saying was indeed plausible, now they just had to prove it. If he was wrong then they would have an unsolved case on their hands. Johnson's theory was easy to accept because there was no other logical explanation for how Michael had escaped his room. People didn't just vanish and disappear without a trace. If he was willing to believe that then he needed to be placed in the same room which Michael had escaped.

Chapter Nineteen

About three hundred miles north of the African Coast Javian suddenly stopped in his flight across the Atlantic and hovered above the waters. Being a descendant of the Viking people, he was colossal in structure and his muscle definition was incredible. His golden blond hair was long and his deep blue eyes were as cold as The North Pole. He could have already reached America, but he was taking it slow, taking his time in his flight. He knew that Julius was expecting him and he'd been looking for another fight with the Immortal since The Crusades. Julius, like himself, was a warrior. A fighter who embraced the prospect of death like a mother embraced a child.

How many times had he reflected on their last fight? Analyzing it over and over again, trying to see it from different angles. Would he have beaten him? He honestly couldn't say and that had bothered him for centuries. He had fought with everything in him, holding nothing back, yet Julius wouldn't be defeated easily. He'd been forced to admit that in him he'd met his equal. There had never been another Immortal who could match him in battle before. He had always hoped that the legend of The Quiet Ones was real, so that he could test his strength against them.

The blood of his ancestors was strong in him. He was a warrior to the code. The idea of war was more appealing to him then life itself. What was life without war? What was nobler in life than obtaining the honor of defeating ones enemy? In the Ancient World his people were well known for their savagery, for their bloodlust. It was a part of who they were, their genetic makeup. God had included it in their physiology and anatomy. It was said that the Viking's lust for war and hunger for blood were greater than their lust for sex. Ancient tribes often marked their passing through foreign lands with their tribal markings or by erecting statues of their gods, but his people left behind the mark of death and total devastation. Annihilation of a place was a sure sign that the Vikings had entered a land.

Many of the Germanic tribes were no different. They were all barbarians. Their last fight would've been to the death if they hadn't been interrupted, but not this time. This time they would finish it. A few months ago he'd began to sense a strange energy and was drawn to it just like the rest of his race. He was familiar with the energy of Julius, but hadn't sensed it in nearly a thousand years. He had instructed his Watcher to look into this and was later informed about Michael, a mortal who fought Immortals. What was even more interesting was the fact that Julius was training him. Had a new challenge finally arrived? He had grown tired of fighting these Immortals who were too young to give him a true fight. Once he defeated Julius maybe Michael would be his next challenge.

A cold chill passed over him as a strong wind drifted by, but he didn't pay it any attention. The night was quiet and still with constellations clearly visible in the sky. They were the same ones that ship navigators had used as maps centuries ago. He looked about, scanning the seemingly endless stretch of water. Something was happening among The Immortals and it went beyond this mortal named Michael. He could feel it. He was sensing restlessness, a stirring of something. Could it be that The Quiet

Ones were real and were beginning to stir from their deep slumber? Or perhaps The Fallen Ones themselves were returning.

He looked down at the calm waters and narrowed his eyes. He could sense movement beneath him. He assumed that it was the aquatic life in the waters, but there was something more to it. Unsure he sent the energy of his mind into the deep waters to scan the bottom for the source of the energy. He didn't pick up anything strange, but he could sense the faint lingering of something's presence. There was energy down there and it wasn't emitting from the fish. He raised his power level briefly, just to flex his energy, as if to send a message to whatever was there. When whatever was down there decided to rise he would be ready.

He put the mystery to the side for now. There was unfinished business waiting for him in America.

***

It had been another rough week for Michael. Julius had drained him of every ounce of energy he possessed. They were going up further and further into the atmosphere. The higher they went the harder it was for him to train. They had already covered the stratosphere and we're now training in the ionosphere. It took so much concentration to breathe that it was almost impossible to focus on fighting at the same time. He'd been light headed and close to passing out more times than he cared to admit. He was also still a little nervous about being so close to outer space. What was born of the earth should remain on the earth.

The more he trained with Julius the more he saw how powerful he actually was. When he was convinced he'd seen the full potential of Julius' power he would prove him wrong. The man could go as far as the Exosphere, where there was not only gravitational issues but gaseous issues as well to deal with. He wasn't too impressed with his own improvement. His power could never match that of an Immortal who was over a thousand years old.

They would often train for three days at a time. After returning to Gray's home, which he had come to think of as his own, he jumped into the shower. Gray had called earlier and informed him that he would be extending his stay with his family for another week. He was in his room stretched out on the bed, with nothing but a towel wrapped around his waist, listening to an old '80s music station. He was allowing the cool breeze coming from the open window to air dry his body.

It was still hard to believe that he now slept in a comfortable bed in a well-furnished room.

Thoughts of his mother had been crossing his mind a lot lately. What had happened to her? He had torn the emotional bridge between them years ago and now he may be forced to repair it. He had never known, there were never any signs of her love. If there had been he'd missed them. His mother had never hated him. She had just been so withdrawn from him or maybe she had just pretended to be. What she done for him was not only bold it was brave and smart. Was it not an act of love? Despite the truth of it he just couldn't bring himself to completely embrace the idea of his mother loving him.

"Hey." Rachel called out from the doorway.

Michael slowly lifted his head from the pillow and smiled. "Hey. When did you get here?"

"A few minutes ago while you were in the shower."

She was wearing a colorful skirt with a thin top that tied at the breast. Her lips held a fresh coat of gloss and green emerald earrings hung from her ears.

"I'm glad you're back." He brought half his upper body up and propped himself on his elbows. The smell of her reached him and sent him straight to heaven. He hadn't seen her in three days.

"Just stopping by. Got a big meeting with Lucas." She leaned against the doorframe and crossed her arms.

"Who is Lucas?"

"The guy that calls all the shots. He's the president over my branch. Cain says that it's important."

She walked over and sat down next to him. She picked up the lotion he had yet to use and gestured for him to sit up. After filling her hands she began to lotion his back.

"We talked about this. My annual break is coming up, if I haven't found out anything by then I'll take my pay and go."

The feel of her hands on his skin was water on the fire of anger that had just ignited within him. He spoke without looking at her. "It's just not safe anymore. They know you're with me and I don't like the idea of Cain protecting you because he thinks he's in love with you. His hand will be forced sooner or later."

She made large soothing circles while applying pressure at the same time. "I'm not alone. We're not alone. They know that too."

Needing to touch her he reached for her hand over his shoulder. She kissed him lightly on the back. He turned to face her. "For twelve years I had a bad dream; a nightmare. When Julius came he shook me from my sleep, but you were the one that opened my eyes. I can't go back to that dream. If I do I will never wake back up."

Still holding her hand he brought her fingers to his lips. "I will die in that dream."

As he gazed into her eyes and became lost in a forest of green. The song "In the Air of Tonight" by Phil Collins came on, the slow intro pulled at them both. Their lips met in the sweetest passion, creating a quiet desire; a silent storm, while his fingers stroked her face. He didn't want to just make love to her, no he wanted to become one with her. He wanted to blend with her until the singularity of his being lost its definition in oneness of them. The Laws of Science stated that no two objects could share the same time and space simultaneously. He wanted to defy that law; to prove it wrong.

"I have never shared myself with anyone, Rachel. I never wanted to." His breathing had become harsh. "Yet, with you I want to share everything."

Her fingers found his chest, his neck, and then his ears. He belonged to her and she would claim all that was hers. She needed him and had been waiting for him all her life. The song took her deeper and deeper into what she was feeling for him. Love? Was that the name of the serpent that was wrapping itself around her heart? As he came to her she opened herself, body, heart, and soul. A seed was placed in her stomach that quickly grew and blossomed in a flower. She didn't just need him, she also needed him to need her. He did.

"We can share each other." She whispered as she tilted her head back and closed her eyes. Inviting him to feast on her as his hands explored and roamed. She was his female. His Eve. The missing rib taken from his body to create his mate. She was a limb that belonged on his body.

The feeling of his fingers roaming over her clothes elicited a quiet moan, a beautiful sigh, from her mouth.

Once her clothes were removed he once again found himself transfixed by the artistry of her body. Suddenly there was an explosion, a volcanic eruption, of desire inside of him. His touches became more urgent. His hands searched seeking to find that which would please them both. Last time he had been hesitant, but not this time. This time he knew what he wanted, what he had to have. He knew what was his. Arching her back she willingly surrendered to him while breathing his name.

The song approached its well-known break, where the drums played and the singer took it too its climax. As it did their love making began its final ascension, a rapture of its own. He could feel his energy building and he knew he would release it into her when the moment came. As the drum's beat faded into silence they fell with a big bang. The explosion had her fingers digging into his back as he buried his face in her neck as they were thrust into a universe of pleasure.

They came together and in that brief breathless moment they were free. They were free from life, from time, from the physical, from pain, from existence, they were free from everything. They entered a dimension of sensations that were unknown; perhaps one of their own creation, until the gravity of reality brought them floating back down. He continued to hold her close, not wanting her to go, but knowing eventually she would. But right now the moment was theirs. They owned it and would enjoy it as long as it lasted.

A few hours later that moment seemed as if it had never existed. Rachel was now being held hostage at Cain's condo.

"Leave us!" Lucas instructed the others in the room.

Before walking out Edgar shot a grin of spite in Cain's direction causing him to hesitate.

"Was I not clear?" Lucas asked standing next to the bed were Rachel was seated.

"But what do you pl..."

His words were silenced as his body suddenly flew back forcefully against the wall nearly knocking him unconscious.

"Don't forget your place, Cain." Lucas said in a voice that was firm, yet still held the illusion of calmness under the danger in it.

"If I decide to slit her throat and toss her out the window there is nothing you can do to stop me. Now leave!"

Feeling a bit disoriented Cain picked himself up from where he had crumbled to the floor. Rubbing the back of his head, he nodded, and left the room.

The only other person in the room was Katrina. She was considered in invalid so she was allowed to remain standing by the window.

"What do you want with me?" Rachel asked as she sat on the bed with her back against the headboard.

The fact that she wasn't bound at the wrist or ankles told her that it wasn't deemed necessary and that escape wasn't an option at the moment.

Lucas stared at her for a moment before speaking. "I have no intention of harming you, Rachel. I only need your cooperation." He glanced over at Katrina before continuing. "Her son is very unique. The information in his blood is all I need. Once I obtain that you, him, or his brain dead mother is no longer of any concern to me. You can depart from this organization and go where ever you chose. You have my word that my people won't bother you."

She glanced over at Katrina. She'd wondered who the strange looking woman was. So, she was Michael's mother. Now looking at her with that knowledge she could see the resemblance.

"Did you give her your word too?"

He shot her a tight smile that didn't reach his eyes and in a voice thick with indifference he said, "I gave her an ultimatum. What you see now is the result of her choice."

"What did you do to her?" Her heart went out to the woman and not just because of Michael.

Lucas sighed. "Rachel, I am not responsible for her condition. She is. Just as you will be responsible for whatever happens to you today."

"You don't need me to find Michael. You already know where he is. Why can't you just let me go?" She asked as she watched him.

"Of course I know where he is. Where he is, is exactly the problem. I need you to pull him away from his Immortal guardian." He said as he tilted his head in her direction.

She almost laughed. "You think he needs Julius to beat you? You can't even fly. There has never been a mortal strong enough to fight the bloodline and you know it. Telekinesis alone won't be enough to stop him. So, what's the point of all of this?"

He took a couple of steps, staying close to the edge of the bed and looking down at the floor as he did. "There will be no fight, at least not a physical one." He said before looking up at her and continuing. "You are going to call him and inform him that we have his mother, but once my people began the process of inflicting pain upon her she'll come to her senses. He will do as told or you'll both die."

The coldness of his voice and his calm demeanor frightened her. The first real feel of cold fear touched her spine. Although she felt a touch of fear it was the stubborn streak and strength of the determined inside of her that made her continue to resist. "And if I don't?"

For a brief moment the expression on Lucas' face genuinely looked sad. He locked his hands behind his back and looked at the laptop that sat at the foot of the bed. Picking it up he tossed it next to her. "Be very careful, Rachel. If you decide to open that and activate it you will start a clock that's irrevocable. It will not stop. I would tell you not to, but it's entirely your choice to make."

She watch him like a cat before looking down at the portable computer. She suddenly felt weak as a sickening feeling crept into her gut. Her hands trembled and hesitated as she fought with the voice in her head. Grabbing the laptop she flipped the screen up and activated it. The reality of what she saw was like a meteorite crashing into her world burning up the air so she couldn't breathe. Her mouth went dry and her entire body froze in shock as recognition of what she was seeing settled in.

It was a live feed so what she was seeing was happening as she watched it.

"You have a beautiful family, Rachel. It's a pity you haven't been in touch with them in so long. As of thirty seconds ago you now have three hours to get Michael where I need him to be. If he's not there in the allotted time they will all die. The only thing that can save them is a call from me. I'll leave you now to consider your options. And by the way, just so you're aware this was all Cain's idea."

Although it was hard focusing in on what he was saying Rachel managed to hear every word that he said as she continued to watch her family on the screen at the park having a picnic. They were all there, her mother, her father, her siblings and their children. Relatives that she hadn't seen since she was little were even in attendance. They all set at a long table smiling and laughing while passing food around.

A strong mix of emotions flooded over her. Was she missed? Did any of them wonder where she was? They looked so happy. How was she supposed to feel? Was she supposed to be angry because it seemed as if they had simply forgotten about her, carved her out of the family portrait? Or should she be happy that they had managed to find happiness without her?

They were her family and that was all that matter. They were being stalked by death and didn't even know it, and it was all because of her. There was no audio, but whoever was monitoring them had to be near, probably even standing very close by.

Whoever they were they were professionals.

She took a deep breath to calm herself and began gathering her focus. Now was not the time to cry or break down. No, now was the time to become angry and to think. Their lives were in her hands and she would protect them or die trying.

Chapter Twenty

The day before Rachel had been taken hostage Alianna had been preparing to head up to Atlanta. After returning back to her hotel room she had called back home to speak to both her father and daughter. She had been glad to hear from them both. She informed her father that she still hadn't found Michael and that she was still looking.

She didn't know why but something, a gut feeling maybe, told her to head to Atlanta. The hotel she worked for had a branch there so she knew that she could easily get a suite there for free, but for some reason she didn't intend to. Instead she would book a room at another hotel on the outskirts of the city.

It was late, close to midnight, when she finally left. Her mind was once again spinning with questions. Why had Michael escaped? Had something happened to him or had he just got tired of being there? Where was their mother? She had told her father about the woman's strange disappearance and he knew nothing of it. Again he warned her about The Ancients, that they were highly skilled and dangerous.

Her adopted father had known her biological father, as a matter of fact they had been best friends. He had also warned him to be careful about when he got involved with The Ancients, yet he had ignored the warning and he paid the price for it. He had shown her the pictures that he still had of them from when they were younger. She had often wished that she had had the opportunity to meet him for herself. The only real connection she had with her biological father was the ability that he'd passed on to her.

She wondered how much Michael knew. Did Katrina tell him what had happened and what their father had done for them? If not he needed to know. She had wanted to come out here and find him years ago, but life had gotten in the way; especially when Angel had been born. She knew they were bound to come together. She'd always known it. It was their destiny.

She reached Atlanta a little after two in the morning. She checked into a room and ate the remainder of the food she'd gotten while on the road before crashing. When she got up it was close to 11:00 am. She didn't know exactly what she wanted to do or would do. She decided to head to the Starbucks located nearby for some fresh coffee, plus she had a weakness for the atmosphere. She hadn't been there long when she felt the strong feeling of being watched.

She was seated by herself at a little table away from the windows. Her eyes scanned the area as she looked around sharply for anything out of the normal. She didn't notice anything. She strained her neck as she checked behind her. She even slightly pulled down her shades to peer over them. When she turned back around she jumped and nearly knocked her coffee off the table.

"You look just like him." Isabella said as she looked at her the way a person who admires art looks at a painting. She was now seated right across from her.

The little girl hadn't been there a second ago and there was simply no way that she could've just appeared. She was the prettiest little girl that she'd ever seen. There was something about her eyes that made them stand out. It wasn't the fact that they were hazel, no it was more than that. It was almost as if they didn't appear to belong to her. They were more like the eyes of a woman than those of a child.

"You're one of them. The Bloodline." She couldn't believe it. Her father had told her about them. He had told her that she would know if she ever encountered one.

Slowly what the child had said slowly began to sink in. "Michael? You know Michael?'

Experiencing a bit of shock of her own Isabella simply nodded before saying, "You're his sister. His twin sister. Wow! Does he even know?"

"I don't think so."

What were the odds of this happening? She could almost feel the energy resonating from her. She had never felt something so strong before.

"What is your name? How long have you been alive?"

"My name is Isabella. I'm almost a thousand years old. Your name is Alianna."

She didn't know which was more shocking, the child's age or hearing her name. "You're almost a... How do you know my name?"

She waved it off with a hand. "It comes with being Immortal. Would you like me to take you to him?"

Alianna raised a brow. "You know where he is? Is he like your friend or something?"

Isabella smiled a pretty smile. "He's more like a big brother, but I've got him by a couple years. Come on. I'll take you to him. He's either training with Julius or hanging with Rachel," she said as she stood up.

"Who?" Alianna asked as she told slowly stood.

"Another Immortal and his girlfriend." Giggled Isabella. "You want to fly with me?"

It took a moment for what she said to register. "Umm… no, I'd rather drive."

Still amazed Alianna glanced over at Isabella several times as she drove. She couldn't wait to tell her father about this.

So, Michael was involved with The Bloodline. Maybe he did know the truth then. She wanted to ask Isabella so many questions. Like what was it like to be an Immortal? To live for so long?

She noticed that they were getting closer to the mountains, so this was where he was hiding. It made sense; especially since the police were still looking for him.

Michael was in the sitting room with Julius and Victoria when he, along with both Immortals, felt her.

Isabella entered first with Alianna trailing slowly behind. The second she lowered her shades and locked eyes with him he knew. But how? How was such a thing possible?

That single moment was the longest he'd ever experienced in his life.

"I was drawn to her the same way that we're drown to Michael." She said speaking to Julius. "They're twins."

Julius, who was seated next to Victoria, looked at her and then looked at the newcomer.

"Twins?"

She could feel the strength of all their energy, but Julius' was by far the strongest.

"My name is Alianna." She said looking at Michael. "I'm your sister."

How could he deny a truth that was staring him in the face? He didn't realize he was shaking his head. "I don't have a sister. I was my mother's only child."

So he didn't know.

"Your mother, my mother, our mother's name is Katrina Flint. Our father's name was Michael Flint."

He had never known his father's name. His mother had never told him. He stood slowly and took a few steps towards her. His brain kept trying to deny what his eyes could see was clearly true.

"But this doesn't make sense."

"Our father had a friend, his name was Jerome Andrews. He took me when we were born. The Ancients never even knew that I existed. Sit down Michael and let me explain." As she looked at him she wanted to embrace him, but now was not the time. She'd known about him all her life, yet he'd just learned that she existed, that he had a sister.

Julius looked at them both. The same strange sense of kinship that he felt with Michael he felt with her. She was telling the truth.

The moment was tense and a brief silence could be heard. Biscuit barked from out back.

Thinking that he might pass out Michael breathed slowly.

"Have a seat." He said as he gestured to the remaining empty armchair on the way back to where he was seated, but didn't sit down.

Alianna viewed them all again and noticed the bond that they shared as she sat down. There was a sense of kinship among them, almost like they were a family. Julius was clearly the leader and the beautiful woman sitting next to him was clearly in love with him. Isabella was the ever active energy amongst them. The child, who had lost one family, and found another. Michael was the nucleus, the glue that held them all together. There was no doubt that they would all stand by one another.

She spoke to Michael. "Our father was born with the Open gene. I'm sure that by now you've heard of it. He was highly telekinetic. He and Jerome worked in construction. Jerome was the only one who knew his secret. As you should know telekinesis is something that has to be controlled, but our father didn't do such a great job of controlling his. One day there was an accident on the work site. There was this heavy piece of machinery, something that weighed close to two tons, and he lost control of his ability and knocked it over. There was a man... he didn't survive."

There had been a spark of joy at knowing he was a Jr, but now hearing that his father was a murderer it died out.

She must've read it in his expression because she said, "It wasn't intentional. It may not mean much to you, but I trust Jerome's judgement and he told me that it was an accident. The company also ruled it as an accident and paid the guy's family a lot of money. He tried to continue with the job, but couldn't. He felt responsible therefore his conscious was torn.

"About a week after he quit he got a strange phone call. It was The Ancients. They told him they were scientist studying his disease, that's what worldly scientist refer to it as. They wanted him to come in and let them run some test on him. Jerome advised him not to go and to just let it go. He was already dating Katrina at the time and she didn't know about his 'disease'. The Ancients told him that they were working on a cure." She shook her head at that. "They had probably been watching him since he was a kid and

216

when the opportunity finally presented itself swooped in. They had been waiting to find someone to give the injections to."

"Injections? What injections?" Michael asked.

Alianna hesitated for a moment before speaking again. "Blood injections."

She looked over at The Immortals. "The Blood of The Fallen. Immortal DNA. They had been conducting experiments with it since the early part of the 20th century. Those that didn't have the Open gene died almost immediately and the ones who did had unusual mental breakdowns. According to what Jerome was told they were only working with a small sample, so they had to choose their subjects carefully. At first they thought the blood sample was simply too potent to bond and merge with human blood cells, but later tests led them to a different conclusion."

"The cell behavior of this blood sample was matched with similar cell behavior that is often found occurring in mad dogs causing it to have a constant state of instability. When the inherent properties of a cell structure becomes unstable the activity of these cells can become...," she groped for the right word before continuing, "chaotic. What this means is that The Immortal that the sample of blood came from experienced some state of insanity. Inherent insanity, it was in his blood like a disease."

Michael glanced over at Julius, who had already made the connection as well and found himself now remembering his long forgotten memories.

Noticing the reaction Alianna waited a beat before going on. "This altered the aim of the experimenting. The subject would no longer be the primary, instead the subject's offspring would be.

Someone born with the exact DNA strand would be in a better positon biologically to stabilize that chaotic cell activity."

"My God!" Michael exclaimed blown away by all that he had already heard.

"What were these people trying to do?"

"Create an Immortal," Julius softly said.

Alianna continued telling them what she knew. "Yes, but this created another potential problem, one they failed to acknowledge to our father. They couldn't be sure if the fetus would survive within the uterus or even if the mother's body could withstand the incubation of the fetus. The body of such a child could have astronomical demands. Demands that a mortal female couldn't meet. To sustain its vital biological demands alone would be a huge risk. I don't mean to sound cruel, but an infant is like a vampire in its mother's stomach."

"The injections went fine for a while. Nothing seemed out the ordinary, but gradually it did. Jerome told me how dad began to act strange. He started talking to himself, making strange sounds, and periodically having uncontrollable violent and explosive outburst with his ability. He even remembered him, out of the blue, shooting straight up like a rocket into the sky. It gets even crazier. He began having blackout spells. In the beginning he couldn't remember what happened, but as they increased he began to realize that he was teleporting. He said the place that he always teleported to was difficult to explain. He was convinced it was somewhere in outer space. He always referred to it as a prison of eternal darkness."

She sighed.

"Jerome kept trying to talk him into stopping the injections, but he wouldn't listen. He didn't know it, but they had also began to give him a drug that has some of the same effects of what is now known as an x-pill. Giving him the pills was obviously meant to increase the sexual activity between him and Katrina. They wanted her pregnant before he had a total melt down." Her expression became very serious. "Michael, for what it's worth Katrina loved him and wanted a family with him. These people took that from them. Took it from us."

The thought of growing up with a little brother crossed her mind and she quickly pushed it away.

"A few weeks before Katrina got pregnant Jerome spoke with one of their scientist. He exposed everything to him because he wanted him to go to the cops, but he wouldn't. It was too dangerous. He had already been threatened by these people. They knew he was trying to talk our father out of it. He had to be careful. This scientist he spoke with mysteriously died a few days later."

"Our father's condition grew worse leading up to Katrina's pregnancy. He became more unstable, teleporting more often to the mysterious place which always had a damaging effect on him. Jerome said he was terrified of the place. He said that he never wanted to go back. Sometimes he would handcuff himself to his car for long periods of time, but it didn't help to stop him from teleporting. Then there was a sudden shift in him. He became obsessed with the study of infant inception. He studied everything he could find on the subject from early embryo stages to incubation, to fetus development."

Frowning slightly Michael asked, "Why was he doing that?"

"Because he was planning to save us, Michael. He was searching for a way to beat them and he did. As you may or may not know twins are hereditary, at least in the genetic sense. A bloodline with no previous generations of twins is unlikely to produce any. It's hard to say what the genetic or biological outcome of a single offspring would've been within Katrina's womb considering the abnormal cell behavior it would've been born with. There could've been mutation or even deformity, but if the cells were divided and split…"

"Both offspring would have a better chance at balancing the chemistry the Immortal DNA introduced; given that they were given an equal share." Julius finished honestly amazed at all of this. He would've never imagined such a thing possible. This wasn't flying or moving at lightning speed. No, this was altering the genetic process of human creation. He looked at Michael and Alianna. "The Ancients failed to create another Immortal. Your father didn't want to create one, so he created something better."

"Both mortal and Immortal," Michael stated with a hint of astonishment. A sudden connection with his father came into being for him. This was his first time hearing anything and everything explained in regards to his father. He could be and was proud of him.

Alianna nodded at them both. "He used the power of The Blood of The Fallen to divide the cells, thus creating twins in Katrina's womb."

Looking directly at Julius she said, "Your blood. That is why I'm drawn to you just as much as Michael is. I thought it was a gut feeling that lead me to come to Atlanta. It wasn't. It was you. I saw the recognition flash in your eyes a moment ago. You remembered something."

"It was this last and final act of our father that killed him. He put everything into this. Into us. His brain simply shut down and he died before we were born." She said, trying not to let her voice crack or show any emotions as she did.

"The only person he told about all of this was Jerome. Our mother didn't even know until the last minute. Jerome swore to our father that he would take one of us and disappear. Jerome took Katrina to a friend's house far away from any hospital to deliver us." She said before stopping and taking a deep breath.

"I want you to understand something, Michael. I have struggled with this all my life. She chose you. She was forced to decide which of us she would keep and she chose you. I have often wondered why. Why didn't she choose me? Why?" Her voice broke again and this time she just couldn't contain her emotions. She shook her head as she attempted to fight the tears that she could no longer hold.

"Why, Michael? Why didn't she chose me?"

A sudden rush of emotion hit him in the gut like a fierce punch from Julius. He felt her hurt as if it were his own. He was moving before he realized it. He knelt down beside her and placed a hand on her knee and lifted her face with the other. "Hey… it's okay. She wasn't given a fair chance. They took that from her. No mother should be forced to choose between her children, but she was. She could have just as easily chosen you just as she chose me. It's okay."

She threw her arms around him and hugged him. He hugged her back. The move was natural, it was instinctive. She didn't realize just how long she'd been wanting to do that until she was actually doing it. Slowly she was restored. She felt the life that had been stolen from her had been returned.

"Thanks." She said as she looked up at Michael who had stood to rub her back.

"Where is she, Michael? They said that she never came to see you. I don't understand it."

Michael was about to respond when his phone rang. He answered it and his facial expression quickly became grim and his hands clenched into tight fists.

Julius stood as he hung up asking, "What is it?"

"They have Rachel," he said before looking down at his sister. "And our mother too."

Chapter Twenty-one

He moved with such blinding speed that he surprised himself. With a ferocious growl Michael launched his fist at Julius. Julius didn't even blink, instead he met the attempted strike with a calm open hand.

Michael then screamed at him, "Why do you continue to allow these people to exist? You could've destroyed them and ended this centuries ago. None of this would've happened and my father would still be alive. Your people allow them to exist, not because they validate your existence but because you don't care. That's the real reason you're an Immortal, because you don't care." Michael's face was contorted with rage and his veins visibly pounded at his temples.

Michael's anger was rational considering all that he had just learned, so Julius kept calm in the face of it. "Bring your power down, Michael, you'll destroy your friend's home." With ease he lowered Michael's fist. "Anger can strengthen you as long as you keep it in the proper prospective. We are what we are. The Ancients exist because they were meant to, just as sickness and death exist. These things cannot be changed. What happened to your parents was unfortunate, but if you want vengeance you won't get it by raising your hand against those who are not responsible for what happened. You need to find your focus." Although he had spoken in a very calm tone there was a dangerous edge that lingered beneath it.

Blinking a few times Michael realized that he had indeed raised his energy. Knowing that it was wrong he slowly lowered it. These people didn't deserve to exist. First they had destroyed his family and now they had the woman that he had fallen in love with. Would they take everything away from him? Would they rip the very heart from his chest? How could Julius justify their existence? If given the opportunity he would kill them all.

"Is Rachel the woman Isabella told me about? Your girlfriend?" Alianna asked from behind Michael.

Victoria answered. "She is with us."

Michael briefly glanced back at his sister before taking a deep breath and looking back over to Julius. His anger wasn't gone it had simply subsided for the moment. "She's with my mother, but they have her family. If I don't go to them then they will kill them. I'll need some help, there may be Immortals working with them. I can't save them all by myself."

Their training had formed a bond between the two of them and now that bond was even deeper, stronger after hearing and remembering all that had happened, so it wasn't that he didn't want to help him. It was just that he knew that Michael could beat them all on his own. He believed in Michael, now it was time for him to believe in himself. He needed to discover who he was and what he could do. He was just about to speak the words aloud when he suddenly sensed something.

He was here. The time had come.

Reading his facial expression Victoria narrowed her eyes at him and asked, "What is it, Julius?"

"He is here."

"Who is here?" She asked as everyone looked towards the window expecting to see one of The Ancients coming.

"His name is Javian."

"Who is he?"

Julius was quiet his focus completely stolen from the moment. He looked at Michael but wasn't seeing him.

"Julius?"

He walked away from him with his hands behind his back. He stopped and looked up at the deer head mounted to the wall before speaking. "I need you to listen to me carefully," he said as he turned back around to face him. "There is a very real possibility that I won't return from this. The information that your sister has provided is very helpful. It is my blood that flows through your veins. Blood that my Watcher stole from me three centuries ago. You have to unlock what's inside of you. You have to find a way to release it. This anger of yours... use it. Don't contain it, let it go. Release it. Remember what I told you. It's all about perspective. Everything is not what it appears to be. You may not be an Immortal, but because of what's in your blood you don't have to be. You have our speed and our power. You are capable of raising your energy just as high, if not higher, than any one of us.

"Immortals will not stop coming to you. As long as you are alive they will come. The stronger you become the more they will seek you out to fight. It is the way we are designed. I cannot go with you. I knew Javian was coming and he will not leave until we fight. Only one of us will survive it." There was no emotion in his voice. He was prepared for this. He was built for this.

Michael looked at the only man who had ever been close to a father to him. Would he now lose him too? He wouldn't allow himself to consider it. He simply nodded in response.

"Rachel is my friend. I will help you." Isabella said as she smiled at Michael. "Where is her family?"

Turning away from Julius to look at her he replied, "North Dakota. We have less than three hours to save them."

"I can get there in thirty minutes." She stated with confidence.

Alianna looked at her. Was she really that fast?

"Good. I'll get the location." He then looked at his sister. "You don't have to get involved in this. You can stay here.""

"But I already am, Michael. I'm a part of this just as much as you are regardless of what's happened she's still my mother too." There was no way that she would just stand by and do nothing.

Michael was surprised at the sudden protective instinct he felt towards her. He couldn't let anything happen to her.

"I'm probably not as strong as you, but I can control my ability," she stated.

He gave a nod to Victoria. He knew she would stand by Julius until the end.

So this was it. It was almost funny. He had stood in this same sitting room a few months ago and listened to Julius talk about Immortals and The Fallen Ones. Now he was here again learning that he had a twin sister and that the blood of Julius was in their veins.

"Our training is not done yet, so defeat this guy, Julius, so that we can get back to it." He said as he locked eyes with his mentor. He almost missed it, but there was a faint grin on Julius' face.

Something passed between the two of them. They both felt it, yet neither would acknowledge it at the moment.

They would both face their adversaries fearlessly. What was in their blood left them no other choice.

***

"None of this was my fault," Cain screamed at Rachel as she set across from him in the SUV. "For the last three years I have been trying to get your attention, and you've done nothing but ignore me. I have been trying to make a better future for us. You think I intend to work for these people all my life chasing after Immortals and trying to solve the mystery of the Bermuda Triangle? No. No one even cares about such irrelevant things in the real world. I've been fighting for us while you've only been thinking about yourself."

She had been trying to tune him out and keep her thoughts clear, but the thread finally snapped. 'There is and never was an us, Cain. I have never once given you an indication that I was even mildly amused by your flirtatious gestures. You are sick!"

She hated him so much that she wanted to spit on him.

He was actually shocked by her outburst. "How dare you? Do you know how extreme the training is for most initiatives for the first three months? Many of them don't even survive it. I spared you from that. I protected you." He said pointing at himself.

"You didn't protect me from anything," she fired back. "I didn't ask for your help. I didn't ask you for anything. You created this fantasy. It's not real, Cain, and it never has been."

He looked like he wanted to erupt. His facial expression underwent several changes before he shouted, "I am in love with you. How can you not see that?"

"You are insane, is what you are. My family has nothing to do with this, Cain. Call your men off," she said in a voice that sounded almost desperate.

He looked at her for a long moment unblinkingly before sitting back and looking at the window and murmuring, "I can't. It's over my head."

She also sat back and allowed herself to calm down. She watched the passing scenery for a moment before speaking again. "Did you send them? He told me that you were the one who sent them." Her voice held an eerie calm with a hint of the danger that was beneath the surface.

He looked at her with a bored look. "What does it matter?"

The SUV drove in a Northwest direction following behind a sedan that was carrying Lucas and Katrina. Both vehicles pulled into the parking lot of a large church that was currently being renovated. There were a few other cars scattered throughout the huge parking lot. The two Immortals who had been trailing them by air came down and landed with ease as well.

Lucas opened the church's doors with his mind and led everyone inside. The sanctuary was made up of a huge open space and housed two long rows of pews that were in the process of being repaired. There were large light fixtures and religious ornaments hanging from the high ceiling. Both sides of the structure were lined with tall stained glass windows. Workbenches, tools, and other obvious signs of reconstruction were scattered about.

Rachel and Katrina were seated next to one another in the first pew while two Immortals stood guard near the doors. Lucas and Cain were engaged in conversation while Edgar wandered over to the piano.

Rachel looked over at Katrina, she was a plump little woman with a pretty face, but her eyes held no focus. Her hair was graying at the temples. She was dressed in a simple gray uniform that consisted of slacks and a short sleeve shirt. It sort of resembled something that a hospital orderly would wear.

Rachel had tried speaking to the older woman several times, but she remained unresponsive. She tried again.

"Hey…," she said as she waved her hand in front of Michael's mother's face. "Your son, Michael, is coming for us. Do you remember him?"

Again she said nothing.

"He really is a sweet person. I know he'll be glad to finally see you again." She said as she laid her hand on the woman's arm, hoping to offer some comfort; some reassurance.

Katrina turned her head and looked away.

She couldn't imagine what this woman had been through or what all they had subjected her to.

The sound of Amazing Grace being played on the piano caused her to look up. Edgar was playing it flawlessly. His long fingers moved over the keys with practiced grace. Despite herself she found herself drawn to the music, pulled into the beauty of its beautiful melody.

He held his hands up and looked at them when he was done. "Such irony, is it not? The same hands that can create something so beautiful can also create something as dark as death itself."

He stood suddenly as Michael entered.

"Michael." Rachel attempted to stand, but Lucas forced her back down with his power.

"Well, the guest of the hour is finally here." Lucas uttered delightfully as he watched Michael approach.

Michael wore a pair of black jeans, a tank top, and a pair of white tennis shoes. He took in the scene as he moved slowly towards them. He noticed Rachel and although she had her back to him he knew that the woman beside her was his mother and his heart instantly cracked. He approached the area that one day would house both the Deacon and Mother's boards, but today his adversaries were there.

"So glad that you could join us, Michael. I wish we could've met up under more pleasant conditions. I brought your mother, I figured that was the least that I could do," Lucas said with a smirk on his face.

"What have you done to her?"

He could sense Lucas' energy, it was strong, but of no concern to him.

"Roughed her a little," he replied with a shrug. "That was a clever little move of hers, hiding you in a crazy house. Who would've ever thought to look there? She's a tough one. Never cracked, did a lot of screaming, but she never cracked."

Michael knew that Lucas was toying with him, trying to get up under his skin. He had to stay focused.

"What do you want with me?"

Lucas raised his arms in a dramatic fashion and said, "What we all want. What the whole world wants. Power. And it's in your blood cells just waiting to be extracted. What is telekinesis compared to the blood of The Fallen? These people are gods. There is no limit to what we could achieve with your power. You're not making a sacrifice, Michael. No, you're making a contribution."

Michael glanced at Cain, who stood beside Lucas like the faithful servant that he was, and then he glanced at the other guy who stood off to the side. "Will you let my mother and Rachel go if I come with you?"

"That depends." Lucas responded and looked over at Edgar. "My dear friend here has requested a fight with you. If you can beat him then they are free to go, but if not… then it's out of my hands."

Michael looked at Edgar again. He was tall and lanky with muscle. His long hair was tied in a ponytail on the back of his head.

"Do I have your word?"

"Of course. There is just one thing though. My friend is an expert fighter and he wants to fight in the traditional style. In other words no telekinesis, just simply martial skill alone. Although he has the ability he would still be at a disadvantage if you were to fight on that level being that you have the blood of Julius in you. This will be a fair fight."

Michael watched Lucas for a moment with narrowed eyes.

"How much time is left before you will call off the hit on Rachel's family?"

He lifted his arm and glanced at his watch and said, "About twenty minutes. You might want to get started."

"Am I allowed to sit my phone down first?"

"Sure."

He walked over to Rachel and handed her his phone. As he did he whispered, "She'll text." With that being said he looked at his mother, who was staring off as if she was unaware of what was going on.

Struggling to keep his focus he suppressed his rising rage.

"Be careful." Rachel said to him.

The area in front of the pulpit was cleared to become a good open space. The two men face each other and waited.

Chapter Twenty-two

The window that Julius was looking out faced the side the mountains. He sighed deeply. The home had a familiar feel to it now. He had developed a small sense of attachment to it. The memories here were few, but they held great value to him.

Victoria was hugging him from behind. Her arms were wrapped around his waist and she rested her head against his upper back where his long hair hung loose.

His thoughts were crowded. Something was happening to him. This experience with Michael had affected him on an emotional level that he wasn't familiar with, had never felt before. He felt almost human again. As an Immortal it was in his nature to remain sociably distant, to avoid the idea of community or anything holding the semblance of family. These were mortal associations and ideologies that had died when his mortal life ended. He felt the stirrings of such things deep within him. He was being forced to admit to himself that Michael was becoming the son that he never had the opportunity to have. Learning that it was his blood that gave Michael his ability to fight the Immortals made him feel... proud? If he was honest he could admit that that was true.

It was the touch of The Great Desire that had stained his blood and driven Michael's father to insanity. This was something that troubled him. He knew that at some point Michael would have to face and battle that same insanity, it was in his blood. He could teach him to fight other Immortals, but he couldn't teach him how to battle this disease. He would have to do it alone.

The last time he had seen Javian was toward the end of The Crusades, shortly after the 6th one. It was led by Emperor Fredrick II, if he remembered correctly, he was a little man that was said to be full of contradictions. He was excommunicated by the Papacy for not going on The Crusade. Then he changed his mind and went and ended up excommunicated again. That was in the year 1228. There was no fighting at all that time. The Syrian Christians wouldn't support him. They had good reasons not to. Fredrick wasn't a military commander, he was simply a diplomat. He ended up signing a treaty with a nephew of Saladin.

Their fight had been interrupted by unwanted allies. There would be no such interruptions this time. This would be the conclusion of a chapter that should've ended a long time ago.

***

Edgar raised a knee and then extended his foot out sideways. He raised it slowly until he was in a split position standing up. The move was meant to intimidate Michael, but it had no such affect. They circled each other and closed the distance.

Edgar struck first with a lightning fast jab followed by a low round house with his front leg. Both were deflected. He was simply testing the waters. He struck out twice more with jabs, advancing towards Michael causing him to step back. He raised his front knee to feign a kick, and in a burst of motion he spun into a spinning back fist. Michael saw it coming and stepped forward at an angle as he ducked. As Edgar was completing his spin he snapped a quick front kick to his midsection.

Edgar absorbed the blow and stepped back. He nodded his approval of the move. He launched at Michael with a series of high kicks. His feet were just as fast as his hands. Michael moved with his defense, while patiently waiting for an opening.

He used his leg to block a low kick from Edgar, with the same leg he struck at his face. The strike was dodged. He pressed his attack briefly, testing Edgar's defense. He spun into a spinning kick, but saw him shift back out of his peripheral so he continued his spin when he missed and spun again. His momentum easily helped him leap into the air and spin out with the second kick. The move generated enough force to knock him out, but Edgar dodged it at the last second.

Edgar was impressed with the well-coordinated maneuver. His opponent was just as fast and agile as he was. They circled again and both took the offensive. There was a brief rapid hand exchange that ended with Michael taking an elbow to the face. In hopes of taking the advantage of the score he leaped up with a flying knee. Michael brought his hands up, but the brute force behind it still knocked him back a little.

Michael growled in frustration as he intercepted another strike and took the offensive. He hit him once, twice, and then a third time before he feigned a hand strike but launched a sidekick to his chest instead. The blow took him off his feet and he hit the ground going into a small roll before coming back up into a low crouch. There was a stinging pain in his chest and it was hard for him to breathe. He rubbed his chest with an open palm.

Edgar stood erect and brought his hands back into position. He struck out again with angry strikes, he was losing focus now, and simply wanting to hit him.

Michael however was bidding his time. He cast his eyes briefly over at Rachel. He was waiting for that text. She shook her head once. His head was beginning to throb from the elbow and he had a cut across the top of his eye that was bleeding.

Edgar was coming at him hard. Michael changed the angle of his defense by shifting his feet, but Edgar moved with him. They both landed blows, to both the body and the face, but neither gave in to the pain inflicted. Their eyes were locked on one another in concentration. A quick sweat had been worked up.

Lucas watched in fascination. Both men were skilled, but it was Michael who appeared to be the better fighter. He noticed he never pressed his attack to hard as to where Edgar would attack with everything until he either landed a blow or received one. Their hand exchange was almost a blur making it hard to follow. He wasn't so sure Edgar would prevail.

Edgar delivered another high kick, but Michael dropped into a low sweep and took him off of his feet. He stood and as he did he pulled two short blades from his boots causing Rachel to scream out.

Michael didn't have time to point out to Lucas he didn't have a weapon as Edgar came at him. The two blades came at him in perfect symmetry, swiping towards his face. The angles changed from diagonal to horizontal to vertical. One blade leading the other. Michael dodged, weaved, and shifted his feet to avoid getting sliced.

Edgar swung one blade wide and followed it with a complete spin. Once, twice, and then a third time. It was the third spin that allowed him to catch the back of Edgar's hand, stopping it inches from his face. Michael was anticipating the other hand as it went for his stomach. He now held both of Edgar's hands. Edgar tried to out muscle him, but Michael was just too strong. They turned about several times, both men fighting to keep their balance. Edgar growled as he pushed with everything he had trying to force both blades into Michael's body.

It was while they struggled that Michael caught sight of Rachel's nod. The text had come. He snatched himself away from Edgar as he shot a front kick to his stomach.

He recovered quickly and came back at Michael who dropped his guard. Edgar knew something was wrong, but kept coming anyway. He completed his swing with his knife and hit nothing.

Michael was gone.

Lucas instantly became alarmed.

A second later he reappeared with Isabella who wasted no time rushing the two Immortals. All three flew straight up through the roof and out of sight.

Lucas cursed and Cain fled the scene.

"Kill him!" Lucas shouted at Edgar.

Edgar released his energy and used it to add force as he slung both blades at Michael, but they never made it.

When Michael released his energy it was far more impacting and devastating. His force alone pushed the front pews to the back and shattered the windows. He screamed as his energy rose. The thrown knives simply lost their momentum against the release the energy.

He charged Edgar with deadly strikes; swinging with incredible force. Edgar tried to resist the attack, but quickly realized that he couldn't hope to match Michael's released energy.

Michael shouted to Rachel, "Take her and GO!"

The instant she tried to move she found that she couldn't. Lucas held her down with his power so with a scream of her own she released her energy against him. He grinned at her as she fought.

"You are a novice, girl. Do you seriously think that you can resist me?"

"Let me go!" She shouted as she continued to push with her mind.

Alianna entered the sanctuary and saw Michael fighting Edgar. She saw Lucas and Rachel staring one another down and knew some exchange of some sort was going on. It had to be Katrina sitting next to Rachel seeming to be oblivious of everything that was happening around her. She went to her.

She knelt in front of her. "Katrina, I need you to come with me now. It's okay, you'll be safe."

The woman said nothing.

Alianna looked over at Michael who was winning his battle with the other guy, but as she looked at Rachel she didn't think she was doing too well.

"Katrina." She tried again, shaking her a little this time. "We really need to leave now."

High above the church roof Isabella easily deflected strikes from the bigger Immortal who had only been alive for two centuries. The other one was barely over a hundred years old.

"Are you serious? I'm twelve and I hit harder than you." She teased him.

The smaller Immortal came from behind hoping to grab her while her concentration was on the other one. As soon as he got close she spun away with her elbow extending catching him in the throat. Like a ping pong ball she sprang right back and hit the older one with an elbow as well. She remained in the middle for a moment, going back and forth with her strikes. She was too fast for them to land a single hit. They tried to work in unison with one another, coordinating their strikes as one, but it wasn't working. They even managed to hit one another in one attempt they hit each other.

She caught a punch coming at her from the bigger one and with a powerful chop she broke his arm while kicking him back down to the ground. In a mad rush the smaller one rushed at her and found his face colliding with her knee. She knew the other one would heal quickly and return.

She couldn't wait.

Rachel almost stood. She was just about fully erect when the force of Lucas' power slammed her back down. She was growing weak and knew that she couldn't struggle with him much longer. "You've got to get her out of here now." She shouted to Alianna in a strained voice.

Alianna tried again, but her mother wouldn't budge.

With a grunt she pushed with all that she had against Lucas who stumbled back from the force. In a fit of rage he snarled as he lifted her clear off the bench with his mind and sent her flying out of one of the windows.

Alianna was still trying to get her mother to move when something suddenly happened. Her back was to Lucas, so she didn't see his approach, but Katrina did.

Alianna watched as her mother's eyes came into focus. In a swift motion she grabbed her and slung her to the side just as the knife was diving down causing the blade to sink deep into her own chest.

They thought she was just a crazy old woman, an invalid, so Lucas didn't bother to search her for any weapons. He didn't think she was capable of plotting, but she had been. She had been plotting for the last twelve years, plotting and waiting for the one moment to strike. That moment had finally come.

Lucas didn't even see the blade that she'd kept concealed slip into her hands. It was too late to stop it when she dug it into his neck. She held him close as he struggled, his blood pouring all over her.

"This is for the husband you took from me." She said as she dug the knife in deeper. "This is for the children you took from me. I have waited for this moment for a very long time. I killed you. You take my life and now I've taken yours." She released him and watched him fall back as she slowly fell to her knees.

Michael heard Alianna scream as he finished off Edgar with an open palm hand strike to the chest that stopped his heart. He hurried over to his sister, who was on the floor holding their mother. Katrina had a knife protruding from her chest and her shirt was covered with her blood.

"Give her to me. I can teleport her to a hospital." He said his voice urgent.

"No!" Katrina held up a hand. "It's too late for that, Michael." She said as she fought to breathe.

"You'll die if you don't get to a hospital." He almost shouted. He had just gotten her back, it was too soon to lose her again.

She was holding one of Alianna's hands with her other one she reached for his. "Come her, baby… let me see you."

Emotions raged high in him. A storm of pain and hurt swirled in his chest. He grabbed her hand and they both held on tightly.

"Don't do this, Mommy. There's still time…"

"Shh… hush child. My mind is broken. I'm too tired to fight anymore. This…" she looked at them both with tears in her eyes.

"This is what I've been fighting for. To see my babies one last time. My babies. I brought you both into this one world. Michael, grab your sister's hand."

He reached for it as tears fell from his eyes.

She looked up at Alianna. "I never stopped thinking about you. I never stopped loving you." She squeezed her hand. "You were always with me. I never gave you up Alianna. Promise me you two will stay together. No matter what. Please promise me that."

They both did.

"Your father would be so proud of you. Both of you. He fought for you, gave his life for you. Don't ever forget that." She coughed. "I love you both."

They were waiting for her to say something more, when a few moments passed and she didn't speak again they knew, it was over. She was gone. They sat there in silence for a long moment. Alianna continued to rock a little with their mother still in her arms.

The church was quiet, but if pain was a sound it would've been heard from miles away.

Chapter Twenty-three

A lonely hawk drifted high above the battleground in large circles. Maybe it was searching for prey or maybe it was aware of the imminent battle. The sun was a ball of fire that sat in a clear sky sprinkled with a few clouds. The temperature was pleasant. The two warriors were not far from the area where Julius trained Michael. As a matter of fact they were just a couple of miles further north. This far up into the mountains they shouldn't be disturbed or attract any unnecessary attention. They stood apart in what was once a green grassy clearing, but was now just some hard earth with scattered fallen leaves about. To their right was a sharp forest incline, a slope filled with dense woods and ancient jagged rocks. A rapid stream was to their south, which was more behind Javian. The clearing was enclosed by the forest, careful digging would probably reveal some ancient Indian relics. No doubt the hidden site was once a place of ceremonial practices.

Ancient Indian warrior spirits probably still lingered about.

The scene was picturesque. It was peaceful and quiet. The only sounds were the sounds of nature. The rapid stream could be faintly heard. They stood at least fifteen yards apart. Both men wore their hair lose. Julius' hair was a bit longer. He wore white clothing while Javian's attire was dark which easily contrasted sharply with his golden blonde hair and powerful blue eyes. Javian was by far the larger of the two. He had chiseled muscles, but Julius was likewise impressive in his physical stature. Both immortals would easily shame any human physical body tone. A cool breeze blew down from the mountain that ruffled their clothes. A few ground animals ran about, stopping suddenly to sniff at the air as if they too were aware of what was happening.

"This will be it for us, Julius. Immortality ends here today for one of us." Javian declared calmly, showing no emotions at all. "Destiny is always inevitable."

"It is." He gave a light nod. "We have experienced death before, but this time The Fallen will come with different intentions. They extended life the last time we saw them, but today they will end it." He flexed his fist several times in quiet anticipation.

Nearly a millennium had passed since these two enemies had faced off, but the animosity between them was still alive and fresh.

The biceps in Javian's arms twitched. His body was strumming with adrenaline.

Julius thought it strange as he stood facing his Immortal enemy. There were some things that not even time could change.

"Why did you go against me, Julius?" He asked. "We could've changed things. We are alike, you and I. I believe even The Quiet Ones would've joined our cause, if they truly existed."

"Or maybe even such beings as The Quiet Ones could see that your views lack reason." Julius countered. "What you speak of is annihilation. We exist because of The Fallen, Javian. It is their blood that now provides the life and power that fills our beings. You are asking creation to defy the creator."

"Is this not what humanity has done? They have defied their creator in every possible way. They worship the gods they created and turn their backs on the God that gave them life. The history of both of our mortal people can attest to this, yet they remain. They haven't been annihilated, as a matter of fact they've been expanded.

They crawl all over this planet like a bunch of rodents and how many times have they spit in the face of their creator?" His voice was thick with passion and conviction.

Julius shook his head. "That is an entirely different matter. The creator of humanity has revealed himself to his creation and communicated with them. They killed him for it. The Fallen has done no such thing. We are not the offspring of The Fallen, we are an alteration... a mutation. They would destroy us before they spent any energy on trying to redeem us. You wanted to declare war on something we don't even understand. We don't even know their origins. We know nothing about them, Javian."

He couldn't refute Julius' logic and in truth he didn't care to either. He simply wanted to exist independently from The Fallen Ones. "I was in love once too, Julius." His voice and expression became nostalgic. He looked up at the circling hawk. "She was beautiful. She hadn't possessed her immortality a whole century yet and they killed her because of our union... our love. My pain probably wouldn't have been as great if they punished every Immortal for this violation, but they don't. They pick and choose. For twelve centuries I have grieved my lost."

And so finally Julius knew the true reason behind Javian's hate of The Fallen. It wasn't for freedom and independence. It was for love. Would his views not be the same if they took Victoria from him?

"I hate them, Julius. They are cowards. I will curse them until the end of time." He continued to look away.

"We cannot declare war on The Fallen." Julius stated plainly.

"Is it fear that makes you submit to their will like some faithful dog?" He nearly screamed it. "I say they are afraid of us. They fear the very power they've given us. We are gods among men brother."

"We were not created to be gods, Javian." He raised his voice. "As mortals or immortals."

"Then what were we created to be? Slaves? I would have rather remained in the warm embrace of my mortal death." The first signs of anger sparked in his voice.

"You are being ridiculous. We are no one's slaves."

"And how do you know this? As you just said we don't even know who they are. The creator of humanity created them for his glory. Perhaps we were created for similar reasons, Julius. To bring them glory." He gave a short crazy laugh. "I will bring them no such thing. At the end of this battle they will appear and if I am the last man standing they will have to force me to my knees.

"They gave us Immortality."

The air about Javian suddenly changed as his power exploded, a light wind generated about him. "They gave us nothing!"

Julius had no choice but to respond, instantly he raised his power level to similar effect. So this was it. "They gave us everything."

In the space of a heartbeat time ceased to exist, the very earth paused in its orbit as The Fallen Ones looked down upon their children. A single tear fell from the heavens.

The blow hit Julius with tremendous force, even with his powerful vision it seemed as if the giant had suddenly disappeared. He stumbled back, not quite entirely dodging the second strike. He suddenly spent outside the extended arm, moving past Javian. He completed the spin with an elbow that landed at the base of Javian's neck. He was now behind the giant, he released a full roundhouse intending to strike the head, but Javian ducked as he spent back around to face him.

Javian blurred again as his knee flew up towards Julius' face. Julius who saw it coming, threw himself into a roll on the ground. He moved right under him as Javian sailed over him. He came up without losing his momentum and jumped towards him with a spinning heel kick. It was pure instinct that brought Javian's hand up to block the attempt. His other hand followed after the block instantly. The intended blow was deflected. Rather than falling back Javian pressed his attack. He took the offensive. Some blows landed others didn't.

The two Immortals moved at blinding speed. No human eye would have been able to follow their movements. The blows that did land were bone shattering. A human body would easily crumble from the impact. They were both conserving their energy, trying not to release too much too quickly. Both men were skilled at this.

Julius ducked another powerful hook, but instantly reversed his motion and became airborne. He shifted back in the air, creating a small distance between him and his opponent, which he knew meant nothing. If he was a hundred yards away Javian could move and still attack him as if it was only an inch of separation. His shoulders rose and fell with his heavy breathing. His hands were up before his face in the guard position.

He was feeling the effect of Javian's powerful blows. He knew he would have to be careful to avoid getting hit. He couldn't trade blows with him. The Viking was simply too strong. He went deeper into himself, strengthening his focus he raised his energy level. His muscles tensed as a low growl began to escape his lips. Flashes of electrical currents appeared around him. A lot of loose dirt and scattered rocks on the ground beneath him began to levitate.

Javian grinned. He came off the ground and resumed his aggressive attack. He knew he was the stronger of the two and he knew that soon Julius' body would begin to tire. Julius snapped out a sidekick, keeping his leg extended he continued to kick out, pumping and swinging his leg in a forward and reverse motion. Javian was able to dodge some, but not all. His opponent was by far the quicker of the two. In a mad rush he took a hit and then moved in, but Julius saw it coming and he spun out and then resumed his attacks with the opposite leg.

With a ferocious growl Javian raised his energy level causing a sonic boom. The act alone pushed Julius away. Javian was pulsing with power. His long hair moved wildly about him and his muscles flexed in anticipation. He raised an open palm towards him and released a powerful blast of energy that shot out at lightning speed. Instead of moving farther up in the air, he moved back down to the ground, barely escaping the attack. The second his feet hit the ground he moved again. If had he hesitated he would've been hit by the second blast that followed and tore a hole in the earth. Javian remained suspended in the air, releasing blasts of energy from his hand like a madman with a gun. Julius moved, ducked, weaved, rolled, and briefly became airborne to escape. He knew he couldn't afford to take a hit.

Still on the ground Julius turned and ran from an oncoming blast, just as it was about to hit him. He turned and slapped it away with one hand then fired a blast of his own with the other hand. Real fear washed over him as he watched Javian absorb his energy as if it were nothing. He had never doubted Javian's potential and or power. He understood that every Immortal grew stronger with time.

He would have to be smart.

The ground trembled and then there was a brief rustle amongst the trees on the slope as some of the deeply imbedded rocks tore loose from the ground. Javian grinned again at this; ever loving the prospect of a challenge. Some of the rocks were massive, the size of small cars. Julius released his telekinetic energy and the assault began. Javian punched out at the first projectile, shattering the rock with ease. He spun suddenly into an elbow hitting then another and another. He continued his spin, elbow leading, shattering rock after rock. He was hit several times, but the pain only managed to fuel his anger. Still facing the assault he shifted back as if running, extending both his hands he released a dual blast of energy into the storm of granite. He roared as he released his energy. His body still receiving hits from the rocks that he couldn't stop. Several cuts began to appear and his blood leaked freely.

Javian's roar increased as he raised his power another level. Again a sonic boom exploded into the air powerfully. The expansion of his energy halted the assault. For a moment there was a brief struggle as Javian's energy pushed against Julius' telekinetic release. The point where the two powers converged at was visible. It was a visible wall of energy that gave in either direction, but Julius was no fool. He knew he would expire before Javian. He released the rocks and before they hit the ground he was in motion, moving to attack. He pushed the giant back with a hard press, but he was careful not to commit, just as Javian took the offensive again he moved to the side. He repeated this, creating a different angle of attack each time forcing Javian to continually readjust his strikes.

Julius spun with another spinning heel. Javian saw it, but instead of blocking it he shifted down. In his descent he grabbed Julius' ankle and slung him to the ground. He quickly followed him down with his fist drawn back intending to crash it into Julius' face upon impact. Julius read the intent clearly, as soon as his back slammed into the earth he rolled. Javian's fist instead crashed into the ground penetrating it several feet deep. The sequence played out so fast it appeared as if it was planned. They were positioned at the bottom of the slope. Javian raised his hand again and begun to fire energy blasts at Julius who disappeared into the dense woods. Javian pursued while still firing blast after blast, barely missing the agile warrior while knocking huge holes into tall pine trees.

He wasn't running from the fight. His intent was to expire the energy of Javian. A single hit from one of his blast could be fatal. He was caught off guard as Javian released telekinetic energy and snatched an entire tree out of the ground. Julius realized his mistake when he veered left, escaping a blast of energy and collided with the uprooted tree. The impact stunned him. That was all Javian needed. In a blink of an eye he closed the distance, coming up behind him and placing a lock around his neck with his massive arms.

Julius knew that he was in serious trouble when Javian locked his arms around his neck from behind. He fought against it immediately, twisting and thrashing about. Already he felt his grip on consciousness slipping away. Darkness was threatening to devour him, but he resisted with everything he had. They slammed against a huge tree, knocking loose leaves, debris, and huge chunks of tree bark everywhere. He became airborne, but Javian brought them back down crashing into the hard earth causing them to roll about as he did. He repeatedly rammed his elbow into Javian's ribs, the blows were powerful, but he still wouldn't release his hold.

Darkness continued to threaten him, but he continued to resist with pure will power alone. Just when he thought it was over a strange thing happened. A memory of Julia entered his mind. It appeared recent, fresh, and vivid, despite the fact that it had been well over a thousand years since he'd seen her. She was standing in a field of flowers, beautiful flowers of myriad colors in the hills of France. She wore a blue dress that was in tune with the style of her day. Her white blouse became visible as she made small circles for him. She waved and blew kisses with a face full of mirth. She clipped off a flower in the high grass and placed it behind her ear. The bright yellow sharply contrasted with the bundle of her red hair that bounced on her shoulder. She mouthed the words 'I love you' and then blew him another kiss.

He heard a strange sound. A growl of something primal and animalistic. It grew and rose in intensity, building, rising, and gathering in strength. Julius realized that it was him. He continued to watch Julia move and spin about in his mind's eye. He stopped resisting the darkness and welcomed it. Not only did he welcome it he embraced it. He allowed the memories of Julia to push him into the deepest hole, the deepest darkness where only rage existed. He knew this place. He'd been here before when he'd battled The Great Desire. This was the place his mind had retreated to to survive.

Julia slowly faded from his thoughts and the Leviathan was awaken. The creature from the abyss arose.

They both shot up into the air as Julius exploded with pure rage and power. Javian was instantly torn loose and knocked several feet away. Like a volcano he erupted with amazing energy. A bright light flashed enveloping him completely as the blast's wave covered a three mile radius. Trees that had stood in the same spot for over a hundred years were blown away. The slope trembled with a violent quake from the pressure of the explosion. The entire time he roared, his voice echoing far out. As the light inverted he came back into view with constant flashes of electricity outlining his form. He was swollen with power, literally leaking with it.

Javian had to fight to stand. He had to shield himself from the initial blast, even by standards of his own it was powerful. Slowly he ascended back up into the air, raising his own power level as he did so. The sky above them was growing dark and not from any approaching storm, but from Julius' power.

"Do you see it Julius?" He asked while breathing heavily. "We are gods. Let's call to them. Let's summon The Fallen, together we can challenge them. What is power? What is life? What is immortality? What is love without the freedom to express it? What is the purpose of having such things if you are without the power to express it? To live it? We live in the shadows of this world. We hide from the inferior race. Why? Why are we instructed not to love?" He laughed. "What gives them the right? Because they made us Immortal? We did not ask for this. They didn't consult us."

"There was never any option. How can you be so blind to this? We were like children blinded by the offering of candy and oh how bittersweet the taste. We were deceived. Immortality is nothing but a bunch of pacifisms." His voice rose in intensity, the passion of his words could be felt. "We are greater than this, maybe even greater than them. We have the opportunity to change the way things are. You and I. To be redeemed. This is the moment of our salvation. We are Immortal for a reason. We too have purpose, but they will never let us realize it. Why, Julius? Because they fear us. They fear the truth of what we are. The truth of what they created. The time of The Fallen has passed… it is now time for us to become the gods that we were created to be."

A flash of lightning flashed between them. Their energy was gravitationally drawn to one another's. The two Immortals hung suspended in the air only several yards a part. Both of their bodies were beaten, bruised, and glistening with sweat. A lot of the ground was held in a levitating suspension, drawn in the air by the gravity of the two powers. Lightning continued to flash between them.

"You are wrong. We are not gods, Javian. We are men. Immortal men. We will not live forever. We will experience death as we once have before. This we cannot change."

Although Javian saw the incoming fist he couldn't move fast enough to dodge it. He tasted blood upon impact. For the first time since the fight had begun Javian became defensive as Julius attacked him. In this new ascended state his strikes were far more powerful causing his body to shake every time he was hit. Julius easily shifted away from a powerful kick. Moving behind Javian he grabbed him and tossed him back down towards level ground where the fight had begun. He followed his flight all the while raining blows on him during his descent. With the last blow he drew back with everything he had and hit him with it causing his descent to be accelerated. He crashed at the base. Slowly he stood, staggering and struggling. He was clearly injured.

So this was it, Javian thought with a resolute expression. His energy was drained. He knew he wouldn't last much longer. If he was to die, he would die fighting. He spread his feet wide, planted himself firmly, took a deep breath, and brought the ends of his palms together. With his long hair hung down over his face concealing most of it he drew his hands back as a low roar rose from his throat as he raised his energy level one last time. A visible spherical shaped ball of energy enveloped him as the intensity of both his energy and his roar rose together. A light appeared at the point where his palms were joined together.

Julius formed the same position. They both waited before releasing their energy allowing it to increase in intensity. When they finally let go two poles of light shot forth, like rams they collided with a boom. For what seemed like an eternity the two powers converged at an equal distance. Both men gave a loud roar, coming from their souls, at the top of their vocal ability. Both men were willing and prepared to die.

It was Julius' energy that finally began to dominate and as Javian saw the blast getting nearer he gracefully accepted his fate.

He didn't want to kill his brother, but he had no other choice. The blast was only inches away from Javian's face when a stranger suddenly appeared. They could both sense him and the fact that his power went beyond both of theirs combined. He grabbed Javian and slapped Julius' energy away as if it was nothing more than a fly.

He locked eyes with Julius for a moment and then he was gone.

Epilogue

Gray finished up the chapter he was working on and sat back in the mobile arm chair. He flipped the laptop down and smiled at the picture of Betsy. He looked over at Biscuit, who was resting his head on his paws.

"Wanna get some fresh air?"

Biscuit raised his head and moved his tail.

"Don't you ever sleep?"

He got up to leave and the dog followed behind, sniffing at his heels. He went out back and stretched his arms wide as he looked up at the beautiful sky. It was the beginning of summer. The few trees that were visible were fully green. In the distance off to the left were some apple trees that were on another person's land. He had none of his own.

He had grabbed a Frisbee on the way out. Biscuit was barking at him to throw it. "I don't get it. What is it with dogs and Frisbees? It's just a piece of plastic."

The dog continued to bounce and bark, so he tossed it out.

He was looking forward to a good summer. His nephews and nieces would be visiting. He had enjoyed his short visit with them. They were really some good kids. They looked a little different, but he loved them the same. They were smart and they would all probably go to college and have good careers. He was proud of all of them.

It had been quiet around here lately. He hadn't seen an Immortal at his home in over a month. Strange group of people, they were.

Michael's girlfriend had moved in. She was a sweet thing, she reminded him of Betsy sometimes. They were young, and they had their whole lives ahead of them. He was happy for them.

He still remembered the night he had met Michael, a naked stranger on the road in the middle of a storm. That night had changed his life, or at least the direction of it. He was living again. He hadn't felt this alive since Betsy was alive. He knew she would want him to be happy.

He didn't view Michael as a son, more like a close friend... a close friend who could fly and teleport. Who would've ever thought?

About two miles down the road from Gray's home Michael and Rachel were walking hand in hand headed back to the house.

"You miss her?"

"Yeah, I do." He looked up as a car drove by. "We talk every day. I met Angel, she sounds nice. I can't wait to see her person. I can't believe I'm an uncle."

She looked at him to observe him. He looked better and the sadness wasn't in his eyes. He had taken his mother's loss pretty hard, he felt responsible.

"You look good, Michael." She said smiling at him.

She was wearing a white skirt with a thin top that had no sleeves, leaving her arms bare. Her long hair hung straight down. "Thank you again for saving my family."

"You should be thanking the twelve year old for that. She packs a mean punch for a kid."

Isabella had taken out the six man unit of The Silent Death in a matter of seconds. He knew he wasn't anywhere near that good.

His expression changed. "I wish I could've saved her. All that time, Rachel, I thought that she didn't love me. I know now that she did. She always did."

"We can't help the things we don't know," she said softly.

He looked in her eyes as the light of the sun reflected in them. She was so beautiful. Her face brought him back from the hole he was falling into. He stopped walking.

"I love you, Rachel."

He kissed her softly. He loved the way she smelled, the way she felt when he held her. To breathe her in was life. He tasted her tenderly, savoring every moment of it.

"So what's next?" She asked after they resumed walking.

His shoulders moved as he sighed heavily. "Julius is still trying to figure out what happened. That may take some time. In the meantime I plan to on finding out who all was involved with the Michael Flint experiment."

"What will you do when you find them?"

He didn't hesitate in answering. "Kill them. Kill them all."

Excerpt

YOLO

The Lovely Little Lunatic

By

Sa'id Salaam

PROLOGUE

"Damn it Philomina, did you have to put these so tight!" Thadeous Frank grumbled straining once more to free himself. His wrist and ankles were secured firmly by thick plastic ties to the heavy dining room chair in the extravagantly furnished dining room. It made no sense complaining to her at the opposite end of the long oak table because she was in the same position.

"She has our baby Thadeous; I did what I was told to do!" his wife shot back in a muted whisper through clenched teeth.

Mrs. Frank wasn't one to sass her husband, especially since he provided her lavish lifestyle. She turned a blind eye to all his indiscretions but had no doubt his insatiable greed was the cause of the current predicament.

Thadeous Frank was about as straight as a circle. In the real world people seek trustworthiness and honesty in a C.P.A. but in the underworld corruption is a virtue. Mr. Frank had a knack for taking duffle bags of dirty, filthy, drug blood money and bringing it back crisp and clean. On average, he ran a hundred mil through his financial washing machine annually.

He took a generous ten percent for his trouble. He proved true the adage of no honor among thieves by skimming a few more points off here and there. He didn't have much respect for his black and Latino customers and assumed they wouldn't miss it. Most didn't but Casper did. He may have been the boss of the Black Mob but he was neither black nor stupid. He wrote the first loss off as an oversight but the next time the money was short he sent someone to collect.

"Please Thad, give her what she wants! She has our Jacinthia!" Philomina Frank pleaded.

"Look she'll never find it. Never! Once she gets tired of looking I'll give her a few grand from the safe and let her scurry along," he shot back. Baby or no baby he had no plans of coming off that cash. He liked the kid and all, but she wasn't worth ten million to him.

"Please, it's been hours. Jacinthia must be terrified," Mrs. Frank moaned looking at the kitchen door where the intruder took her child.

"Stop bitching, you're making too much out of it. What can that girl do?" he said curtly. Thadeous was smug like that, confident, always in charge. The silly man had no idea who was upstairs in their home searching for stolen money.

"You're good! I still can't find it!" the intruder sang in the singsong manner of an eight year old as she breezed back into the dining room.

The couple both frowned at the sexy maid outfit she had changed into but for different reasons. The high priced item was cut low in front and high enough in back to show the pert caramel ass in a thong underneath. Thadeous recalled the one time his pasty white wife wore it for him and it didn't look like that.

"Is she wearing my lingerie?" Mrs. Frank complained to her husband then turned to the girl. "Where did you get that?"

"Same place I got this," she giggled and produced a large brown dildo. Brown from the porn star who modeled for it. The white lady turned beet red from embarrassment.

"Well I never!" she huffed indignantly.

The intruder frowned dubiously, sniffed the vibrator, and gave it a flick from her tongue. "Yes you have," the girl giggled sheepishly. She looked at her target and covered her mouth suddenly coy. "Oh I see you!"

"Frank!" Philomina shouted seeing her husband's stubby little erection standing up.

"Here relax," the uninvited guest said turning the knob at the base of the dildo. She giggled again when it began to vibrate with a soft buzz. She shoved it under the woman's vagina and tuned towards the kitchen with Thadeous' eyes glued to her ass.

"How's Jacinthia? She must be hungry," Mrs. Frank asked desperately.

"I doubt it," the girl laughed over her shoulder as she left the room. "We'll talk more after dinner."

"Just give her what she wants! I said nothing about your affairs and...stuff," she demanded trying to ignore the building pleasure the vibrator was creating.

"She said we'll talk after dinner. She hasn't found anything in the..." he paused to look at the grandfather clock, "four hours she's been here! I'll give her ten grand and she can run off and buy some crack and colorful clothes those niggers love so much!"

Mrs. Frank missed the last sentence from the buzzing between her legs. She shook her head 'no' as she tried in vain to stave off an orgasm. It was futile and she came with a loud grunt. It was the best orgasm she'd had with her husband in the same room. Then she concentrated and went for seconds. Her pleasure was cut short before she got to bust another nut.

"Dinner is served," the girl announced pushing the sterling silver dinner cart into the dining room. On it were two plates topped by silver domes to keep the food warm.

"Would you mind loosening our hands so that we may partake in this wonderful meal?" Mr. Frank requested sweetly. He attempted to hide his devious plan behind the kind words and pasted on smile.

The fifty-ish out of shape white man figured he could over-power the little girl. Boy was he wrong.

"Um...ok but one at a time," she relented. Thadeous again watched her firm ass shift as she skipped into the next room.

She returned a few seconds later with the black satchel she came with. Before she opened it, she pulled the blonde dreadlock wig off and stretched her neck in relief. It made a dense thud when she placed it on the table. She un-zipped the bag and pulled out a long chrome pistol and even longer chrome silencer. "In case you try anything."

The girl next pulled a pair of wire snips and danced over to the Mrs. She cut the plastic tie that had broken into her skin from her movements. The woman immediately snatched the vibrator from between her legs.

"Ladies first," the server said placing the plate on the table in front of her. She removed the dome with an air of flair complete with, "Ta dah!"

"Oh!" Mrs. Frank uttered at the attractive meal on the good china. She also noticed how pretty the girl was now that her face was no longer obscured by the dreads. She was the exact same shade that the lady took her coffee with milk, not cream. Although her features were delicate and defined, she had an odd look in her eyes. The far-away gaze of a lunatic. The curious gape of the deranged.

"We have wild brown rice with slivers of almond. Braised Brussel sprouts in butter-garlic sauce and I'm sorry but I can't pronounce the meat. Jaza or jasm? Something like that," the girl explained.

Philomina was scared the food would be poisoned but she was more afraid of the big pistol on the table. After a second of contemplation, she decided to eat. She popped a whole Brussel sprout in her mouth and chewed. A slow nod of approval began as she savored the flavor. Next, she sampled the rice and finally the pretty kabobs of meat and peppers.

"How's my baby?" Mrs. Frank asked after swallowing.

"You tell me," the chef asked in return.

"I don't follow?" she frowned curiously.

"You said how's my baby and I said you tell me. That's what you're eating. I didn't over cook her did I?"

"Noooo!" the mother screamed as the nightmare was multiplied times infinity. She pulled and tugged at the plastic tie cutting deeply into her wrist. "You're sick! Sick!"

"Me? You're the one who ate her baby lady," the girl shot back sarcastically. With the woman busy trying to cut her own hand off she turned her attention to Mr. Frank. "Have some? It's thigh, I hear that's the best part. I wouldn't know cuz I don't eat kids. Well…"

"Mm mm!" Thadeous declined squeezing his mouth tight and moving his head from side to side to avoid the forkful of baby thigh meat, she extended.

"Ooh, I know what will make you open up," she exclaimed cheerfully at her bright idea. She grabbed the gun a fired a silent round into his calf. Harmless, but it got him to open his mouth wide in an opera worthy high note.

"Good?" she asked shoving the meat inside the open mouth. She didn't wait for an answer and went back into her black bag. Thadeous took the opportunity to spit his kid onto the marble floor.

Both Franks were dealing with their problems but the next item out of the bag took precedence. She stopped thrashing about and he longer felt the burn of the gunshot.

"What the hell is that?" Thadeous demanded as its mere presence offended him. Actually, it should have.

"This," she began, holding up the circular wire contraption, "it's the D.C. 2000! That's short for decapitator 2000. I saw it in a movie and had to have it!"

She went on to explain how the spring-loaded wire hoop snapped shut to a zero circumference when activated. It was strong enough to cut through a 2x4 so skin and bones were no problem at all.

"Now I'm going to cut both of your heads off," she said plainly, as if it were no big deal.

"Why both of our heads? I don't have anything to do with any of this!" Mrs. Frank pleaded in an attempt to save herself.

"No, both of his heads I meant," the girl explained going back into the satchel. The garden shears she produced needed no explanation.

"Wait! Wait! Wait!" Thadeous appealed as she approached. "I'll tell you where the money is!"

"Too late," she said slipping the D.C. 2000 over his head. "I'm glad you didn't give it to me."

"Go to hell!" he shouted and in a final act of defiance, spit in her face. The lovely little lunatic smiled, licked the saliva from around her mouth, and picked up his flaccid penis.

"Ok, bye-bye," she sang and simultaneous hit the switch and closed the shears. The tiny dick head popped off and rolled under his chair. A second later, his big, bald head fell into his lap.

Mrs. Frank stared on in stunned silence as her husband was decapitated. Whoever the girl was, she was a killer. A killa, a real animal. She let out a sigh of contentment and accepted her fate.

"Well, time to go with your baby, but don't tell her you ate her," she whispered conspiratorially.

Mrs. Frank lifted her chin prepaid to die with dignity. Instead of shooting her or cutting any parts off, the girl prepared to leave. She packed her pistol and D.C. 2000 into the bag along with the shears. She took the wire cutters into the kitchen and cut the gas line leading to the restaurant size stove. Then she breezed back through the dining room ignoring the confused woman.

The girl made a stop in the family room and lit the fireplace. Once the gas made it that far the house would be leveled by the explosion. A sly smile spread over her face as she stepped over the body of the butler. He had smiled brightly when he opened the door for her and she shot him in it.

When she got into her SUV and drove away, she added the two kills to her tally. The total was now 99 and she wasn't quite 21. She pulled her cell phone out to report in to the boss.

Casper smiled brightly when he saw the name on his caller ID.

"Yolo! Did you get it?" the white boss of the Black Mob asked eagerly. He didn't need the money but didn't want anyone to have the satisfaction of stealing his and enjoying it.

"No, he wouldn't tell me," she replied sadly. "Good news though. The D.C. 2000 works like a charm!"

"That is good news. Have fun?" Casper inquired.

"I did. I did," Yolo said bouncing in her seat.

A thunderous roar rocked the SUV and shook the earth. A glance in the rearview mirror showed a huge orange fireball where the house once stood.

"Yay! One hundred!" she cheered knowing Mrs. Frank was in the debris blown sky high.

You may wonder why a girl would derive such joy from killing people and the answer is because she's crazy. You may also wonder how she amassed such a high body count at such a young age. The answer to that is simple too; she started early.

CHAPTER 1

"Here we go again!" the ER doctor groaned as the patient was wheeled in near death. The middle-aged white man didn't care much for black people and he particularly loathed poor people. So this poor black woman was the scum of the earth to him. The fact that she was pregnant only made matters worse.

"Great, another ghetto bastard! World get ready, here comes Leroy Johnson!" he quipped to the amusement of one of the two nurses present.

The white nurse didn't necessarily like the racist jokes but she did like the doctor so she went along with his jokes. The black nurse hated him, his jokes, and his cavalier attitude. And since her peer thought it was funny, fuck her too.

"She's in labor," Nurse Marquita announced hoping to spur some urgency in her co-workers. They stood back while she attempted to wash the emaciated little crack head on the gurney.

The dirt on her skin was clearly visible once her filthy clothes were cut off. Even the smell emanating from the woman could be seen like the ripples of heat emanating from an Arizona highway. Her frail body housed a misshapen lump, the body of her premature baby that was near death, in her belly.

"Her blood pressure is through the roof!" Nurse Nancy said after inflating the arm cuff. She pulled yet another mask over her mouth and nose to avoid the suffocating stench coming from between the patient's legs.

"Why prolong the inevitable? Just let them die," the doctor suggested in violation of both the Hippocratic Oath and humanity.

"If you don't attend to this patient like you would any other patient I will report you!" Marquita growled.

"Oh ok!" he relented before doubling his mask and gloves and moving in. He shoved his whole hand inside the woman's beat up vagina to see how far she had dilated. Her vagina was so loose that it was laid open like a baked potato therefore his hand went in to the wrist with no problem. "Huh?"

"No way!" Nurse Nancy said as the Dr. pulled out a whole condom, a piece of another, and a bottle top. She just shook her head at the mess on the stretcher. The crack addict still had twigs and leaves in her matted hair from sleeping in the woods like a squirrel.

"Yes, it's in labor. The baby's coming," he said as he backed away.

The bells and whistles began going off as the mother's life slipped away. That gave the doctor an excuse to sit back and watch them die. Nurse Marquita couldn't sit idle. She rushed over and shoved her hand inside.

"It's breached, I have the feet!" she screamed just as the mother flat lined.

"One down, one to go," the doctor mumbled dryly. Marquita didn't respond, instead she snatched the child out of its dead mother by its feet. She was then faced with yet another dilemma upon seeing the umbilical cord was wrapped tightly around its neck. The child's face was blue from lack of oxygen. The nurse quickly grabbed a scapula to cut the cord away. Then risking her own life she breathed directly into the child's mouth.

"Marquita that woman is a registered HIV patient! She has full blown AIDS and hasn't picked up her meds in months!" Nurse Nancy warned.

The blue baby took her first breath just as the mother took her last. Nurse Marquita cut and tied the cord to prepare the child for the incubator where she would spend the first few months of her life.

"Well, congratulations, another ward of the state is born. Welcome yet another burden for the tax payers," the doctor bitched.

"Guess you can do the honors and name her. She certainly can't," Nancy said as she pulled a sheet over the corpse.

"Oh, here we go with another 13-syllable ghetto name!" the doctor cackled.

"Oh do you remember the twins?" Nurse Nancy reminded as she cracked up.

"Denise and De-nephew! How could I forget!" he howled. Even Marquita had to stifle a chuckle at the memories of the gold tooth patient who birthed them.

"How about Ephemeral, since it probably won't survive," Nancy offered seriously. The baby was weak, underweight, malnourished, and most likely HIV positive.

"Well you only live once," Marquita said finally noticing the sex of the baby. "Isn't that right Yolo?"

"Yolo Jackson!" the doctor repeated with a decimating nod as if checking the sound of it. "Nice ring to it."

"Yolo Jackson it is," she said and took the child to the neo-natal unit to die.

Only she didn't die. To everyone's surprise, the child was spared from the deadly virus that killed her young mother. She gained weight quickly and grew healthier by the day.

However, the stoic infant never smiled, laughed, or cooed. Instead, she wore a perturbed look on her face as if she wanted to curse.

Nurse Marquita wanted to adopt the child but her busy schedule had no room for an infant. Besides, it wouldn't be much of a story if she had since the nurse would have provided the loving home and proper guidance a child needs to be well balanced. Instead she was going into the fucked up foster care system of New York. Blame them; it's their fault that she grew up to be a lunatic.

www.ingramcontent.com/pod-product-compliance
Lightning Source LLC
Chambersburg PA
CBHW070848250626
47159CB00003B/987